FRANCES HARDINGE

Verdigris Deep

MACMILLAN CHILDREN'S BOOKS

Many thanks to the members of all the writers' circles I have attended over the years; Nancy for swooping in to become my agent, and keeping me sane when the world went mad; my editor, Ruth Alltimes; Kathy Norman and her biro of power; Rhiannon Lassiter; Richard Ridge, with whom I have eaten blackberries in Magwhite. And, of course, Martin.

First published 2007 by Macmillan Children's Books
a division of Macmillan Publishers Limited
20 New Wharf Road, London N1 9RR
Basingstoke and Oxford
www.panmacmillan.com

Associated companies throughout the world

ISBN: 978-1-4050-5537-6

Text copyright © Frances Hardinge 2007
Illustrations copyright © Peter Ferguson 2007

The right of Frances Hardinge to be identified as the author
of this work has been asserted by her in accordance
with the Copyright, Designs and Patents Act 1988.

1 3 5 7 9 8 6 4 2

A CIP catalogue record for this book is available from
the British Library.

Typeset by Intype Libra Limited
Printed and bound in Great Britain by Mackays of Chatham plc, Kent

Contents

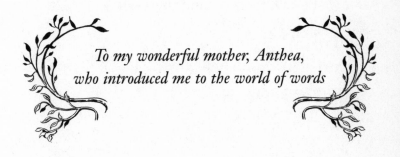

To my wonderful mother, Anthea,
who introduced me to the world of words

Verdigris (Ver-di-gree) **n.** a blue-green rust that tarnishes ageing and forgotten copper coins, altering them entirely . . .

1

The Flight of the Trolley

For a wonderful moment Ryan thought Josh was going to make it. When they had turned the corner to find the bus already at the stop Josh had burst into a run, scattering starlings and shattering puddles. The bus's engine gave a long, exasperated sigh and shrugged its weight forward as if hulking its shoulders against the rain, but Ryan still believed Josh would snatch success at the last minute, as always. Then, just as Josh drew level with its tail lights, the bus roared sulkily away, its tyres leaving long streaks of dull against the shiny wet tarmac.

Josh chased it for about twenty yards. Then, through the tiny crystal specks of rain that freckled his glasses, Ryan saw his hero stumble, slow and aim a kick at a lamp post.

The bus seemed to have carried away Ryan's stomach, and the last of the summer daylight. Suddenly the dingy string of shops seemed much colder, darker and more dejected than before. Ryan could still taste the chocolate milkshake that had cost them their ride, and the flavour made him feel sick.

Behind him he heard Chelle's asthmatic gasping and turned to find her fumbling with her inhaler. She took a deep breath, her round eyes becoming even wider for a second so that he could see the whites all round them. She stared at Josh's slowly returning figure.

'He said . . . Josh said . . . he said that the bus was always late, he said there was time for a milkshake . . . I am sosososososo dead . . . my mum thinks I'm baby-sitting . . .' Her pale eyebrows had climbed up her forehead in panic to hide behind her blonde fringe.

'Shush, Chelle,' Ryan said as kindly as he could. It was hopeless. Chelle was unshushable.

'But . . . it's all right for Josh, everyone expects him to get into trouble. I . . . I don't know *how* to be in trouble . . .'

'Shush,' Ryan said with more urgency. Josh was almost within earshot. Whenever Josh felt bad about something he had done he got angry with the whole world, became playfully vicious. Ryan did not want to be stranded in Magwhite with an angry Josh.

They were not meant to be in Magwhite at all.

Magwhite was an almost-place. The gas towers and the railway made it almost part of Guildley. The lurid fields of oilseed rape that stretched away to the east were almost countryside. The sad little strings of houses, the minimart and the bike shop were almost a village. The towpath walks were almost pretty.

Someone had once been knifed there, or maybe a

finger with a ring had been found on one of the paths, or perhaps the local rugby club came to pee in the canal from the bridge. Nobody could quite remember which, but something had happened to give the name 'Magwhite' ugly edges. If Magwhite was mentioned, parents' faces stiffened as if they had picked up a bad smell. It was very definitely Out of Bounds.

There was nothing much to do there, but its out-of-boundsness made it exciting. Feeding chips to the jackdaws outside the boarded-up Magwhite post office was more interesting than feeding ordinary birds in the park. So, ever since the summer holidays had started, the forbidden excursions to picnic by the Magwhite canal had become almost routine.

Magwhite was their place, but now there was nothing Ryan wanted more than to be out of it.

Josh trudged back towards the others, his head bowed, the rain darkening his fierce, blond, scrubbing-brush hair. He seemed to be grimacing at his foot. Maybe he had hurt it against the lamp post. Then he looked up, and Ryan saw that he was grinning.

'S'all right.' Josh shrugged and wiped the rain off his yellow-tinted sunglasses with his sleeve. 'We'll catch the next one.'

Chelle was biting her lower lip, her upper lip pulling down to a point, like a little soft beak. She was trying not to disagree, because she worshipped Josh more than anybody else in the world, but words always seemed to dribble out of Chelle like water from a broken tap.

'But . . . we can't, that was the last Guildley Cityline

bus, our return tickets won't work for the Point-to-Point bus, and we haven't got enough money for new tickets for all of us . . . we're stuck . . .'

'No, we're not.' Josh was still smiling. 'I have a plan.'

It was a simple plan, an odd plan, but it was a Josh plan, so it had to work.

Behind the wall of the minimart car park, there was a long tree-tangled slope that ran down to the canal side. In this wood roamed escapee supermarket trolleys, stripped grass trapped in their wheels, 'sweetheart' creepers trailing from their wire frames. Josh's plan was to find one of these, take it back to the minimart car park, attach it to the chain of trolleys outside the entrance doors and reclaim the pound coin deposit in the handle slot.

Suddenly everything was an adventure again. The threesome dropped over the wall into the wood and started hunting through the trees.

It was a strange wood, stranger still now the light was fading. Ryan loved it for its litter. Yellowing newspapers nestled in branch nooks, like a crop of dead leaves strangely patterned with print. A sprawling throne of rotten oak trailed dark ivy and coddled a treasure trove of crushed cans. The twigs of one wavering branch had been carefully threaded through the fingers of a red woollen mitten, so that the little tree looked as if it was waiting to grow another hand and start applauding.

'Ryan, you're our eagle eyes, find us a trolley,' said Josh, and Ryan felt an uncomfortable swell of pride and doubt. He was never sure if Josh was making fun of him. 'He sees everything different to us, Chelle. Cos his eyes, right, they're in upside down. You just can't tell looking at them.'

Chelle gave a faint giggle, but in the darkness her dimly visible face looked uncertain. Her eyes were large and widely spaced, windows into a world full of doubt and surprise.

'It's true,' insisted Josh. 'He blinks upwards, you know. Not when you're watching. But right now, in the dark, I bet he's blinking upwards, aren't you, Ryan?'

Ryan wasn't sure how to answer, so he plunged on through the trees and pretended not to hear. Scaring Chelle was easy, and Josh seemed to find pleasure in teasing her. It was often hard for Ryan to remember that Chelle was older than he was. Ryan himself had been 'moved ahead' and dunked into the icy waters of secondary school a year before everyone he knew. It did not help that he was small, skinny and full of sentences that seemed fine in his head, then came out sounding over-adult and clever-clever. He had formed an alliance of desperation with Chelle. She had an air of kitten-tottering helplessness, and the pallor of her hair and skin made her look as if she had been through the wash too many times, losing her colour and courage in the rinse. All this made her an irresistible mark for the bullies in their class. Both Ryan and Chelle had been glad to find someone willing to talk to them, even if in Chelle's case she apparently lacked the ability to *stop* talking.

Josh had been their salvation. He had the advantage

of age – there is a world of difference between a first year and a second year – but, in any case, no bully knew what to make of Josh, with his Cheshire Cat grin and knuckleduster humour. Taunts seemed to bounce off the shields of his yellow sunglasses, leaving his attackers winded by the ricochet. He won people round somehow, as if everyone wanted in on the private joke that kept him smirking. Josh had remembered Ryan from primary school, much to Ryan's surprise, and suddenly both Ryan and Chelle were taken under his capricious wings. For the last year, his friendship had protected them from the worst school-time persecutions like an invisible amulet. For all these reasons, Ryan guessed that Chelle did not truly mind Josh's teasing, but he never felt comfortable joining in with it.

Usually there were half a dozen trolleys in the little wood. This evening, however, the trolleys seemed to know that they were in danger of being taken back to captivity and had all gone into hiding. At last Ryan cornered one down by the canal. It was lying on its side as if it had fallen in its hurry to get away and been unable to get back on its wheels. The three of them dragged it over to the wall, feeling the trolley catch at every bramble and tussock, trying to jolt itself out of their grasp.

It was only when they reached the car-park wall that they started to see a small flaw in Josh's plan.

The ground on the woodland side of the wall was much lower than it was on the car-park side. They'd scrambled up and down the wall themselves so often that they no longer noticed how high it was. Now they stared sadly at the trolley, then up at the wall, which loomed above and laughed at them.

'We can do this,' Josh said after a moment. ''S just mechanics, that's all.'

Following Josh's new plan, the three scavenged materials for a makeshift rope – a loose-flapping ribbon of plastic cordon tape, a mouldering abandoned T-shirt, a length of wire. These were knotted together, and one end tied firmly to the trolley. The other end was thrown over a low branch, and Chelle and Ryan grabbed it as it tumbled down on the other side. Josh, who was by far the strongest of the three, clambered up on to the wall and waited to grab the trolley when Chelle and Ryan had hauled it high enough.

This can't work, thought Ryan as he started to pull on the 'rope'. But then the trolley raised its handle-end, swung to and fro, and took to the air. The plan was working.

The flight of the trolley was a beautiful thing to see. It bucked repeatedly against the tree trunk, and its wheels left dark scars across the lichen, but it rose, a few inches at a time. Then just as it was almost within reach of Josh's fingertips, it bumped up against one of the lower boughs and half disappeared among the leaves. They tugged and tugged, and the foliage shivered and shook, spilling sleeping raindrops on to their upturned faces. But a thin branch had pushed its way up under the trolley's blue plastic child seat and would not release it.

At last Ryan and Chelle stopped tugging. They stood sucking their burned palms and stared up at the triumphant trolley.

'I think . . .' began Chelle, tumbling helplessly into the silence, 'I think if we sort of stuck a stick up under that wheel and levered it, swayed it to and fro, then it might . . .'

'It's stuck,' said Josh. They had all known this in their souls, but Josh saying so made it true. Josh's tinted sunglasses had dulled with the setting of the sun, and behind them Ryan could see the pale flicker of eyelids as he blinked twice and narrowed his eyes. He was biting both lips together so they were quite hidden – a bad sign with Josh.

Without another word, Josh dropped from the wall and strode away down the slope towards the canal. Ryan and Chelle exchanged a look and then followed.

He's not going to run off and leave us, is he? . . . but what did Josh have to lose if he went home late? Being in trouble meant something different in Josh's home and sometimes Josh seemed to have no fear of that anyway. Ryan caught up with him.

'Where are we going?' he tried.

'The well.' Josh sounded too calm.

They followed Josh's ruthless pace, struggling through dead-nettles and ducking the drooping purple fingers of the buddleia, until they reached the moss-covered steps that led down to the canal bank and path. Trainers sliding against the wet slate of the steps, they descended until the glitter of the canal was just visible through the trees; then Josh stopped. To one side of the steps was a small dimple in the ground, and at the bottom of the dimple was a stark ring of concrete, with a wire mesh covering the hole in the middle. Several crisp packets had been pushed through the wire and stuck in the mesh.

Josh got down on his hands and knees. Only when he got out his Swiss Army knife and pulled free the screwdriver attachment did Ryan realize what he was doing. Soon Josh had unscrewed three of the bolts fastening the well cover in place and was starting on the fourth.

'It's a wishing well, isn't it?' Josh explained, continuing to wrestle with the rusty bolts. 'And that means coins. Got it!' The wire mesh came away. 'All right, who's going down? Chelle, you're thin and wriggly. Want to go?'

Chelle's only answer was a thin squeak of alarm.

Josh grinned at her. 'All right then.' He swung his legs over the edge and, to the others' dismay, started to lower himself in.

'Josh, look, um . . .' began Ryan. He exchanged a worried glance with Chelle as Josh disappeared into blackness.

'Josh, what if you get stuck? Shouldn't we make another rope and tie it round your chest, cos—'

A sharp cry echoed in the darkness below them.

'Josh!' squealed Chelle. She threw herself on to her hands and knees beside the well and stared down into the murk, her pale hair falling around her face.

'It stinks down here!' Josh called up suddenly.

'Josh, you scared us!' Chelle's nervousness melted helplessly into giggles.

'That's right, you go ahead and laugh. Here I am . . .' Josh's echoing tones were interrupted by a sudden splash. 'Oh bollocks.'

Chelle peered quickly down into the well again.

'I think he's fallen in,' she managed through her laughter. 'I can hear sploshing.'

'Can't be that deep then,' whispered Ryan. He was pretty sure that if Josh was drowning he would be spending more time screaming and less time swearing under his breath.

'Right, I've got some,' they heard at last. The well's echo gave Josh's voice a solemn and impressive sound. 'Coming up.' Josh whistled to himself as he started to climb, the tune interrupted now and then by the scrape and splash of dislodged masonry. At long last he reappeared and clambered out. He shook one leg then the other, trying to dance the water out of his trainers. Even in the dusk light, however, it was obvious that his trainers were the least of his problems.

Chelle fumbled a small white something out of her pocket. She looked at it, and then at the sodden wreckage of Josh's clothes, and her shoulders began to shake uncontrollably.

'I've got a tissue!' she squeaked, and somehow this was much funnier than it should have been.

Five minutes later they were running down Magwhite's high street just in time to catch the last bus to Guildley.

Open-mouthed, the driver looked at the green that slicked Josh's hair and smudged his sunglasses, took in his clothes, dark and clinging with water from the waist down, contemplated the slimy puddle of blackened coins in Josh's outstretched hand.

'You just pulled all that lot out of the well, didn't you?'

'No,' said Josh, with his best brash, unblinking stare.

It was the total shamelessness of this lie that seemed to throw the driver off balance. He gave Josh a long look, as if to say that he wasn't fooled, that he'd be watching him. Then he jabbed at a few buttons on his ticket machine and a loop of three tickets curled into Josh's waiting hand.

Josh sauntered to the back of the bus and waited while Chelle spread the seat with newspapers for him, then settled himself with a grin, as if he would face no inquisition when he reached home half-drowned, with rust under his fingernails.

He did it. At that moment Ryan would willingly have taken a bullet for Josh. He would have followed him over deserts or waded across leech-infested rivers for him. Ryan hugged the surge of feeling, as Chelle talked and Josh wiped his sunglasses with her tissue. Suddenly he wanted to face some great danger or difficulty and prove himself to his hero in turn, and he was so full of the wish that it seemed it might split him like a conker shell.

If Ryan had known as much about wishes then as he came to know later, he would have been a lot more careful with his thoughts.

2

Upside-down Eyes

The first faint signs of the Change became apparent about a week after the robbery of the Magwhite well. Ryan was the first to notice them, but that was not surprising. Ryan was always the first one to notice anything.

He woke up that morning sensing that he had just lost his hold on a dream. It had left him with an uneasy feeling, as if a cold hand had slipped out of his just as he started to wake. Then his head cleared, and the lingering sense of clamminess passed away. He surfaced to the smell of coffee, and knew that the house was going to be invaded again.

His mother had a rigid drill for whenever anybody came to interview her. She believed fanatically that the best way to make a house seem welcoming but elegant was to fill it with the smell of expensive ground coffee. Downstairs three coffee-makers would be growling their hearts out in the kitchen, the living room and the conservatory.

Ryan reached for his glasses, and his finger touched

an empty case. Clearly his mother had already been in his room.

Only when the back of his hand brushed against his night-time glass of water did he almost remember something of his dream. The memory smelt like greenhouses and damp blots on walls. It felt cold and silvery, and Ryan knew that he had been dreaming about the Glass House again.

Ryan had been dreaming of the Glass House about three times a year for as long as he could remember. He had never spoken about it to anyone. The truth was, the Glass House dreams left a strange, acrid flavour in his mind that made him want to forget them as soon as possible. Today, however, the lingering memory seemed slightly *damper* than usual, as if dew had settled on it.

He struggled out of bed and felt his way on to the landing and down the stairs. His father glanced up from his crossword as Ryan stumbled in.

'Hello. Where are your glasses?'

'I think Mum's got them,' Ryan confessed.

'Oh, not again.' His father glanced over his shoulder towards the kitchen door and decided as usual that his voice could travel the distance without him. 'Anne!' he shouted.

'It's all right,' Ryan said quickly. 'Mum doesn't like to be interrupted when she's percolating.'

'Anne,' his father called out again, 'your son is running up and down stairs blind and likely to break his neck. We only have one child – can we try not to kill it, please?'

There was the faint hushing of an aerosol can, then Ryan's mother's voice: 'Tell him to put in his contact lenses, Jonathan – he has to get used to them.'

'Particularly when there's a danger of a photo opportunity, it would seem,' called Ryan's father. Ryan knew that other families took the trouble to enter the same room before talking to one another. His parents, however, thought it perfectly natural to hold conversations from opposite ends of the house at the top of their voices. They carried this conviction with them everywhere they went. 'Which of your victims are you being interviewed about today, anyway?'

'Jonathan, don't call my subjects victims.'

Ryan did try not to think of the people his mother wrote about as victims. Sometimes it was quite hard. She was an 'unofficial biographer', which seemed to mean working hard to meet famous people at parties, then writing books about them without asking them first. His mother's books had shiny lettering on the front, and words like 'sensational' and 'uncompromising' on the back, and the famous people were usually very unhappy about them. One artist called Pipette Macintosh had been so upset that she had spray-painted their front hedge pink. Ryan's mother had been very excited about that, partly because it made even more papers want to interview her.

'Anyway, it's *Curtain Call*, wanting to talk to me about

the book I've started on Saul Paladine. You know, the actor.'

'Oh, *him*.' Ryan's father was a drama critic, although he had narrowly failed his exams for law school. Ryan thought he would have made a very good lawyer, tall, spruce and handsome in scarlet robes with a crisp white wig, pausing mid-stride to fix the jury with a slow, knowing twinkle. You often got the feeling that he was sharing a clever joke with somebody you couldn't see, picking the words most likely to amuse them.

'Delivers his lines like a postman,' murmured Ryan's dad. He was thinking theatrical thoughts now, and Ryan had slid out of his mind. Ryan took his cue and slid out of the room, quite literally. The floor of the hallway, living room and kitchen was polished wooden tiles, with grain lines that ran into each other at loggerheads. Ryan had long since discovered that he could skate along these in his socks.

He glided into the kitchen on one foot and had to put a hand out against the wall to balance himself. The wall was clammy with condensation from the coffee-making, and again his dream ran its cold fingers across his mind for a moment. Briefly he thought of a wall of steamed, dripping glass pressed against his palm. His dream-self had, he half remembered, been skimming through the Glass House with a sense of urgency . . .

But he blinked, and the kitchen showed no sign of becoming glass, even if the outlines were a bit fuzzy in places. His mother was standing at a table, pulling and poking at an orchid in a vase as if she was straightening the uniform of a child. Her face was a blur, but he saw the long sweep of her black hair swing and tremble with the brisk little head-shake she often gave when impatient or excited.

'Mum, can I have my glasses back, please?'

'You look much better without them.' The mother shape approached. 'Let's have a look at you.'

Ryan could feel his mother's fingers pulling and poking him around as they had the orchid. He sometimes wondered whether she thought that if she tugged at him for long enough she would end up with something more interesting. But his hair and eyes remained mud-coloured, and no amount of tweaking could make him larger or more impressive.

'Oh dear, now, what's that?' She was turning his hand over and holding it closer to her face. The pad of her thumb rubbed at something between two of his knuckles, vigorously but not painfully. All the same, Ryan found himself wanting her to stop. The skin there felt odd and sensitive. His mother scratched at the place very gently, and he could feel that her fingernail was catching on some slight bump on the skin.

'Mm. I think it's a wart or something. Ryan, if you get any more of these, let me know and I'll take you to a specialist.' Ryan's mother liked specialists now she had money. She often showed love by buying Ryan specialists. He sometimes wondered if he would come down on Christmas Day to find one struggling out of wrapping paper with a ribbon festooning his head.

Ryan skated slowly out of the kitchen and along to

the back door. Wearing his contact lenses was an easy way to please his mother, but he always felt stubborn about them. He knew he would put them in soon, but he wanted to delay it for a moment. The back door slid sideways, racketing its blind, and the sun patted a hot palm against his face.

He hopped from one warm paving stone to the next, until he reached the little green-painted bench beneath the cherry tree. He squatted on it, facing the back, and then let himself down backwards, until his hands were resting on the grass and he could see the house upside down. Somehow he felt more in control of things when he could turn the house upside down like that.

Josh was the only person he had ever told about this.

When Ryan had joined the Waites Park Primary at age seven there had been so many scary boys. Ryan had ducked his head and blinked behind his glasses and hoped that none of them would notice him. But somehow, by the time the summer field had become too muddy for football and the guttering clogged with fallen leaf mulch, Josh seemed to know his name, and would call it out familiarly.

And then, by the time the hay-fever season returned, it seemed inexplicably that they were friends. Ryan realized this one day when he was hanging upside down from a climbing frame in the corner of the school field. Josh was hanging beside him, and Ryan was telling him about the woman with upside-down eyes, something he had told nobody else.

When Ryan was six he had owned a book of optical illusions. On one page there had been an upside-down picture of a woman's face. She looked like she'd be pretty and smiling until you inverted the page. Then you got a shock as you registered that the photo had been adjusted so that her eyes and mouth were upside down compared to the rest of her face. The smile was only a smile when the book was the right way up. When you inverted the picture the thing that *had* been her smile became a terrible clenched-teeth down-turned frown, and her eyes were upside down.

Josh was the only person Ryan had ever told about the way this picture had frightened him. It had shown him that if you looked at things from a new angle they could suddenly become unfamiliar and scary. It became important to see things in as many different ways as possible, so they couldn't catch you by surprise.

While Ryan had been telling Josh this, he had realized two things. The first was that Josh would not tell everyone and lead them in teasing him about eyes. The second was that Josh was really interested in what Ryan was saying. From time to time he would laugh as Ryan explained that upside-down cypresses looked like a rush of green liquid pouring out of a hole in a field, and that you had to think of people walking around with very sticky feet like flies to stop them falling away into the sky. He had laughed, but then he had asked more questions and thought about the answers.

'Cool,' he had said at last.

Josh understood. Ryan would have worshipped him

for that alone. And when Josh occasionally mentioned 'upside-down eyes' in passing, he would meet Ryan's eye to show that he wasn't teasing, it was just a secret they shared. That gave Ryan a warm, uncomfortable, strangely uneasy sense of pride.

He stood, and teetered slightly as the blood rushed from his head. He padded back to the house and felt his way up to the bathroom.

'Ryan!' His mother had obviously heard the creak of the stairs. 'Coffee saucepans in the bath! Be careful, darling.'

The poinsettia pot which always sat in the bath when it wasn't in use had been moved on to the flimsy wooden stand with the slender column and the lion's paws at the bottom. It was so delicate that Ryan knew one day he was bound to knock it over and break everything. It seemed unfair to have to feel guilty about something he hadn't even done. Ryan moved around the stand very carefully and felt along the window sill for his contact lenses case.

The mirror was clouded with steam from the coffee saucepans, and Ryan could only make out a faint ghost-Ryan craning his head forward to peer. He prised out the first lens, worked out which way up it was and balanced it on the tip of one finger.

Ryan reached out with his free hand, and wiped an arc of glass clear with his sleeve. A streak of the other Ryan's face became fuzzily visible. It almost seemed to Ryan that there was more steam in the bathroom in the mirror than in the room where he stood, and again the memory of his dream briefly slithered through his thoughts. He beat the memory back, and held his eye open as he dipped his face to his finger and felt the contact lens's hard strangeness against his eyeball. He straightened, trying not to screw up his face, and for a moment saw clearly out of one eye. He gasped.

The Ryan face that he could see in the streak of clear glass had both eyes closed. The lashes were dark and spiky with moisture, and beneath them tears flowed freely down the face. The eyelids, both upper and lower, were trembling as if they were struggling to open or fighting to stay closed. Then both eyes started to open, and murky water flooded between the lids and bubbled down the cheeks.

Ryan leaped backwards, banging the back of his knee against the edge of the bath and completely losing his balance.

3

The Cavern

Three hours after the mirror incident, Ryan tried to phone Josh. There was a fault on the line, however, so instead he phoned Chelle's house.

'Hello?' Chelle's voice always sounded even higher and more chirrupy on the phone.

'Hullo, Chelle.' It was almost impossible to go straight to the heart of the matter. 'Chelle . . . I've broken the Poinsettia Stand. It's OK though, cos I fell over at the same time and banged my head and burned my hand on a saucepan of coffee, so nobody minded so much.'

In fact, rather than being angry with Ryan for his clumsiness, his mum had been furious with herself. For a while she had been quite insistent about driving Ryan to casualty in person, she would either cancel the interview completely or leave Ryan's dad to tell the journalist that she was a terrible mother who liked to boil her own child alive in the bathtub. But seeing the disappointment in his mum's face Ryan had, of course, persuaded her that the scald was not serious, almost liking how brave he sounded. Eventually she had agreed to go ahead with her interview.

'Anyway,' Ryan continued, 'Chelle – do you think I could come over this afternoon? And can you invite Josh too?' The mirror incident was something he wanted to discuss face to face. Chelle ran off to ask her mum and returned almost immediately.

'She says yes. She says it'll stop me getting under everyone's feet while Miss Gossamer's visiting.'

Miss Gossamer had been an old friend of Chelle's grandmother. Somehow, after Chelle's grandmother had quietly snuffled herself out of the world, Miss Gossamer had slid into her place within Chelle's family. Ryan supposed this was probably very good-hearted of Chelle's parents, but there was something eerie about it, like one of those dreams where a familiar face is replaced with that of a stranger with no explanation. Although Chelle never quite said so, he was sure she felt the same way.

Ryan's mum still felt guilty enough about the accident to give him a lift instead of leaving him to walk through the park.

Chelle lived in one of a long line of terraced houses. It had tall, thin windows with broad, deep sills which made perfect cat-balconies. Like a lot of old houses, it had an 'area', a little square pit in front of the house with steps going down to it, as well as two steps rising to the front door.

The two lowest windows opened on to the area, below street level. At one, Ryan saw Chelle's face appear. She smiled and waved to him just as the front door opened.

'Hello, Ryan,' Chelle's mother said, scarcely glancing at him before looking towards his mum's car. 'Isn't your mum coming in for a cup of tea?'

'She has an appointment, um, somewhere, um, quickly.' His mum was waving from the car with the bright, wide smile she kept for people who made her feel uncomfortable – people like Chelle's mother, who liked having Ryan's mum in the house talking about the famous people she met.

'What a shame . . .' Chelle's mother said, then looked down at Ryan absently as if to see whether she had been delivered the right package.

Chelle's mother's name was Michelle. As a child she had liked being nicknamed 'Chelle', so much so that she had christened her third daughter 'Chelle', on her birth certificate. Ryan thought Chelle's mother looked like the sort of woman who would think this was a good idea.

She had big, vague eyes and a big, vague smile, and was always very busy in the way that a moth crashing about in a lampshade is busy. When she heard that Chelle's schoolmates were calling her 'Barnacle-head' she said things like 'Aren't children funny?'

Ryan followed Chelle's mum into the hall, and the handle of Miss Gossamer's umbrella in the stand went for him with its parrot beak, as it always did.

Chelle's house was always so full of sound that Ryan never understood why anybody bothered talking there at all. The radio was on in the kitchen, and the television had been left on in the next room. Upstairs two people were arguing. Somebody seemed to run up or down the stairs every few minutes.

Chelle was waiting for him in the kitchen. Her greeting was lost as the upstairs argument ceased abruptly and her oldest sister, Celeste, thundered down to the front door in her cycle helmet. Someone else, presumably Chelle's other sister Caroline, retaliated by slamming a door.

Supplied with drinks, Ryan and Chelle descended the narrow stairs to the Cavern.

'. . . and is it horribly burnt under your bandage?' Chelle's nervous, rapid patter only became audible as the door closed behind them. 'Oh, but don't show me, I hate scars and things, they make my stomach feel like it's unpeeling . . .'

Neither of Chelle's sisters had wanted the basement room, with its mostly lightless window, the annoying pic-pic-pic that emanated endlessly from the light fitting and a creeping yellow edge of damp that drew maps on the ceiling. So Chelle had won the whole wide, chilly, dungeon-like room and loved it with a passion that would have made her sisters jealous had they known.

It was wonderful for secret meetings. Ryan liked looking up and seeing the feet of people passing in the street, not knowing they were being watched from below.

'. . . and it's tricky because she always makes me feel

like, well, you know what it's like, when somebody's watching you and you can feel it like dead leaves down the back of your jumper . . .'

Ryan had no idea what Chelle had been talking about. But the good thing about talking to Chelle was that she never really expected anyone to listen to her properly. When you were used to her you could just let her ramble, and it gave you a nice long space to think about what you were going to say next.

Ryan and Chelle always felt slightly odd together when Josh wasn't there. In some ways it was easier, because Josh was a firework and you never quite knew which way he was going to explode. When he was absent they talked more freely, and often caught themselves agreeing with each other. Somehow both seemed to become a bit bigger and louder to fill the gaping hole left by Josh. But that chasm was a scary thing to fill. Sooner or later one of them would wonder aloud what Josh would say about something, then they would talk happily about him instead, and the absent Josh would swell up to stop the gap again.

And Ryan knew that soon he would mention Josh's name, but first he wanted to hear what Chelle thought about something, not what Chelle thought Josh would think.

'. . . and at first I assumed it was the radio but it turned out to be me and I still don't know what I was talking about.' Chelle paused to grimace, and Ryan leaped into the pause.

'Chelle . . . there's something I want to tell you. It's about why I fell into the bath.'

Chelle waited, her own story forgotten.

'Mum and Dad think it's because I couldn't see, and the floor was slippery with steam, but it wasn't that. Chelle . . . I *saw* something, and I was jumping back to get away from it. It was when I was trying to put my contact lenses in. OK, my eyes were running, and I didn't have my glasses, and there was steam everywhere, but I could still see my face in the mirror. Only it wasn't.'

'Wasn't what?'

'Wasn't my face.'

The bulb filled the silence with its pic-pic-pic, while Chelle chewed the air and then swallowed.

'I mean, it looked like me,' continued Ryan, hearing the pitch of his voice rise, 'with my hair and my eyelids, only I shouldn't have been able to see both of my eyelids, should I? My eyes were open. And then when the reflection's eyes did open, they began pouring water. Not just tears, rivers of water. And the wrong colour. Any kind of a colour is wrong for tears.'

'That's really creepy,' Chelle said in a small voice. She did not try to tell him that he had imagined it. Ryan felt a surge of relief. 'I wish Josh was here,' she added.

'Isn't he coming?'

'Yes, but he'll be late. He's serving time, didn't you know? Because he came back all sludgy and green from the well and wouldn't tell them where he'd been.' Josh's parents thought that the most enlightened way to punish him for his escapades was to trap him in useful tasks that would make him a better person. Often this involved staying with the elderly aunts his mother hated, gardening and cleaning out their sheds. Instead of 'grounding' him and refusing to let him out of the house, his parents refused to let him *into* his own home. His key was taken from him, and he had no access to any of his own possessions until he had served his time.

Anything to get rid of me, Josh had said once. *They'd send me back if they could find the receipt.*

Ryan could not imagine how he would feel if his own parents sent him into this kind of exile. Josh, who took most punishment with fierce good humour, tended to react to a stint in Merrybells – the name of the house where his aunts lived – with a weird, glowering craziness unlike any of his other moods. His aunts, whom he despised, he obeyed with a sullen, dangerous taciturnity – it was that or face an extension of his exile – but his conversations with everyone else became a forest dense with tripwires.

Somewhere a phone rang, and then they heard footsteps approaching the door to the Cavern. Chelle's sister Caroline opened the door, phone in hand.

'It's Josh. Five minutes, OK? I'm expecting a call.'

Chelle waited until Caroline had closed the door before uncovering the receiver.

'Hello, Josh, we were just starting to wonder where . . . oh no, but Ryan had a weird thing . . . no, he's right here.'

Ryan took the phone with a sinking heart. If Josh

was cutting short Chelle's sentences, he was in a bad mood.

'It'll take less time if I tell you,' Josh began ungraciously enough. There was a hard, knuckley edge to his voice, muffled only by a faint whirr in the background like a washing machine. 'I'm at the Aunts'. I can't get to the Cavern. If there's anything important, tell me now before they come back.'

Ryan tried to tell Josh what he had told Chelle, but quickly, so that Josh wouldn't get impatient.

'Make a better story if one of the eyes fell out of the socket on a string and swung about a bit,' Josh said, unimpressed. 'Uh-oh, the Aunts are back.'

Ryan suddenly became aware that something other than Josh's tetchiness was setting him on edge. Something was bothering him, like the feel of fingers drumming on the back of his neck. It took him a moment to realize that the familiar, repetitive pic-pic-pic sound from above had accelerated.

'I've got to go. If your face is too scary for you, stay away from mirrors.'

'Josh . . .'

Pic.

Pic.

Pic.

Pic. Pic. Pic. Pic-pic-pic-picpicpicpicpicpic . . .

The filament of the bulb started to pulse slightly with each faint chink. As Josh hung up on the other end, it flared blindingly and died, leaving the tiny red scrawl of the wire floating in darkness.

4

Running Down the Clock

Ryan slept badly that night. The invisible stranger who had sat tapping the back of his neck while he listened to the bulb die was back every time his eyes closed. Now sitting on his bed, it tip-a-tapped on the skin between the knuckles of his burnt hand. His hands moved of their own accord to brush away the tickle. His questing fingernails discovered a cluster of small bumps on his skin and scraped over them, waking a sleeping itch.

It was too hot. Whenever he got close to sleeping, the tickle would spread into wide red pools of itch bigger than his hands and pulse like the bulb in the Cavern had before it died. The bandage tightened with every throb. At last he staggered to the bathroom and peeled back its edge.

The swellings on his hand were not part of the burn. They were white and tight like new nettle stings, but swollen as dewdrops. There was a slight slit down each, like the first narrow split in a conker shell, and the slits were fringed with tiny black hairs. With each throb, the tiny hairs fluttered.

Ryan turned on the cold tap and pushed his hand into the sink. *I didn't see that, nothing could look like that; I'm asleep; if I don't look at them, then they didn't look like that* . . . There was a penny of panic in his throat.

Only when his hand was so numb with cold that it hurt did he dare take it out of the sink. Between his knuckles were clustered five white, shrivelled warts, nothing more.

See, they didn't look like that. Ryan went back to bed, resolving to tell nobody about it so that it wouldn't have happened. He settled himself with his hand dangling into a mug of water. Someone had told him once that if you were asleep and someone wet your hand, you wet the bed. He hoped it wasn't true.

The next day, his 'dreams' preyed on his mind.

'Well done,' his mum said when she saw him surrounded by his textbooks. He did not tell her that he was actually trying to bury himself in maths. The cold, smooth lines of numbers always took over his mind so completely that he couldn't concentrate on anything else.

But today even maths felt hot. Just as he was starting to concentrate, he was jarred by the phone's ring. When he answered it, there was nothing at the other end but a fuzzy grinding noise, and a high note that cut through his brain like a cheese-wire.

'It's probably somebody's fax machine,' said his mother. 'We had about three messages like that on the answering machine this morning.'

Ryan went to open the window. The leaves of the

trees outside gleamed like coins. The invisible stranger had followed him and was still tap-tap-tapping at the back of his bandaged hand.

'Ryan!' called his mother. 'Chelle on the phone for you.'

When he held the receiver to his ear, he hit a wall of incoherent words.

'Chelle, c'mon, slowly,' Ryan interrupted as kindly as he could.

'It happened again! Only this time it was really bad because Miss Gossamer was there and she *looked* at me, I'm sure she thought I was talking about her . . . and I don't even know if I was or not.' Her breath had a faint woollen rasp to it, and Ryan knew that something had worried her into asthma again.

'Chelle, *what* happened again?'

'You remember, I . . . I told you about it yesterday . . .'

With a sick, guilty feeling Ryan realized that at some point the day before Chelle must have trusted him with something important, and that he had no idea what it was.

'Well, tell me what happened *this* time,' he said gently.

'Oh, it was just the same, only we were out shopping, and then suddenly all this strange rude stuff was coming out of my mouth about somebody pushing in a queue and somebody else having a fat bottom . . .'

Then again, perhaps if I had listened to her it still wouldn't have made much sense.

'. . . and I tried to phone Josh, only when someone

picked up the phone there was this weird noise like they were standing next to a digging machine, and I couldn't hear them properly, only I could kind of hear a bit of a voice and I think it was Josh. And I think he said something about how we had to do something before we grew more heads, but at the end he just gave up and kept saying "Merrybells" over and over again, like he wanted to make sure I'd heard it.'

'He's still on aunt duty.'

'Ryan . . .' quavered Chelle, 'what do you think he meant?'

'We've got to talk to him.' Ryan hesitated. 'We'll mount a mission. To Merrybells. Let's find out if the Water Clock plan works.'

Before heading out, Ryan discreetly checked the answering machine and found that another message had been left. It was filled with the same rush of static and ear-splitting note, but there *was* a voice drowning in the grey noise.

'. . . it's not funny any more . . .' It sounded a lot like Josh, but Josh without his usual confidence.

An hour later Chelle and Ryan were gingerly climbing up the back of an enormous clock.

Josh's family lived surrounded by a garden called The Haven. At one end of the grounds stood his parents' great house, and at the other stood the little thatched cottage known as Merrybells. The Haven was more of a park than a garden, Ryan had decided. People spent time in gardens. People showed each other around parks. Gardens had spots: a sunny spot for basking, where the flowers have been crushed to the shape of a cat belly, a shady spot with ruts from a deckchair. Parks did not have spots. They had 'features'.

One of the features of The Haven was the Water Clock, designed after a famous one in a square in Munich. You could see right into its innards, where jets of gleaming water spilt down a series of tiny steps from a high vat to a great basin at its base. It was made of bronze, coated in a 'verdigris finish'. Ryan knew that 'verdigris' was the greenish colour that old metal some-times took on after years of exposure to damp and air. It was a nice-sounding word for a nice-looking sheen that was really a kind of mouldy tarnish. 'Verdigris finish' was an expensive kind of fake tarnish, and Mr Lattimer-Stone, Josh's father, was very proud of it. A big central rod pounded up and down as if it was churn-ing butter, and its motion nudged cogs, which turned big grooved cylinders, which from time to time rang bells or set little metal figures dancing merry-go-round style.

'If I ever rob a bank and get sent to Merrybells for ten life sentences,' Josh had sometimes said, 'then you two bring the getaway car and park it near where the Water Clock's built into the wall. Then you can climb up and throw me a file or a Kalashnikov or something. Only signal with a mirror first so I know you're there.'

So here they were, perched on top of the wall.

'Are you sure this is a good idea?' asked Chelle, but she did not wait for an answer. *Josh will know what to do*, she was no doubt thinking, and that thought was enough for her to be hunched in a tangle of clematis, angling a little mirror towards Merrybells. 'How am I even supposed to know if it's shining at the house? I'm just flashing it all over the place just in case – oh, there he is . . .'

Josh strode over. He wore wellingtons, and there were grass stripes like camouflage paint on his arms – presumably the result of gardening duty. His tinted sunglasses hid his eyes.

He looked behind him for a second. When he looked back up again his face was set and certain.

'It's bad. There must have been something down the well. I don't know what, but I think someone dumped something radioactive down there, and now I keep – look at this.' He flipped back the buckle of his watch-strap, and snatched it off. 'You see this? Dead.' He waved it at them, though they were too far up to make out the tiny digital screen. He flung the watch into the basin, where it hit the water with a reproachful plop.

'It's been like that ever since . . . I'm giving off some kind of . . . radiation . . . and the bulbs keep blowing and the television screen's kind of pink on one side and green on the other. And by now everybody thinks I'm *doing it on purpose*.'

'Then we'd better tell—' began Ryan.

'No!' Josh bit off his sentence. 'We're not telling anyone. I've decided. If we told them they might never let us hang out together again. We just need to take care of this ourselves. Milk's good for radioactivity. We need to drink lots of milk. And take showers. And just phone me, will you?'

A bubble rose from the water basin as if Josh's watch had been holding its breath and had finally given up. Ryan thought he could make out its tiny, ghostly face dancing beneath the surface, but there were so many lights skimming across the water that he couldn't be sure.

Ryan blinked and suddenly felt sick. The curving arc of water from the spout by his head gleamed like a twist of metal. The drops that sprang from the corners of the cogs looked heavy and he expected them to chime and clatter as they dropped. He half closed his eyes, and his lashes filled the world with soft gold discs that floated around Josh like ghostly coins. Josh nestled in the middle of this phantom treasure trove, tinted yellow pennies on his eyes.

Josh, he thought, *get out of there . . .*

'Josh!' It was Chelle's squeak. 'Get away from there!'

The rod at the heart of the clock had started juddering and jerking. The cogs of the inner works jumped in sympathy, and resumed their positions with a crunch, forgetting how they had locked smoothly together. A screw punched its way out of its socket with a 'pock!' and Josh leaped back just in time as a large metal piston fell towards him and bounced off the grass. A pipe hissed, and water sprayed outwards.

'We didn't do it!' shrieked Chelle.

'I didn't touch it!' Josh shouted at the same time.

As they scrambled backwards through the clematis,

Ryan could hear Josh running away with the watery, lolloping sound that wellingtons sometimes make. Chelle and Ryan dropped to the ground and walked quickly away, so that nobody would connect them with the sounds of the Water Clock dying behind them.

5

The Glass House

The lasagne at dinner seemed as heavy as cement, but Ryan struggled to wash it down with as much milk as he could manage.

He wasn't at all sure about milk helping with radio-activity, but the medical encyclopedia was in disguise again. His mum hated the way the dust jackets of books always got torn, so she took them off and kept them safely in a drawer. When an important guest visited she would hastily slap the jackets back on, but randomly, on to any books of the right size. At this moment, the medical encyclopedia was probably masquerading as *The Decline and Fall of the Roman Empire* or something.

All the while that he ate, Ryan was wondering about radioactivity. Maybe it would all just get better and then nobody would ever need to know . . .

At least he hadn't started making bulbs explode or TVs go green. Of course, he hadn't gone down the well like Josh . . . but he had tried to help wring out his jacket, and maybe that was why the weird warts were sprouting on his hand. The fork was warmed by his fingers and he set it down. Didn't radioactive people make things around them radioactive? He glanced with a sudden pang at his parents, talking just across the table from him.

'I . . . think I'll go to bed early.' Both parents looked up as Ryan's chair scraped backwards.

'What's the matter? Are you ill?' Ryan flinched away as his mum reached out a hand to feel his forehead for a temperature.

'I'm fine, just a bit tired.' He wished he had just said that he wanted to do some homework in his room. As he climbed the stairs he told God that God could make him radioactive just as long as it didn't hurt his parents. At the same time he knew that he was partly saying that so God would be impressed by his bravery and decide not to make him radioactive either.

He took a long shower. The soap stung the warts on his knuckles, and he could not help noticing that another small bump was starting to form on the back of his unburnt hand. He wrapped wet flannels around both and went to bed.

It was bad enough lying awake, but everything got worse when his mind became foggy with sleep and he couldn't control his thoughts. The rest of his body seemed to disappear, leaving only the nagging red itch on the back of his hand. For a while he had the sleepy notion that if he opened his eyes he would see the warts gently glowing in the dark. This was followed by a growing certainty that he had left the shower on.

He would have to go and check, because he was sure that the house was filling up with steam, and water was running down the landing into the bedrooms. Eyes still closed, he sat up and lowered his feet to the floor. The surface beneath his soles was ice cold and impossibly smooth, and with that chill moment of contact Ryan knew where he was.

He opened his eyes. Sure enough, he was back in the Glass House.

His bare feet left prints in the steamed glass of the floor, and through them he could see the living room, where his father sat on a glass sofa turning the leaves of a glass book. Ryan did not try to skate along the landing. In the bathroom he found the shower silently pouring steam and turned it off.

Above the ceiling he could see a hazy tangle of rafters, and beyond that a sky the colour of old paper. Down through the surface of the stairs he could see the translucent outline of the vacuum cleaner in the understairs cupboard. The air around him smelt like greenhouses and damp blots on walls.

In her little office his mother was cutting clippings from a newspaper sheet so transparent that the print seemed to float in the air.

Ryan's fingers slithered against the back-door handle, then found a grip. For once, the door opened.

Outside, Ryan's garden was nowhere to be seen. Instead there was a rough plain of tarmac like a school-yard or car park. The colours here were old and faded like those in Victorian photos. There was a wall at the edge of the tarmac, and Ryan had a weak-kneed edge-of-cliff feeling as if the earth just dropped away beyond it. A chain gang of trolleys gently swayed and strained against their bondage, and Ryan thought he glimpsed two or three dark figures chained among them, moving to and fro in the same restless, useless way.

He walked to the wall and pulled himself up so that his chest rested on the top and his feet dangled. He looked down and found himself staring down through the tumble-thicket of Magwhite. The trees were strange to him though, older and crusted with fungus. Yellow moss oozed from their bark like custard, dripped to the ground and grew back again as he watched. Swaying in the breeze, the twigs lost their grip on their dying leaves and then somehow caught them again.

A long way down amid the dripping trees he could see a dark dimple that could only be the well. It seemed to be drawing a spiral of shadow and leaf-whirl down into it like a ragged plughole. Beside the well someone sat almost motionless. It was a woman, Ryan thought, for the figure's hair was very long. She had her back to him, or at least he could see no gleam of a face. It seemed that on either side of her head something was in motion. Ryan thought that it must be hair snaking in the wind, for the motion was too liquid and supple to be gestures of her arms, and yet the movement was so slow that she might have been underwater. Strangely, it was only when she shrugged her head down to her chest and started to turn towards him that Ryan began to realize how large she was.

He pushed back from the wall and spun around. He could still see his house, with the tiny coloured shapes of his parents inside it, but it was a fragile glass toy in the middle of a creeping, dripping forest.

He felt one of the wandering newspapers wrap itself around his calf, and the shock of the touch woke him.

Ryan had a ritual for making sure he was awake after nightmares. He blinked hard three times, clenching his eyes tight each time so that he could not fall back into sleep without knowing it. Then he picked out the arrow-slit of dark silver sky between the curtains, the luminous display on his alarm clock. It was not enough.

He got up and went to the bathroom, let the light fill his world with colour, saw the soap glisten creamily in the belly of its holder on the bath-side. It was still not enough. There was now a slight tingle in the knuckles of his unburnt hand, and when he pulled off the flannel to stare at them there seemed to be new tiny bumps pushing up under the skin.

Ryan sat up all night on the window sill, reading by the growing daylight that fell in through the curtains. By morning he felt queasy with sleeplessness.

When he came down to breakfast his mother took one look at him and told him to go back to bed, he wasn't well. She brought him up a soft-boiled egg with soldiers, and a grapefruit. She'd used a knife to cut the grapefruit in half with a zigzag line, and put a glacé cherry on top. Ryan felt guilty, but not too guilty to eat it. He knew his mother well enough to guess that she was worried about him but had to go out, and the zigzag grapefruit was meant to make up for that.

It felt strange sitting in bed all day, his stomach turning over and over like a tumble-dryer. He almost started to wonder whether he might be ill after all.

Ryan's father did not look up from his crossword when Ryan came into the living room fully dressed.

'I'm feeling a lot better,' Ryan explained quietly. 'I thought I might go out in the garden.'

His father looked up blankly for a moment. 'Good.' There was a pause while his brain hopped back and actually heard what Ryan had said. 'Good,' he said again, with more sincerity.

As Ryan's hand closed around the back-door handle the cold of the metal chilled him with the memory of his dream. For a moment, he was afraid that he would find himself looking out on a windswept tarmac plain in sepia shades.

The door opened to show the garden, his garden. He looked over his shoulder, and his home had not paled into glass, but somehow he kept feeling as if it had each time he turned his back on it. And that just beyond the fence, there might be a windswept stretch of tarmac, or the litter-tangled slopes of the Magwhite wood . . .

He walked to the end of the garden, through the gate and down the familiar footpath that led along the backs of all the adjoining gardens. But perhaps the end of the footpath would be where the painted page ended and the strangeness began . . .

No, there was the road, sweeping under the bridge in the most sensible manner possible. He would not go far, Ryan told himself, just up on to the bridge so that he could look out and see that there were no fences where his world suddenly stopped. There was a man up on the bridge, washing graffiti off the cement with a high-powered hose. Ryan would wait until he had finished, slip up to the bridge, then go home.

Under the bridge the road ran between two concrete walls. On one wall someone had pasted a poster of a young woman sitting at a table. She had long straight hair that shone in the way that hair only shines in adverts, as if it was polished wood. Her dress was green. She was smiling and her eyes were lowered, as if some-one had said something that embarrassed her but made her happy at the same time. On the other side of the table one could just see the edge of a man's face and shoulder. From the bulge of his cheek you could tell he too was smiling.

Water from the hose above was running down through the cracks in the concrete and over the poster. Ryan was just turning away when the woman in the green dress moved. She dropped her chin to her chest, then angled her head away from the smiling poster man until she was facing Ryan. She started to open her eyes.

Her eyes were fountains. Ryan could not see if there were actually eyeballs there at all, the water gushed so fiercely from between her lids. Her lips trembled and parted, and water rushed from her mouth too, as if she was a churchyard gargoyle.

Ryan made a small noise. He was not sure what it was meant to be. It choked up out of him as if his own lungs were full of water.

A terrible bubbling sound came from the poster woman's throat, and Ryan realized with horror that she was trying to speak through the torrent.

'Thlphlllay . . .'

'No . . .' It was all that Ryan could manage. He felt as if everything inside his chest had vanished. *No, make this not be happening . . .*

'Schlllaayyyy . . .'

It was only when she held out one hand, fingers spread, that Ryan understood the word. *Stay*. He realized that his hands were gripped in his own trouser pockets, as if holding his legs motionless. Out of the corner of his eye he could see the sunlit road beyond the bridge shadow, but it seemed as unreachable as a vista on a cinema screen.

'Phlook . . . fomm . . . mlee . . .'

'I don't . . .' Ryan shook his head, terrified.

'Phtook . . . flrom . . . mee . . .'

Took from me. Was that it?

'Phlphllllischlesh.'

'I don't . . . I can't underst . . .' Ryan's words came out in broken, husky squeaks. He covered his eyes with his hands and clenched them tight into fists. There was a sting as the bandage dragged back from the tautened skin. Something between the knuckles on both his hands quivered and loosened, and then suddenly, despite his covered eyes, Ryan could see the poster woman more clearly than ever before.

She was swinging her head angrily from side to side in a slow snaking motion, and her hair followed the movement of her head draggingly, like reeds in the tug of a wave. The poster man had vanished now, and yellow leaves were tumbling past her, fumbling across her face. Behind her a soupy darkness was striped with pale tree trunks. The woman turned to face him again, and Ryan recognized her. It was the figure from his dream, the one that he had seen sitting in the woods of Magwhite.

He felt sure that if he ran she would drag herself dripping from her poster and come after him while the world around him turned to sepia. She would walk through his parents without even seeing them, shatter the walls of his bedroom like glass and find him.

And with his strange new sight Ryan suddenly noticed that an ooze of darkness was bubbling up through the leaves at her feet. Beneath the oily surface of the black water he glimpsed a dull, coppery gleam. Coins, coins, hundreds of them, some bright, some verdigris-dappled, some blackened almost beyond all recognition.

There must have been something down the well, Josh had said.

Something down the well . . . The figure in his dream had been sitting near the mouth of the well . . .

Took from me . . .

Oh no . . .

'We'll get you all the coins you want!' Ryan cried. 'We will, we'll get you better ones than the ones we took . . .'

'Noooo! Hhwwhphhhhischessss . . .'

Ryan realized that his own lips were pursed, trying to help by mouthing the bubbling word. She opened her mouth again and released a long, hissing waterfall of words, pointing at him as she spoke. She was giving an order. She finished, and waited. She waited for him to agree.

'I can't . . . I can't understand, I'm trying but I can't . . . I can't . . .'

Her mouth made angry shapes, and water spattered Ryan's shoes, his T-shirt, the backs of his hands. She leaned forward with a menacing hiss.

'All right! All right!' Ryan clenched his fists uselessly into his eye sockets.

A sudden roar at his back made him jump. He looked over his shoulder in time to see a moped slice through the darkness under the bridge before curling away down the daylit road. When he looked back at the wall, the woman sat flat and demure in her poster, her paper face darkened and rippled by the dying trickle of water from above.

Slowly, he stretched out his trembling fingers. For two cold, dark seconds he stared at his knuckles, and at what the warts had become. Then, at long last, he remembered how to run.

6

Crook's Baddock

'Get a grip – there's a snuffly yelpy noise coming from your end. Is that you or the phone? It'd better be the phone.'

'Josh, listen, it was this woman in a picture, but she moved and there was water coming out of her eyes, like it did with my reflection before, but much worse. And it's my *hands*, Josh – the warts've gone normal again now but right after I could see what they were and they're *eyes*! I've got *eyes* growing on my *hands*, it's just mostly they're closed . . .' Ryan was curled on the window sill in the lounge, behind the curtain. From his hiding place he could watch the garden path to make sure nothing was making its way from the gate.

'Hey.' Josh's voice was sharp but not unkind. 'C'mon. Don't lose the plot.'

'Josh, *it's the well*. There's something down the well, and it wants . . . I don't know what it wants, I couldn't understand it because of all the water . . .'

'I went down the well. There was nothing living

down there. Just some old wrappers and muck in the water.'

'She was there, Josh, even if you couldn't see her . . . Josh, this is real, I swear . . . it's . . . we're not radio-active, she's *doing something to us* . . .'

The line made strange churning noises while Josh thought.

'Did you catch *any* of what she said?'

'I don't know. Bits. There was something at the end that sounded like . . . Crook's Baddock.'

'Crook's Baddock. Ryan, have you told anybody else about this?'

'No . . .'

'Then don't. We're going to sort this out. I'm going to find a way out of here, and Chelle and me will come and get you. We'll get a bus to Crook's Baddock, and on the way you'll tell us everything that happened, and when we get there we'll have a plan, OK?'

And, sure enough, an hour later the three of them were on a 'homework research trip' on the Crook's Baddock tour bus, and Ryan was recounting his ordeal blow by blow. And this was where everything went wrong.

'You said *yes* to her?' Josh asked for the sixth time.

'I told you how it was.' Ryan felt hot and miserable as he stared out through the bus window. 'I thought she was going to throw a flood or something . . .'

'But you don't say yes! Idiot! You don't agree to

things like that! You know what you've done, don't you? You've only gone and promised this whole . . . wet-spooky-puking-god-thing . . . that we'll all go and do something – and we don't even know what it is!'

Chelle for once said nothing. Her expression was damp and crumpled, as if she'd left it out in the rain overnight.

'But I didn't!' protested Ryan. 'I didn't say anything about you two . . .'

'Oh, wake up!' The seat back huffed as Josh dropped his weight back against it. 'Ryan, she must know about all three of us, but she only appeared to you. Don't you get it? She picked you as a representative.'

And that, Ryan realized, was the real problem. Josh was angry that someone else had made a decision for the group, but he was far, far angrier that he had not been the one asked.

'It's just because of these,' Ryan said quickly and apologetically, running his fingertips over his knuckles. There were now undeniably three new warts on his unbandaged hand. 'It's not like I'm a leader or anything. She just wanted one of us to have these so they could see her properly and take her orders, I'll bet. '

'Ooh, that's really creepy and horrible.' Chelle shuddered, and then brought herself up short. 'Oh no, I didn't mean it to sound like that, I just meant to say, *eyes* on your *hands* – that's really, really weird. In a *horrible* kind of way.'

Ryan swallowed, fighting back a memory of his

knuckles blistering with oozing, greenish-brown orbs, a little star of slick light trembling in each.

'Yeah,' he murmured. 'Look, maybe she just decided to affect us in different ways. So with you, Josh, there's all this business with phones and TVs and watches going weird around you . . .'

'Yeah, right,' snarled Josh, while Chelle stared nervously at her feet. 'She wants someone to take her orders, and somebody else who can make toasters go insane. *That* makes sense. You can't promise things for other people, you know. Chelle and me don't even have to be here.'

It was about the third time Josh had said this, and yet he was still on the bus as it entered the old town.

Crook's Baddock was only a handful of miles north of Magwhite. However, unlike Magwhite, which had the outskirt shabbiness of many villages entangled on the edges of Guildley's sprawl, Crook's Baddock lay amid true countryside, nestling pristinely among soft, duvet-fold hills.

To begin with, Crook's Baddock had been just a small weaving village. Some of the oldest houses still survived, with surprised thatched eyebrows above their windows and doors, but now they had little signs outside saying how old they were, and history leaflets in brackets on the wall. Most of them had become museums, with tiny model looms inside, and posters about weaving and dyeing. Nearly everything that had not become a museum seemed to have become a tea shop.

Once a year, towards the end of the summer holidays, coachloads of children were brought down for the Crook's Baddock Festival and forced to look at hundreds of spinning wheels and make sketches of timber-frame houses.

Across the aisle a girl of about five, half buried under her mother's shopping, watched Josh with frightened fascination, her lower lip pulled down at the corner by one tiny, curling finger. Josh noticed her and stared back for a bit, then pushed his sunglasses down his nose and bulged his eyes as if the little girl was the most alarming thing he had ever seen. The free corner of the little girl's mouth twitched, then turned up. For some reason small children tended to like Josh, however outrageously he behaved.

'Do you know what you're looking for?' Now that Josh was happily occupied by a new audience, Chelle had shuffled a little closer to Ryan. 'I mean, did she say anything else, I mean, any more instructions . . .'

'Ki-i-i-nd of . . . Something like, "Hlaarrlley Daarrrridphum."'

'Harry Daddy what?'

'More like, Hhhlllaar. Leee. Daarrrrid. Phum.'

'Kind of hhhhlll . . .'

'Hhhhllleeeugh . . .' Josh joined in suddenly, making it sound like a vomiting noise. He grinned. In his usual unpredictable way, he seemed to have recovered his temper in less than a minute. 'No, go on, show us again.' Ryan demonstrated, and the other two tried to imitate him. The three of them rasped and gurgled like coffee percolators until Chelle could no longer breathe from giggling.

'Do you think . . .' Chelle began when she'd recovered, 'do you think we could get some rolls and things, just small ones, and go to the park maybe? Last time there was that stand by the park which did crushed ice and lime, only they just had paper straws and I hated that because they go soggy and tear – but you can't just drink crushed ice because it makes your teeth hurt so you have to wait for it to melt and then it goes all funny like the goo from ice lollies when you lick the wrapper and that's ten pound seven don't give me a tip then you mean-faced old harridan . . .'

Ryan stiffened. Chelle's voice had become much louder and had a new, hard edge. The accent was not her own.

'. . . what have they been doing with this table, playing football on it, we'll need another tablecloth oh God it's Moaning Minnie and the Banshee child back again for chocolate yes yes I know chocolate with double cream for the screaming little horror I've served you a hundred times and you don't even remember me do you . . .'

'Chelle?' Ryan stared at her.

Chelle's eyes were wide and panicky. She shook her head slightly but her mouth kept moving, spilling out words.

'Chelle, get a grip!' Josh leaned forward and peered into her face. 'Hey, Chelle! Hey!'

What was it that Chelle had been trying to tell Ryan

the day before? Something about words pouring uncontrolled out of her mouth?

'. . . Oh that God-awful child's using the coffee pot as a gong again TAKE THE TEASPOON AWAY FROM YOUR CHILD TAKE THE TEASPOON AWAY FROM YOUR CHILD BEFORE I DO SOMEBODY A MISCHIEF!' Chelle was shouting now, her face turning bright red as everybody else in the bus turned to stare at her.

Hastily Josh pressed the button for the bell. As the bus slowed at a stop Ryan and Josh seized an arm each and guided Chelle to the doors.

'Thank you!' Josh called to the bus driver with manic enthusiasm.

'Sorry!' called Ryan as they reached the pavement.

'FOR GOD'S SAKE USE A NAPKIN!' Chelle shouted as the doors closed.

'What do we do?' hissed Ryan.

'I don't know . . . walk her somewhere until it stops happening. And stuff something in her mouth.' They had to crumple up several leaflets about the Crook's Baddock wool trade and bung them in before Chelle's words became truly muffled. 'Give us a nudge if you start to choke or anything.'

After the relative darkness of the bus, the sunlit street was brilliant. Outside a green-painted pub, a fleet of motorcycles dazzled Ryan with the shine of two dozen wing mirrors. Next door, an ice-cream sign swung outside a pale pink tea shop with curtains printed to look like patchwork.

'So what the hell was that? Is she picking up local radio or something?' asked Josh.

Chelle shook her head. She waved her hands in frustration.

'How many words?' asked Ryan.

Chelle held up one finger, then tugged her ear lobe to mime 'sounds like'. Then she hesitated and made a vague clutching gesture at the air.

'You're rubbish at charades, Chelle, don't even bother. Write it down. Got a pen, Ryan? C'mon, we'll go find one.'

When they pushed open the door of the tea shop it struck a trail of wind chimes which hung so low that Josh had to duck beneath them.

'Here.' Josh put some money in Ryan's hand. 'Go get us three milkshakes and a pen – the guy at the till is bound to have one – and I'll look after the Amazing Mouth here.'

All the tables in the tea shop had plastic-coated table-cloths patterned in the same bright patchwork colours as the curtains. Behind the counter stood a thin young man with a floppy, blond fringe and shaky hands.

'Three milkshakes . . . take a seat while I make them.'

Ryan borrowed a spare pen from a pot by the till and returned to the table.

Fortunately, no one seemed to have noticed Chelle's strange appearance. A toddler a few tables away was trying to sing along to the radio and was attracting far more attention, and annoyance, from the rest of the customers.

But as Ryan pushed a biro and napkin towards Chelle, her eyes were mad with surprise and excitement. She pointed towards the man at the till.

'What?'

She snatched up a teaspoon and waved it triumphantly in her friends' faces, then pointed across at the songful toddler. They stared at the infant in bewilderment, and then realization dawned. The little boy had a teaspoon gripped in his fist, and was using it to beat time on the coffee pot in a loud and infuriating way.

'That's what you were talking about before, wasn't it?' whispered Ryan.

Chelle scribbled a few words and pushed the napkin towards him. It read, 'Man behind the counter – his thoughts.'

'You're . . . speaking his thoughts?'

Chelle bounced ecstatically and touched herself on the nose. Charades language: right on the nose.

'We've got to get out of here and talk about this,' Josh said under his breath. 'Looks like you're right, Ryan – the well-thing's changing all of us in different ways. Now we just need to work out why she needs Chelle to be able to read minds.'

On Ryan's suggestion they left what they hoped was a generous tip even though they hadn't actually had their drinks. They waited until they were out of earshot of the tea shop before pulling the sodden wad from Chelle's mouth.

'. . . one decent tip of the day anyway,' she began, sounding somewhat mollified. 'Stuff this, though, that sounds like Sarah coming in at the back. I'm due a fag break . . .'

Ryan glanced over his shoulder and saw the man come out of the tea shop behind them and pull a crumpled pack of cigarettes from his apron pocket. Then he sauntered over towards the front of the neighbouring pub and stood gazing around him while the breeze dragged a streamer of smoke from his cigarette.

'. . . Suzuki toys over there . . .' murmured Chelle quietly. For the first time her borrowed tone of voice sounded almost happy.

Josh stopped dead.

'Oh, I'm a genius,' he muttered.

'What?' Ryan was still trying to lead Chelle away.

'Look how many motorbike stands there are out there,' Josh whispered. 'The local bikers must come to that pub all the time.'

'. . . Triumph,' murmured Chelle softly. 'Thought I recognized the sound of the engine. And look at that, 1000 cc, what a beast. Honda 500, needs new tyres by the look of it . . .'

'And I bet he comes out here every fag break he gets. I know I would.' Josh grinned. 'You see what that is over there? Behind the yellow Kawasaki? C'mon, you can't miss it. What was it that the well-thing was trying to say again?'

'. . . Harley-Davidson . . .' whispered Chelle in tones of love.

7

A Dream in Steel

For about ten seconds all three of them felt extremely pleased with themselves. Then the feeling faded.

'I don't know what it means,' said Josh, answering the unspoken question, 'but I'm going to find out. You two stay here and listen to his thoughts.' Before Ryan could say anything, Josh was striding away with his hands in his pockets towards the man from the tea shop. The man was busy brushing cigarette ash from his limp orange T-shirt and did not see Josh until he was quite close.

'. . . that's one of those kids who were in earlier.' Chelle's borrowed voice sounded anxious and uncomfortable. 'Hope he hasn't come to beg a fag, I always feel so feeble saying no . . . got the same sort of face as Donny Sparks back at school, always made me buy cigarettes for him because I was taller . . .' Tea-shop Man was staring determinedly at the end of his cigarette and looking nervous. Now Ryan could imagine him as a loose, gangly teenager being bullied into a shop by a smaller boy. It made Ryan feel sorry for him and rather guilty, as if he had been reading someone's private diary.

Josh pushed his sunglasses up on to his forehead, grinned and said something to Tea-shop Man. Chelle's monologue paused and then resumed.

'What does he mean, which bike is mine? Does he think I look like a biker?' The borrowed voice sounded surprised now, but pleased. 'So that's it, lucky kid. Having an older brother with a Harley . . . Seems OK . . . Perhaps his brother would let . . .'

'I'll get a pen ready in case he says something useful,' sighed Ryan.

'. . . good to talk to someone who actually cares about . . . intelligent questions . . . mmmphwpphh . . .'

Ryan looked up from his scribbling to realize that Chelle has pushed the leaflets back into her mouth. A female traffic warden was hovering nearby wearing an expression of concern. Wishing that all traffic wardens were as cold and uncaring as they were supposed to be, Ryan took Chelle firmly by the sleeve and led her further down the street so that they could huddle at the window of an antique shop.

'. . . if I had to choose a Harley-Davidson, it'd have to be a Road King Classic,' Chelle continued in hushed, happy tones, as they pretended interest in pearl-handled cutlery and pink-faced porcelain milkmaids. 'Though the Ultra . . . what does it matter, I'll never get one. It's a dream. That's the thing about a Harley, it's a dream in steel. If you're sitting on a Harley, the horizons must look eager, as if they were itching to swoop towards you . . . I'd give just about anything just to feel . . .'

After glancing up and down the street, Ryan started jotting Chelle's comments on a napkin.

'. . . I could tell this kid about that competition in the latest issue of *Silverwing*,' Chelle went on, 'the one with the Ultra as first prize . . . not that *I'll* be entering. Even if I won, Mum would never let me keep a bike, let alone a beast like a Harley . . .'

In the shop window several prints of Victorian posters were spread out in a fan shape. Ryan glanced at the uppermost poster for a moment, and as he did so he seemed to feel something click into place in his brain.

It was a print of an old drawing, at the centre of which a man in ragged, old-fashioned clothes stood bent backwards in dismay. He was lifting a small round something out of his tankard, and staring at it aghast. Beside him a puff-chested, moustached soldier was pointing with jeering triumph at the object in the old man's hand.

The caption's crumbly woodblock letters read: 'Slipping Him the King's Shilling: Liberty Lost for the Price of a Pint Pot'. The man had been tricked into picking up a tankard with the King's Shilling hidden in the bottom of it. Now he'd be dragged away to fight . . . Ryan remained motionless, as if moving too suddenly would dislodge his thoughts from their new positions.

'. . . well, that's the last of the cigarette,' Chelle said reluctantly. 'I suppose I'd better get back to the till . . .

Hang on though, that must be the kid's brother coming out of the pub there . . .'

Ryan turned sharply. Four men in bulky leathers had emerged from the pub and were approaching the motorbikes. One of them straddled the red and black Harley and started putting on his helmet. *Oh no, Josh,* thought Ryan, *you told him your brother owned that bike, didn't you?*

Josh pushed his sunglasses down in front of his eyes, possibly to hide his expression. He gave a long upwards stretch with his arms, then brought his hands down to clasp them behind his head. The gesture always made him appear relaxed and usually meant that he was thinking fast. Then he said something with a grin, turned and sauntered off in the direction of the bikers.

The biker on the Harley was fastening his gloves as Josh drew close. For a few minutes they stood talking, then the Harley man slowly swung his leg back over the machine to stand beside it and heaved it on to its stand again. Then he stood back with a hand on the body-work to steady the bike as Josh climbed on to it, getting into the high seat with some difficulty. Josh waved at Tea-shop Man, who still watched from a distance. He waved to Josh and walked back in through the door of the tea shop.

'. . . idiot idiot idiot I'm such an idiot . . .' muttered Chelle under her breath. 'I'd only look like an idiot if I went to talk to them what do I know about bikes except what I read I've never even ridden one . . .'

Ryan stared back at Josh in mounting disbelief. In a

few short minutes, Josh seemed to have become the bikers' mascot. They dropped a crash helmet on to his head, laughing when it slid down past his chin and wobbled around. At last Josh climbed off the Harley and strolled back towards Ryan and Chelle. One of the bikers started up his bike, and the engine gave off a tearing rak-ak-ak-ak as if the air was being beaten flat by rapid hammers. Another engine lifted its voice, and another, and another, and then four motorbikes curved carefully down to join the main road, where they became roaring coloured streaks and vanished.

'Did you get all his thoughts?' asked Josh when he rejoined the pair on the pavement.

'Most of them,' answered Ryan.

'. . . we're all out of mustard on this table I'll swear everyone goes away with sachets in their pockets just to make more work for me . . .' added Chelle conversationally.

Josh raised his eyes to heaven.

'Let's go. We need to find somewhere we can talk properly. Where *all* of us can talk properly,' he added meaningfully.

A couple of streets from the tea shop, Chelle abruptly 'lost reception'. One moment she was voicing Tea-shop Man's annoyance with a fly at the window, the next she was in control of her own mouth again, at least in so far as she ever was. Twenty minutes after this all three of them were sprawled in one of the parks, playing Jenga with cooling chips.

'You told him you were there with your brother and he owned the Harley, didn't you?' Ryan was lying on his stomach on the grass and wheedling a chip from the unconvincing Jenga tower. He usually won through a maddening patience that the others yearned to disqualify.

'Course. Had to get him talking about it, see if he gave away anything useful.' Josh grinned. 'Might even be true. We don't know, do we? I might have a brother with a Harley-Davidson.' Ryan was never sure why Josh always grinned when he made sidelong references to his own adoption. Probably just Josh wanting to make people uncomfortable, as usual.

'And he let you sit on it,' breathed Chelle, still impressed.

'Yeah.' Josh's grin grew broader.

'Poor Tea-shop Man, he was so jealous,' Chelle said. 'His thoughts felt all different when he was thinking about the Harley-Davidson, all strokey instead of pointy . . .'

'I got his name too, when we were in the tea shop,' added Ryan. 'Will Wruthers. He had it on a little badge.'

'Speed it up, Ryan. At this rate the chips'll evolve and start playing Jenga with us.'

Ryan tweaked his chip free triumphantly, held it up for general approval, then ate it ceremonially.

Josh took his turn next, found a chip jutting from the

'tower', hesitated for a fraction of a second, then yanked it free with daredevil recklessness, showering chips into Chelle's abandoned drink.

'Bollocks, they always stick when they go cold.' As loser, Josh let the others 'tidy' the 'rubble' of the tower into their mouths and sat watching Ryan narrowly. 'You've got that little flat voice on again. You've worked something out, haven't you? You've got something,' he added with an odd air of pride.

'I might have. Yes. I *think* I've got something. But . . . I'm not sure you want it.'

They both looked at him expectantly.

'All right. I think it's like the King's Shilling.' Ryan glanced at the others briefly and saw no sign of comprehension. 'You know, in history people joining the army were given a shilling and if they took it that was like promising to be in the King's army, and they couldn't get out of it. And it didn't matter if they took it by accident, not knowing what it was, they still had to go and fight. They couldn't just give it back. It wasn't the coin, it was what it meant. And, well, we kind of did the same thing.'

'And what was that?' asked Josh quietly, all sign of mockery gone.

Ryan took a deep breath and held his hands out in front of him, palms towards each other, as if he was holding the space between them steady. Doing that often helped him arrange his thoughts into calm, straight lines.

'OK, wishing wells. People come and drop in a coin

and make a wish. That's what they're for. So . . . there's this thing living down the well, a well spirit, and she gets given all these coins with wishes attached, and maybe she's supposed to grant them in exchange. And then we come along and take the coins . . .' Ryan gave the others a wince of a smile. 'There was this word the well-thing kept saying over and over, but it just sounded like she was sneezing through soup. Only I'm starting to think it might have been "wishes".'

Josh gave a sudden low groan as if stricken with indigestion and doubled up so that his forehead rested on the grass. Clearly he had guessed what Ryan was about to say.

'I think . . .' Ryan continued. 'I think when the well accepts the coins that's like promising to grant the wishes . . . and I think us taking the coins means . . . that *we* have to grant them.'

8

How to Make a Miracle

A few seconds passed in horrified silence.

'What . . . all of them?' squeaked Chelle. 'Can't we just . . . give her some more coins instead?'

With a shudder, Ryan remembered the Well Spirit's hissing response to that suggestion. 'I think that's a definite no,' he murmured.

'But we *can't* grant all the wishes – there were *dozens* of coins, and we've only got three weeks before school starts, and they ought to have a warning sign over the well cos just anybody could pick out some coins by accident . . . maybe the council have to do something . . .'

Josh heaved himself up into a sitting position with a resolute snort of breath. 'All right, everyone shut up and let's think. She sent us to Crook's Baddock, right? And it must have been to find old Wet Will.'

'He must have dropped a coin in the Magwhite well,' said Ryan. 'I mean, you're not reading everybody's thoughts, are you, Chelle? If I've got extra eyes so I can take orders from the well-thing, maybe your mind-reading is so we can work out what the wishes are and how to grant them. So you're probably picking up his thoughts because we stole his wish-coin.'

'Yeah, and I don't need to ask what he wished for,' Josh muttered. 'Could have been worse, though, couldn't it? Could have wished for a moon sandwich. At least Harley-Davidsons exist.'

'Do you think we could just maybe wheel a Harley-Davidson from one of those stands outside the pub and kind of lean it up against the tea-shop door?' asked Chelle.

'Doubt it. He wants a Harley. Finding one on the step, then getting beaten up by an angry biker who thinks he's trying to nick it, isn't really the same, is it?'

Josh swung his legs around in front of him on the grass, then held out both hands as if gripping invisible handlebars. With an expression of concentration he clenched an unseen something with his left hand and moved his right thumb as if pressing a button. Then he tapped his left foot on the turf, and twisted his right hand slowly back on itself. 'That guy at the pub showed me how to start up his motorbike. Just trying to remember the controls in case we need to nick one and change the number plates.' He grinned as Chelle's eyes became pools of awe and fear. 'Relax, I'm mostly joking.'

'Even if we had one, we couldn't just drop by and give it to him,' added Ryan. 'He'd probably call the police.'

'What about . . .' Chelle hesitated. 'What about that competition in the magazine that he was thinking about entering, only he hasn't because he doesn't think his mum will let him have a motorbike, well, what if we entered the competition with his name and he won, then maybe it would count, wouldn't it?'

Ryan was looking for a kind way of pointing out the hopelessness of this plan, but then he wondered if perhaps it was the least silly idea they had had so far. It probably wouldn't work, but it wouldn't see them all taken away in a police car either.

'We'd need him to win.' Josh's voice was speculative, not scornful.

'But we can't *make* him win, can we?' Ryan pointed out.

'I dunno. Can we?' Josh narrowed his eyes.

Silverwing stood out from the other magazines thanks to its bright yellow cover, and the black and silver title with wings built into the 'g'.

Once they were back out on the street, they flicked through it until they found the competition page.

'I was hoping we'd just have to cut out a coupon and put his address on it,' whispered Chelle. 'I didn't know there'd be so many questions . . .'

'How big was the engine of the 1902 Harley-Davidson prototype?' read Ryan.

'We can look that up somewhere,' Josh murmured uncertainly.

'I suppose we could guess. I mean we could just say, "quite big" or "big as a coconut" and that might be close enough . . .'

'Don't be thick, they want it in cc.' Josh's neck was flushing as he looked further down the page.

'What are all those?' Chelle prodded a sequence of fuzzy photographs with her fingertip.

'Match these photos with the correct model names.' Ryan looked at the speckled pictures. One of them looked like a bicycle with extra bits stuck on, and a couple seemed to be close-ups of parts of engines. 'How are we supposed to look that up?'

'There's a bit at the bottom too,' Chelle said. 'They want a written piece about why you want to win the motorbike. But we could just put some of that stuff Will Wruthers was thinking for that, couldn't we?'

'Not for five hundred words,' Josh muttered. 'Useless idiot – why didn't he just enter the competition him-self?'

The traffic lights next to the pavement where they stood flickered slightly, and the bleep of the pelican crossing dropped a semitone. Josh did not seem to notice.

'Because he's worried he'll win,' Ryan said quietly. 'And then he'd have a Harley and he'd have to tell his mum he wanted to keep it.'

'He should just tell her to lump it.'

'Yes, but he's afraid of her. You can tell from the sound of his thoughts. I think he's really scared of lots of people he seems angry about. He's even a bit scared of you, Josh.' Ryan regretted letting the words out as soon as he saw Josh's face. He felt as if he had betrayed a confidence.

'Give me the magazine,' said Josh. 'I'm going back. I'm gonna make him fill it in.'

'How?' Ryan said nervously.

'Don't look so scared! Go wait for me at the Cross.' Josh stalked off with the magazine under his arm, and Ryan obediently followed Chelle across the cobbled square to the bus stop at Market Cross.

'Do you think we should go back and like maybe listen in and see what Will Wruthers is thinking?' Chelle asked suddenly. 'I mean, I could, it's OK, I really don't mind . . .'

Ryan looked up at Chelle and was suddenly startled by how happy she seemed. His mind had been so full of ways to work miracles, he had not noticed her pleased smile. The only other time he'd seen her look quite so happy was during a cricket match in the school field the year before. As usual she'd been exiled to fielding out by the fence. But somehow a ball had curved her way. She'd put up a hand to shield her eyes from the sun, ducked in panic and then straightened to look at the ball cupped in her hand, with a disbelieving smile. *I helped*, said her smile. *I was useful.*

'Maybe in a bit,' he answered gently. 'If Josh doesn't come back soon.'

Josh came back half an hour later without the magazine. 'It Is Done,' he said in a low-pitched voice as he approached them at the bus stop, the capital letters clearly audible.

'What did you . . . ?'

'It wasn't easy. I had to wait till the tea shop was

empty. Then I went over to the counter like this . . .' Josh made a little backwards motion of his shoulders, like a gunfighter limbering for a draw. 'Dropped the magazine *slap!* in front of him, and put a pen next to his hand. And then I grabbed him by his weedy tie and told him, Either the answers or your brains are going to be on this magazine, it's your choice . . .'

There was a devastated silence.

'. . . and you two are beautiful,' continued Josh. 'You've got no idea what you look like; you both look like . . .' He dragged off his sunglasses, bulged his eyes and dropped his jaw in dead-carp astonishment. 'Yeah, really, I forced him at fork-point to fill in the answers, and then *Matrix*-kicked him through a wall . . .'

Chelle's open mouth managed a single squeak of outrage, and Ryan remembered how to breathe again.

'No, course I didn't . . .' Josh broke off, possessed by one of his convulsive fits of silent laughter. The other two had to wait while he laughed into his fist. 'What happened was, I went up and sat at the table right at the front, with the magazine open in front of me. And he could see I was putting answers in in pencil, and he kept turning his head upside down trying to see what the questions were, and what answers I was putting.

'And he could see I'd put things like the prototype engine being "about as big as a coconut". And he started to twitch, like this.' Josh gave the eyelid of one eye a neurotic, twitching flutter. 'I swear, I thought he was going to grab me round the neck, wrestle the pencil out of my hand and fill it in right.

'So then I looked bored, and asked him if he'd seen the competition. And I said, Ooh look, the twenty best entries get to go to the Golden Oak Rally in Guildley, pity I'm too young to enter. And he jumped right over the counter to take a look at the questions. Well, he almost did – you could see he wanted to.'

'And you left it with him?'

'Yeah. He's hooked now he's started.' Josh yawned. As far as he was concerned, the matter was already over. 'And if anyone can rant on about Harleys for five hundred words, it's him, right?'

'What if he doesn't . . . ?' Ryan stopped himself. 'I mean, nice one, Josh, but what if he doesn't send the answers in?'

'Bet you he does.' Josh peered at Ryan and clicked his fingers in front of the younger boy's frown. 'C'mon, let it go. We'll come back in a week and see if Wet Will's heard anything. Forget it for now.'

Perhaps Josh was right, Ryan thought. Josh seemed able to snatch up any sort of a plan and trust himself to it full throttle, like James Bond surfing down a snow slope on half a door or someone's cello case. Ryan had a mind full of 'what ifs'. His brain never wanted to let go of something when he could feel the holes in it.

'Come, my friends,' Josh announced in deep, super-hero tones as their bus approached. 'Let us leave. Our Work Here Is Done.'

'The "big as a coconut" bit was my idea, wasn't it?' said Chelle as she followed him on to the bus.

*

Josh insisted that they ride on the top of the open-top bus back to Guildley. They blinked in the breeze and found the pigeons skittering after a paper cup strangely funny. They would be back a little later than promised, but no parents would mind. Crook's Baddock was the very opposite of Magwhite. Parents thought that if you went to Crook's Baddock and breathed in, you would come back better educated.

At Guildley Market stop they got out, and Josh revealed that he had been hatching another plan.

'C'mon, we're going back to Ryan's bridge. The one with the poster.'

'What? Why?' The sun above Ryan lost its warmth.

'We're going to report in, tell her we're doing what she wants. Maybe get some info on our next mission.' Josh paused, seeing the look on Ryan's face. 'Look,' he said more quietly, 'she's going to have orders for you sooner or later, right? Do you want her popping out of walls when you're not expecting it? No? C'mon then.'

I don't think I can make myself do this, thought Ryan as he turned his feet towards the bridge. *But perhaps I can just . . . let go, like Josh, just let the plan happen quickly so I don't have time to think.* He set his face hard and dropped into a trot so that he was ahead of the others, and they wouldn't see his face.

'Hey.' Josh caught up with Ryan. He lowered his voice so that it couldn't be heard by Chelle. 'It's paper really, OK? Remember that. If she tries anything, I'll tear her face off.'

Ryan nodded, dry-mouthed.

The sun was lower than it had been that morning, and the bridge shadow had swung away to one side, allowing one corner of the poster to be illuminated. Ryan could get quite close to it before he had to step from lighted pavement to shadowed ground, and felt his steps falter. Josh, of course, moved past him straight into the shadow to stand directly before the poster. Ryan had assumed that Chelle would hover out in the sun, so he was surprised and grateful to see that she was at his side.

Josh unscrewed his plastic bottle of lemonade and peered at the poster.

'This one?'

'It wasn't so wrinkled before. I guess that's the water and maybe the heat.' Ryan's heart was still beating furiously, but now he was feeling sick with a mixture of relief and embarrassment.

'What did you do to set it off before?' Josh leaned forward and held his face so close to the poster that Ryan took several involuntary steps towards him into the shadow. He had suddenly imagined watery hands thrusting out to grab Josh's head.

'Nothing. I just stood in front of it. Like we are now.'

'Was anything else different?'

'Well . . . it was wet.'

Josh took a long drink from his bottle, paused for a second, and then threw the rest of the lemonade over the poster.

'Josh!'

'You wanted it wet. It's wet. Hey, do you think now

she'll start pouring with lemonade instead of water? We could get some cups and set up a stall or something.' A long pause followed, during which little runnels of lemonade ran down to the pavement. Apprehensively Ryan tugged back the bandage around his hand, but the warts on both hands showed no sign of swelling into eyes.

'Can we go now?' asked Chelle.

'Not yet. O-ka-a-ay. Let's try this.' Josh locked his hands together in front of his belt and bowed to the poster. It looked a bit martial-arts film, but very polite. 'Great Lady of the Well, we are obeying your bidding. We shall bring more news soon.'

The poster did nothing but drip. The lemonade had left a splash in the shape of a question mark, and the question mark seemed to hover in Ryan's mind as he trudged along the footpath to his own back garden. The coffee burn had faded, leaving only a pink, shiny place at the base of his thumb, but Ryan tugged the bandage back into place to hide at least some of his little wart colony from his mother's probing eyes.

It was only much later in the evening that he realized his warts had stopped itching.

9

The Tyrant of Temple Street

Ryan slept well that night, the coolness of his knuckles a blessed relief. In the morning his warts were soft rounds and he felt a painful throb of hope. *Maybe our plan with the competition worked. And maybe she'll let us off with granting just one wish.*

'Legal,' said Ryan's mum, picking an envelope out of her morning post and scrutinizing it with an expert's eye. She sounded almost excited.

'Saul Paladine?' asked Ryan's dad as she opened it.

'Oh.' Ryan's mum looked disappointed. 'No, just Pipette Macintosh again.' She paused to read. 'Oh really, not again! She's still banging on about my chapter on her temper tantrums. It's been two years – you'd think she'd be getting tired of trying to sue by now. It's not even good publicity for either of us any more.'

'I was wondering . . .' Ryan hesitated, not sure how to finish the sentence. 'Someone I know was . . . was thinking of getting a Harley-Davidson, and I was wondering what the best way was to get one . . .'

'Tell Josh that he will find it a lot easier in three or

four years,' Ryan's dad answered, carefully spreading his toast with pâté. 'I daresay he'll find a way to persuade his parents to buy him one then.'

'If you talk like that you'll have Ryan expecting one when he reaches seventeen. And he'll be far too young.'

'Neither of us knows how mature Ryan will be six years from now, but in any case . . .'

'Well, that's splendid then. When some day the hospital phones to let us know that Ryan has driven his motorbike through the central reservation of the A32 I shall try not to remind you of this conversation.' Ryan's mum heaped and shuffled her mail with rather more aggression than it deserved.

'Well, when he does it will probably be because his mother has stolen his glasses,' Ryan's father muttered darkly, laying down his knife.

'I don't actually want a motorbike.' Ryan's belly was twisting, the way it always did when his parents' sparring started to look like a real row.

People's personalities took up space, he sometimes thought. When they were trapped in a house or a job or a school together they rubbed up against each other, squeaked like balloons and made sparks. Ryan's parents both had large, gleaming, hot-air-balloon personalities. Sometimes it was hard to fit them into the same house, and Ryan had learned the art of suddenly making himself take up less space, demand less, so that his parents were not chafing against each other as much.

As usual, it worked. His dad reached across the table towards the lawyer's letter and fluttered his fingers to show he wanted it. Then they talked about Pipette Macintosh and the day she lost her temper and pushed one of her statues made of cutlery off its podium and on to the museum caretaker, because he'd tried to take a spoon from it to stir his tea. The tale even stole a smile from Ryan's mother.

Ryan felt the knot of tension in his stomach loosen, but increasingly scenes like this left him with a slightly sick aftertaste. Suddenly he remembered Josh sitting on the motorbike and chatting with the bikers outside the pub – and he felt a throb of jealousy. It wasn't that he harboured any desire to sit on a motorbike, but . . . he wanted to be allowed to *want* to sit on a motorbike.

While he was trying to reason himself out of this, the doorbell rang and Ryan's dad went to answer it.

'Ryan!' The shout resounded from the hallway.

Ryan reached the door to find Josh standing on the step holding a big kite in the shape of a bird. A little behind him stood Chelle.

'There's a wonderful wind out today.' Josh had a 'talking to parents' voice that he could pull out from time to time. It made some parents call him 'intelligent' and 'engaging'. It made Ryan's father raise his eyebrows and smile, as if he was trying to catch an expert magician palming a card.

Ryan's suspicion that the kite-flying was a cover story was reinforced as soon as he noticed that they were not heading towards the park.

'So . . . ?' Ryan trailed off questioningly. 'It's Will Wruthers?'

'Oh, that.' Josh looked bored. 'Nah, forget about him for the moment. We've found another one!'

Chelle nodded vigorously, a broad smile on her face.

'It was me.' She sounded slightly incredulous about this. 'I'd been shopping for my mum, and it was just after, going back down Temple Street, it came over me again, loud as anything, and I had to use a scouring pad and the green bit scratched my tongue.'

'You mean . . .' Ryan tried to pull the loose loops of Chelle's sentence into sense, like the cord of a drawstring bag. 'You mean . . . the thought thing happened again? You've found another wisher?'

'Yes!' Josh sounded elated. 'So if it's a good wish, we can forget about Wet Will for now and do this one.'

As they walked towards the town centre, they passed East Guildley Secondary. Ryan looked away, but he could smell the tarmac cooking on the netball pitch. The field would be parched yellow by the long summer. The changing rooms would smell of new trainers and fear.

It seemed impossible that he could be walking past with this freedom. And it seemed impossible that in three weeks he would be walking back through the school gates, desperately picking over forgotten facts and fears in his head. One night a year before he had realized, really realized, that some day he would die, and had spent hours sleepless and paralysed with leaden, desperate horror. The feeling had been strangely familiar, and Ryan had eventually recognized that he felt a version of this every time he thought of starting a new term.

'We need to get this sorted,' Josh muttered under his breath. Ryan knew that he was thinking of the new term as well. If they had not paid off the debt to the Well Spirit by then, how long would it be before someone saw Ryan's knuckle-eyes flutter open, heard Chelle gushing borrowed thoughts or noticed that the strip lighting always blew out when Josh walked underneath it? Even Josh, with all his bravado would be unlikely to brazen his way out of that. Whereas for Ryan and Chelle . . . the torment of their first term would begin all over again. The scalding sense of isolation, the 'accidental' brushes in the corridor that knocked them off their feet, the disappearance of their possessions . . .

Josh was right; they had a deadline.

Soon after, the threesome turned into Temple Street. There were no ordinary shops here, just two long rows of terraced brick buildings, with intercom buttons and business plaques next to the doors.

'It was just over there.' Chelle waggled a finger down the street vaguely enough to take in most of it.

'Well, we've got our Chelle Geiger counter.' Josh grinned at her.

Interrogation of Chelle revealed a number of things. Her ability to read Will's mind in Crook's Baddock had been either 'on' or 'off' – within a certain distance she had had 'reception', but it had been no clearer two feet from him than it had been twenty feet away.

'So we can't just walk her up and down and find out

where she's the most weird.' Josh did not seem unduly demoralized. 'No problem, I've got another plan. It's blinding. We're going to walk down the road, and when the Radio Chelle thing cuts in I'll stop walking. You both keep going, and when the weird stuff cuts *out* you stop walking, Ryan. And then you and me'll walk towards each other, Ryan, taking steps at the same time, and see where we are when we meet in the middle.'

At Chelle's insistence they waited until the street was more or less clear.

'And I'm keeping this ready.' Chelle brandished a scouring pad. 'I mean, while I'm being all weird I might meet somebody I know or something . . .'

Ryan wondered how Chelle's definition of 'being weird' could include gabbling loudly, but not include walking around with a kitchen sponge sticking out of her mouth.

'I think it was just after the step with the orange cat, cos I remember thinking about going to stroke it, only it was flicking its ear and I thought it might have fleas so I didn't, but it was just after that my mouth ran off, so I think it might be up by that tree stump, only I s'pose it might have moved – the cat, I mean, not the step – because sandalwood is more expensive but re-energizes the body, and you can leave just a drop of it to evaporate and it fills the whole room . . .'

Josh's steps became slightly uncertain, and then he halted altogether.

'She's off again,' he hissed.

'. . . and Greenspell incense to ensure personal

growth . . .' Chelle's eyes were wide but her voice continued low and expressionless, as if she was uttering an incantation.

'. . . and that's another order for a box of zodiac paperweights, which reminds me, let's look up Cancer for this week. I'm back again. Ryan, it's me, I'm back . . .'

Ryan stopped walking. A little ahead of him, Chelle stopped as well and stooped to stroke the cat. Ryan revolved on the spot and began a stately stride back towards Josh. Josh mirrored him until they halted face to face with the tips of Josh's trainers just resting lightly on Ryan's toes.

'Well, let's have a look at it.' Josh started up the steps of the nearest building. Beside the door there was a panel with several intercom buttons, each with a different name next to it.

'They're all different businesses, aren't they?' Ryan said, glancing quickly at the names.

'Yeah, looks like it. But Chelle was spouting hippy crystal-waving stuff. That rules out most of these – they're nearly all surveyors and dentists . . . look, it's got to be this one: Jeremiah Punzell, Holistic Soul Repair. Holistic means psychic.'

'I think it sort of means to do with everything all being linked.' Ryan racked his brain.

'Yeah, well, that's the same thing, isn't it?' Josh pushed the button next to Punzell's name.

The intercom spat like fat in a pan before a female voice answered, 'Holistic Soul Repair.' There was something accusing in the tone, as if she suspected the visitors on the step of having no souls to repair. 'Donna Leas receiving messages for Mr Punzell, can I help you?'

Josh wrinkled his expressive face and mouthed a silent swear word. Ryan could feel his own face drawn up in a wince. The name was familiar to both of them. *Is it definitely her?* Ryan mouthed back. Josh nodded. They became aware of the intercom crackling impatiently between them.

'Who's there?' The voice was sharp now, despite the fuzz of static. 'Look, whatever you were going to say, take it from me, it wasn't funny. The sole-repair-cobblers joke is getting old, and the load-of-cobblers joke is getting really old. And "going holistic" wasn't even funny the first time. So let's just accept that you're sad and pathetic and then we don't have to talk to each other.' The intercom went dead.

'You're right,' Ryan whispered. 'It *is* her.'

'Course it's her.' Josh stepped back and glared up at the windows. 'She's probably up there with her feet on the desk, like when she was in charge of the library, remember?' He clasped his hands behind his head and leaned back. 'OK. We've got to get past the . . . the poison-toad-woman of Guildley to get to our wisher.'

It was at this very moment that the door beside them opened, and a man stepped out.

His hair was black and curling and crept out into square-cut sideburns. His black cashmere coat was impressive in length, which was a shame since its wearer was not impressive in height. He wore a midnight-blue silk shirt, open at the neck. It made his eyes look particularly blue and interesting. One of his ears was pierced, and a small silver dragon wound round the buckle of his belt.

The man strode past them and off down the street in the direction of Chelle, who was still petting the cat.

'D'you think that's him?' Josh asked through the corner of his mouth.

'Looks pretty holistic to me,' whispered Ryan.

The man was twenty yards from Chelle when she looked up and saw Ryan pointing desperately towards him, and Josh miming for her to stuff something in her mouth. She fumbled with her sponge and dropped it. As she crouched to the ground to pick it up, covering her mouth with her hand, the stranger strode past without giving her a glance.

Ryan and Josh ran to join her.

'That's him!' exclaimed Josh. 'But we're going to have to find a way to talk to him while he's not in his office. Maybe we should go after him now? Listen, Chelle, don't freak, but he's got that witch Donna Leas working there as some kind of secretary . . .'

'I know . . .' Chelle's voice was small and she was twisting her fingers. 'I know, and . . . and . . . Josh, it's even worse. That man isn't the wisher – he walked right past me and I didn't get any of his thoughts. In fact . . . I think *Donna* is the wisher.'

10

The Library Witch

One summer, four sixth-form girls from another school had signed up to spend two weeks as 'Helping Hands', assisting the teachers of Waite's Park Primary. One of these, Donna Leas, had entered school folklore.

She had slouched in through the school gates when Ryan had been there less than a year, when everything still blinded and dizzied him with its newness. Thinking about her now was like looking into a painful light. She brought with her too many memories of self-consciousness, mortification and fear. In any case, Donna had been papered over with countless stories since then, and Ryan could not help thinking of her as the 'poison-toad-woman' Josh had described.

Ryan could remember her sitting by the window on library duty, one hand holding a paperback bent back on its spine. When she read she forgot about her tongue, and it peeped out at the corner of her mouth. This corner was rubbed red, and Ryan always found it hard not to stare at it.

Sometimes she searched your bag when you left the

library to make sure you weren't smuggling out books (some said she confiscated your sweets and crisps and ate them herself), and if your book was late she gave out detentions (some said she also pulled out individual hairs from your head and kept them).

Ryan had been lucky and had not come into much contact with her over the two weeks. However, he still remembered the one time circumstances had forced him to approach her. He'd found a battered library book down behind the radiator, with its front cover buckled from the heat, and taken it to the library to hand it in. Donna had pushed her curtains of blonde hair back from her slab of a face and glared at him as he tried to explain.

'This book's five months late.'

'I didn't borrow it,' Ryan had said. 'I found it.'

'What are you doing with a book that hasn't been signed out to you?'

'I just found it . . .'

'It's the book your class was reading last term, isn't it?' She obviously did not believe him.

'No, I mean yes, but Mrs Parthogill is letting *me* read *next* year's books. I'm . . . they're going to move me ahead a year . . .'

For what seemed like ten minutes Donna had skewered him with her unblinking, spectacled gaze.

'Put your name down here, and if your story doesn't check out your parents will be getting a serious bill for this book fine. A *serious* bill.' She glared at him as he wrote his name. 'So . . .' The bitter words almost seemed to push their way out of her. 'So you're supposed to be clever then, are you?'

Ryan stared at her with a crashing sense of embarrassment, but not for himself. It was the stupid spite of her tone which shocked him, coming as it did from an adult.

Nearly everybody at the primary school had a worse story, of course. Indeed, at the end of the two weeks Josh had taken on the role of archivist and collected many of the best ones. As he walked with Ryan and Chelle away along Temple Street he recounted some of them with vicious verve.

'So what makes you so sure that it's Donna you were picking up on Radio Chelle?' he asked at last.

'Well, after you left me, Ryan, I thought I'd sneak back into range and see if I could be helpful and hear anything. And at first I was just getting stuff about her looking through this magazine for her star sign, and then looking up another star sign, but then when you two were pushing the intercom button her thoughts were all about it ringing and her answering, and her being angry about all the kids who pushed the button and said things like *is there anybody theeeeeere*, and then . . . well, she thought her name when she said it out loud . . .'

Josh swore under his breath. 'She *is* the wisher then.'

'Oh, *great*,' muttered Ryan with feeling.

'Like she deserves to have her wish granted.' Josh wrinkled his nose. 'I mean, what's she going to ask for anyway, a new face?'

'I don't want to find out more by listening in. I don't want her thoughts in my mouth, eeugh . . .' Chelle tangled her fingers up in a knot of squeamishness. 'I mean, it's *Donna Leas*, and he's put the stamp on upside down again, I expect his mind is half-astral today, it always is when he's been working too hard . . .'

It took a moment for Ryan and Josh to realize what was happening. It took another moment for them to realize what it meant. Josh clapped a hand over Chelle's mouth, and Ryan peered anxiously down the street, looking for the dreaded Donna Leas.

To his great surprise, he could not see her. Across the road a young man in denim was tucking flyers under car windscreen wipers. And not far away a young woman with a russet bob slowly sorted the envelopes tucked into the crook of her elbow and pushed them into a postbox.

She wore a soft green jacket, a long skirt and a white blouse with a Victorian-style lacy collar. She seemed trim and smart, and as if she might be pretty when she raised her head. Then, as Ryan watched, she held one envelope up to the light and peered at it intently. Her tongue poked out with the effort of concentration, and she pushed her swings of hair back in an all-too-familiar gesture. It was Donna Leas.

Ryan felt a plunging sense of unreality. He was still boggling at the transformation when Chelle snatched Josh's hand from her mouth and took to her heels. Ryan took half a step after her, but Josh caught his arm.

Donna was walking towards them in a way that was

like and unlike the monster Ryan remembered. She had lost her slouch, but she planted her feet squarely apart as if she was used to having wider legs and was still making room for them.

Josh started walking slowly towards her, his head lowered and his eyes fixed with fierce concentration on the holes in his kite, as if he had only just noticed them. Ryan fell into step with him and joined him in glaring at the poor kite.

As Donna drew closer he could see that her face was the smooth, dead, peach colour that meant layer upon layer of make-up. Dark green eyeliner rimmed her eyes, extending into long painted bars at the outer corners so that she looked a bit like something from an ancient Egyptian painting. As she stalked past, Ryan kept his gaze downwards.

And then she was past and clipping away from them. Grimacing with suppressed laughter, Josh half capered behind the postbox and crouched, peering round it at her retreating back.

'She didn't recognize us!' Josh's voice was half choked with hilarity and excitement. 'C'mon, let's tail.'

'Um, Josh? We kind of stick out. I mean, we've got this great big kite . . .'

Josh stared blankly at the kite, then pushed its beak through the slot of the postbox. When he let go it dangled sadly, as if the bird had crashed cartoonishly into the postbox and got its head stuck.

'And now we haven't,' Josh said, with a note of

lunatic calm. 'Come on!' They crept along behind the row of parked cars.

At the end of Temple Street, the strange new Donna took a left down Marvel Hill and clipped up the steps to the Eastgate Library.

Even though Ryan knew this library well, he felt a moment of hesitation. In his imagination Donna was the hulking monster haunting all things library. Shadowing her into one seemed a bit like following the dragon into its private cave.

They waited a couple of minutes, then followed her in. Unlike the grand Guildley Central Library, with its broad, brightly lit aisles and computer desks, the Eastgate Library smelt like somebody's attic. The furniture was a jumble-sale mix. The shelf stacks rose to various heights like a set of tower blocks. Ryan loved the way you had to weave your way through this mad book-city maze, trying not to catch your clothes on jutting nails or rough-cut splinters.

Into this maze Donna Leas had vanished, and now they listened in vain for the sound of a step.

'Is there a psychic-holistic-dippy-hippy section?' Josh asked in a whisper.

'I think folk dancing and yoga are over there some-where,' Ryan whispered back, and led the way.

Halfway between World Dance and Buddhism, Ryan halted, hearing a faint, stealthy floorboard creak. On a shelf a little above his head was a row of books marked 'Self-Help and Happiness', each bound in a different soothing shade of blue. Peering over these in a far less soothing fashion were two large, green-lined eyes, terrifyingly intense without the glasses they had once worn. The next moment they were gone.

Josh turned to find Ryan mouthing silently at him.

Donna was right there! She saw us!

They peered around different corners, but she had disappeared again. Then they heard quiet, firm steps approaching.

Mrs Corbett, one of the librarians, put her grey head around the nearest corner and looked at each of them with a stony deliberateness. She knew Ryan well, but for once she did not smile. She withdrew her head and the footsteps receded.

With a seething sense of embarrassment, Ryan pulled a book of folklore from the shelf at random and walked towards the desk. Something had been done, something had been said and suddenly he was not welcome in his library. He did not meet Mrs Corbett's eye as she stamped his book, and he only looked around to see if Josh was still with him when he was out in the street.

Josh was still beside him, biting his lips together tightly.

'That was a trap,' he said after a while in a thin, angry voice. 'Just her sort of trap. It must have been Chelle running off like that, made her guess it was us ringing the intercom. Bet she led us in there so she could take a look at us and to see if she could get us in trouble with someone. Bet you.'

'She's a library witch,' Ryan said. 'We should never have followed her in.'

Chelle was nowhere to be found. Josh and Ryan retrieved the kite and parted at the park.

As soon as he skated into the lounge Ryan knew that something was wrong. His dad was sitting in his chair with the paper in his hand as usual, but he looked up as soon as Ryan entered, instead of taking minutes to register his presence.

'Did you have a good time at the park?' The tone was carefully casual, but Ryan recognized that, for whatever reason, he was being given an opening to choose his story carefully.

'We kind of gave up on the park,' Ryan answered quietly. 'Josh's kite's a bit broken.'

Ryan's father looked at him for a few moments and then folded his newspaper.

'About half an hour ago I had a phone call from a woman who claimed that you spent the afternoon ringing her doorbell and running away, following her through the streets calling out names and chasing her around a library.'

Ryan collapsed under a wave of mixed outrage and shame.

'We didn't! I mean . . . we did ring the doorbell once, and we kind of walked along after her a bit because it was someone we knew, but we didn't shout anything or chase her . . . it wasn't like we were trying to scare her or anything . . .'

'So what was Josh trying to do?' His dad stared into his face for a few more moments, then sighed and lowered his eyes. 'I'm sure whatever his reasons were they were ingenious and compelling. Josh is a very clever boy.' Ryan's father laid stress on the word 'clever' as if there was a danger that it might be confused with a similar-sounding word of very different meaning. 'However, cleverness is all very well, but trusting *everything* to one's wits is as dangerous as trusting everything to one's luck. If I were Josh's friend, that would worry me.'

Ryan wanted to understand what his dad meant. This seemed to be one of the rare occasions when his father was really serious.

'I just hope,' his dad said, scratching at his own ear lobe with a pen cap, 'that Josh is clever enough to appreciate how lucky he is to have you as a friend.'

Sadly Ryan watched his faith collapse like snow in the rain. He wanted to believe in his father's all-penetrating wisdom, but that one sentence showed that his dad understood nothing of the way things worked. Josh, who could win friends in a minute, had decided to take notice of a timid outsider. There was no doubt of who had been generous, and who was lucky.

Mrs Corbett must have given Donna my name and number, he thought as he climbed the stairs to his bedroom. *Well, at least Mrs Corbett won't have recognized Josh. If Donna had phoned his parents as well he'd go crazy for revenge . . .*

11
The Paranormal Punzell

As it turned out, although Mrs Corbett had not recognized Josh, Donna had. Perhaps it was his trademark sunglasses that had given him away, but Ryan rather thought not. In the short fortnight of the 'Helping Hands' Donna and Josh had clashed repeatedly.

The bitterest episode had been the incident with the helmet. Donna always chained up her bike, but left her cycling helmet slung loosely over one of the handlebars, and this proved too tempting to Josh's sense of mischief. Later, everybody agreed that Donna had probably seen him slipping off with it, and that her insistence on the police being called was pure malice. The headmaster had convened the whole school in the hall so that the visiting officer could impress upon them the seriousness of the offence. Gradually, those nearest the door became aware of a faint, choking smell of burning plastic. Needing to hide the helmet somewhere, Josh had pushed it behind the heater in the school airing cupboard. When it was found the back part of the helmet's dome had melted and flattened.

Josh had been spotted leaving the airing cupboard, and his parents were called in to talk to the police. He had been exiled to Merrybells for a month.

Even after three years, Ryan could well believe that Donna would remember Josh as clearly and bitterly as Josh remembered her.

Donna did not phone Josh's parents after the library incident. Instead she turned up on his family's doorstep that evening, and was invited in. The conversations that followed went so badly that it was two days before Ryan and Chelle heard from Josh. During this time, Ryan was haunted by the uncomfortable sense of being watched with increasing impatience, the same tingle he felt when a teacher lurked behind him to watch him write. Ever since the day his reflection had become a stranger to him he had regarded it with suspicion and fear. Once as he was hurrying down the street he thought for a tiny second that he glimpsed it in a shop window, standing stock still, water damping the lashes of its closed eyes and leaving glistening snails' trails down its cheeks. He became nervous of crossing puddles, afraid of the other Ryan that walked inverted below him, touching its soles to his and watching him with upside-down eyes.

He was on the point of sharing these fears with Chelle when word from Josh finally arrived. To their great surprise, it took the form of an invitation to tea at Merrybells.

'It looks like Josh's handwriting, but it doesn't sound like him,' Chelle said on the phone. 'Maybe it's a trap . . .' Not for the first time, Ryan was glad of

Chelle's habit of speaking all his most shadowy thoughts aloud so he could hear how silly they were.

They both accepted, of course. They were planless without Josh. Ryan's warts had stopped subsiding and were keeping him awake again. And besides, neither of them had been to Merrybells before.

This time they approached The Haven by the black wrought-iron front gates. A gardener led them past the big house where Josh usually lived with his parents. They followed him down a crisp gravel path, which weaved past two totem poles carved from red wood.

At the end of the gravel path they found that a table had been set up outside Merrybells. Around it stood six chairs in one of which sat Josh, hunched with a knee drawn up to his chin. He showed no sign of noticing Chelle and Ryan, but as they approached an elderly woman in a pale grey woollen jumper hurried out to meet them. Her eyebrows were drawn in with pencil, and there was a necklace of knobbly amber beads around her neck.

'You must be Ryan and Michelle. Do come and join Joshua, he's been so looking forward to your visit. We made a little bargain – he could invite friends over for tea if he planted out all the winter vegetables and removed the dead heads from the flowering hedges.'

Ryan peered at Josh in an agony of sympathy, not unmixed with perplexity. What was the Merrybells spell that turned the ever-rebellious Josh into a flower-plucker and jam-maker?

'Now, do help yourselves,' the Aunt continued. 'The

sandwiches are cucumber, and the sausages with the little forks in them can be dipped in the satay sauce. The saucer there is for the forks – I'm trying to keep the set together.'

Chelle and Ryan each obediently picked up a sausage, and waited while the Aunt disappeared into the cottage.

'Who's the sixth chair for?' Although there were a hundred things Ryan wanted to ask, somehow this question found its way out first. The excess of chairs made the whole thing even more like the Mad Hatter's Tea Party than it was already.

'You'll see,' Josh said grimly. He was using his fingernail to scratch spirals into the tablecloth.

'If you're in Merrybells, Josh, does that mean . . .' Chelle glanced furtively at the cottage, 'does that mean you're being punished for something?'

'Donna Leas came to talk to Mr and Mrs Lattimer-Stone.' It always made Ryan's blood run cold when Josh stopped talking about them as his parents. 'They brought me into the Indigo Room with her there, smiling, while they repeated all the things she'd been telling them. She lies – she just makes stuff up.'

'But . . . didn't they believe you when you told them that?' Chelle had forgotten to chew her sausage.

Josh continued slowly drawing his nail across the cloth. *You didn't tell them*, thought Ryan. *I bet you just sat there making spirals like that.*

'Oh no, it's horrible that everybody always believes her. Did they yell at you lots?' Chelle looked distressed.

'They told me I'd be in Merrybells for three days.

They told the toad-woman they were very sorry and told me that I had to apologize to her. And then the lights went out. All over the house. Fuses blown. Both circuits.

'And when they got the fuses changed they'd forgotten about me saying sorry, because Donna was talking about feng shui, and how important it was to get everything all lined up with natural energies because otherwise things broke down and bits fell off people's souls and lots of rubbish like that. And they bought it. Now they're paying Holistic stinking Soul Repair to feng shui the grounds, and that cow is going to be around all the time.' Josh emptied the cucumber out of his sandwich, spooned the satay sauce into it, then closed and bit it.

'That's really tough.' Ryan tried not to imagine how he would feel about Donna Leas stalking around his own garden. 'Only . . . it does mean we can get closer to her, doesn't it? So we can do this wish thing.'

'You think I'm going to grant her wish?' Josh looked up fiercely. 'Whatever it is, it came out of her foul mind and I'm not touching it.'

'Oh, but we know what her wish is, don't we?' Chelle leaned dangerously across the table for another sausage. 'I mean . . . don't we? She was looking at *two* horoscopes. And everyone knows what that means.' She sat back triumphant, apparently unaware of her companions' expressions of bewilderment. 'My sister Caroline only ever looks up two horoscopes when she's got a crush on somebody. I think it's the kind of thing you can't help doing when you're in love.'

'Who . . . oh.' The answer dropped into Ryan's head before he could even finish the question.

'And her thoughts were all like, I hope Mr Punzell doesn't see my blonde roots, and won't he be pleased to see I've done his filing for him, and doesn't he have piercing eyes . . .' Chelle carefully threw her fork at the saucer and missed it completely.

'Oh no.' Ryan thought of the spiteful, green-rimmed stare in the library. 'We can't! Nobody deserves that!'

'You haven't met him,' Josh said with feeling.

A second Aunt tottered out of the cottage with a tray, on which a tea set shook and rattled with every step. This Aunt had a long face with deep lines running between the nose and mouth, and a side-parted bob that made her look oddly little-girly. She set the tray down in front of Chelle.

'Since you're the lady, I shall make you an honorary daughter and you can be mother,' the Aunt said, in a breathless, hollow sort of voice. Chelle's face was a picture of bewilderment as the second Aunt walked back into the cottage.

'Pour the tea,' Josh muttered, by way of explanation.

While Chelle was trying to manage the heavy pot, the mystery of the sixth chair was answered. Ryan became aware that a man was walking along the gravel path towards them. He wore a white shirt with full sleeves that made him look a bit piratical and a dark blue waistcoat with silver buttons. It was unmistakably the dragon-belted man they had encountered at the intercom a few days before.

As they watched he halted, held up something that looked a bit like a spirit level and peered down it towards the totem poles.

'Mr Punzell! Mr Punzell!' The Aunts had magically materialized at the door. 'Tea, or perhaps some sparkling wine, Mr Punzell? We have some chilling.' Josh had gone back to making spirals, but the buzz of a distant lawnmower turned guttural for a moment, then lost power with a groan.

The way Jeremiah Punzell walked across the grass towards them reminded Ryan of seeing the lead actor in a play walk on stage. Nobody told him to put his forks in the saucer.

'You are both to be congratulated,' he told the Aunts, fixing one then the other with an intense but friendly stare. 'You do realize, of course, that your vegetable garden and rose walk are perfectly and auspiciously aligned?'

The Aunts looked delighted. Chelle looked less happy, since she was still holding a hot and heavy pot and waiting to find out if he wanted tea.

'Well . . .' The Aunt with the bob exchanged a glance with the Aunt in the amber necklace. 'I do not think we ever spoke of it in such terms when we arranged the garden, did we, Sophia, but I am sure that we both felt . . .'

'Oh yes, I think so,' the other Aunt agreed quickly, placing a glass of fizzing wine by Mr Punzell's plate.

'Do you know how rare that is?' continued Mr Punzell, looking from one Aunt to the other as if they were the most interesting people he had ever met. 'Though I'm afraid I have often wished that my sense of the energies were less acute. Sometimes it is almost painful.'

Ryan put down his sandwich, and quietly slid his hands under the table where they could not be seen. Perhaps this was all rubbish, just as Josh had hinted, but . . . what if it wasn't? If spirits lived in wells and posters could talk, maybe this man really did have some kind of psychic power. And if he could sense malign energies, then perhaps he could also sense the new strangeness of the children around him.

The teapot rattled, and Ryan glanced at Chelle, wondering if she felt the same worry, but her hands were just shaking under its weight.

'Forgive me!' Mr Punzell noticed Chelle at last and stood to help her pour tea into his cup, then set the pot down on the cloth. 'You are very kind,' he said, half bowing a little theatrically. Now Chelle suddenly seemed to be the most interesting person he had ever met. Perhaps he looked at everybody that way. Or perhaps he had seen something odd about her. Ryan squirmed.

'Wow – I love all your rings,' Chelle exploded, her voice shrill and sudden. 'Are any of them wedding rings?'

'No, as it happens.' Mr Punzell looked a little surprised.

'Good!' exclaimed Chelle, and then went bright crimson.

Mr Punzell blinked a few times, and then looked amused and flattered. 'I can show you what each of these rings is though. Now this one, shaped like a twining silver snake, is an old symbol for wisdom . . .'

Ryan was wondering if the Holistic Soul Repair man could say anything without making it sound as if he was telling someone something terribly wise and important that might save their life some day. *Oh God*, he thought, *he thinks that Chelle's got a crush on him. He thinks people get crushes on him as soon as they meet him, and he just laps it up.*

The Aunts really did seem to be hanging on his every word. *Oh Chelle, Chelle . . .* Ryan thought in sudden dismay, *don't be like them, don't start gushing or going all round-eyed.* Bracing himself, he stole a glance at her face.

Chelle could no more control her expression than she could her speech. She was looking up at Mr Punzell with incredulous and fascinated dislike. Ryan could have hugged her. The 'psychic', however, did not seem to have noticed this at all.

He can't be all that psychic then, thought Ryan and risked reaching for another sandwich.

Aunt Sophia clearly felt that Chelle had hijacked the conversation, and she started to talk loudly about the party that Josh's parents were to hold the next day.

'It is so kind of you to agree to perform palm readings for all the guests, Mr Punzell. I know that you find it so draining. Josh, perhaps you and your friends could bring the bowls in ready for the charlotte russe?'

All three children hurried with alacrity into the sunless kitchen, which was full of great hanging twists of onions and garlic cloves and the smell of hot strawberries.

'See?' hissed Josh, pulling off his sunglasses.

'Yeeeurrgh!' Chelle scrunched up her face. 'He's so . . .'

'Yeah! Isn't he?'

'He thinks you're off home to check his star sign, Chelle. He thinks you're his latest groupie . . .'

'Yuck! Stop it! Yuck!'

'He's . . .' Ryan hesitated, still groping to understand why the 'psychic' was so annoying. 'He's probably not bad. He's just . . . awful.' All three grinned at each other, with the delight of complete agreement.

'Yeah. And my parents let him go everywhere. I can't get away from him. He came in my room and took *measurements*.'

'You know it has to happen, don't you?' Ryan said as calmly as he could, then started to giggle in spite of himself. The hideousness of the thought was like laughing gas. 'Mr and Mrs Punzell . . .'

'Oh . . .' Josh shoved a parsley-strewn chopping board out of the way, and swung himself up to sit on the sideboard. 'Oh, now that would be vengeance . . . on both of them.'

That one irresistible idea caught them like a wave and bore them sniggering out to sea. Usually it would have been Ryan's job to point out the difficulties of matchmaking two grown adults, one of whom would distrust anything they said. But at this moment Ryan, like the others, felt that they really could do this.

'So . . . how?' he asked.

'Well, she's his secretary, isn't she?' said Chelle. 'I mean, maybe she could do that thing? You know, that thing, with all the . . .' She paused, raised her hands to pull off imaginary glasses and then tipped her head back, shaking out her hair. For a moment she looked most un-Chelle-like, quite a lot older and more confident. 'Type of thing,' she added, dropping back into her usual expression again.

Josh tipped over with laughing and nearly put his elbow in one of the puddings.

'Joshua!' There was a call from outside.

'Bowls!' hissed Josh. By the time Aunt Sophia reached the door, three children were filing out with a little crystal bowl in each hand, faces red with smothered hilarity. Perhaps it was the Alice-in-Wonderland effect of the tea party, but they all seemed to have gone a little mad.

In particular Chelle, who was usually extremely timid when meeting new people, wriggled gleefully into her seat, then jumped up again when the charlotte russe was brought out.

'Mr Punzell, you must let me give you some!' The Aunts watched aghast as Chelle carved enthusiastically into the pudding, heaping Mr Punzell's bowl until it seemed to defy gravity. 'It's so nice to meet you. I knew you had to be lovely, because Donna is working for you and Donna always gets everything right, you see . . .'

'You . . . you know Donna . . . ?'

'Yes!' Chelle gave him a big, bright, mad smile. 'She came and helped with our school ages ago, and she was really, really . . . everybody really . . . liked her, particularly us. Because she's wonderful.'

Ryan had to put his hand over his face as a dribble of cream escaped from the corner of his mouth. He nodded vigorously.

'Yes,' choked Josh. 'Yes . . . she's really *great* . . .'

'Yes, and my parents always say: I wonder what happened to that nice girl Donna? And I told them, now she's working for a real psychic, and they said, wow, I bet that's really interesting . . .' Chelle was trying to pour cream on top of Punzell's charlotte russe, and little rivulets were escaping over the brim of the bowl. 'I expect she's coming to the party tomorrow, isn't she? I wish I was coming because she was really really great . . .'

'I am not sure if Donna is coming. She has a very busy schedule . . .'

Ryan saw Mr Punzell's eyes flicker slightly as he spoke. *I bet he never even considered asking her*, thought Ryan. *But now he's wondering about it because if there are lots of parents at the party that like her, she might persuade them to give him lots of money for feng shui like Mr and Mrs Lattimer-Stone.*

'. . . but if she can, I will have a talk with Mr Lattimer-Stone, and see if your families can be added to the invitation list as well.' He performed the same old-fashioned bow to Chelle.

Ryan listened to this with a mixture of hilarity and misgiving. Was this good? Was this bad? It did not seem to matter. They had no plan, but there the three of them were, trusting themselves to impulse, surfing down the snow slope on a cello case.

12

The Collectors

Ryan's mum said that she thought the last-minute invitation from the Lattimer-Stones was very rude.

'They might just as well have said, "Somebody we really wanted to come has just pulled out, and so we're inviting you to fill the holes."'

'I agree,' said Ryan's dad. 'Let's phone back and say we can't come.'

'I've half a mind to do just that,' said Ryan's mother, dropping to her knees in front of the wine rack, and pulling out bottle after bottle with a harassed air. 'I knew we should have saved some of the San-Luisha-whatever-it-was-called. We can't take any of these to the party.'

'You clearly don't want to go, Anne. I'll call back and cancel.' Despite these words, Ryan noticed that his father was setting up the video machine to tape his favourite programme for that evening.

'Well, I would.' Ryan's mum pushed her hair back from her face. 'Only . . . I thought that feng-shui man sounded interesting.'

'No, you didn't. You thought that the Lattimer-Stones would invite lots of famous people, some of whom might not realize that the world desperately needed to know their deepest secrets. But since we're clearly going to suffer this party, I'll go and track down some wine and find some small gift from the Cobbled Market that won't embarrass you.'

'Angel. Could you?' Ryan's mother looked up at his father with a dishevelled little smile that made her look young and worried. Ryan's dad touched the tip of one of her ears, smiled briefly and left. Ryan went with him to get out of his mum's hair.

Now that the tea-party madness was wearing off, hosts of problems were clearing their throats and waiting for his attention. Yes, this evening Chelle, Josh and himself would be in the same house as Donna and Mr Punzell . . . but he no longer felt entirely confident about engineering true love now that all three of them would have their parents in tow.

While his father was in the off-licence Ryan noticed a familiar cover in a magazine stand on the street. It was a new issue of the motorbike magazine *Silverwing*.

Quietly Ryan flicked to the competition results. Twenty finalists had reached the 'shortlist', and won free tickets to the Golden Oak Rally, where one of them would be declared the overall winner and receive the prize motorbike.

Near the end of the list Ryan found Will Wruthers' name.

*

Ryan's family drove up to the gates of the Lattimer-Stone house as the late light was fading over the grounds. Ryan's glasses had been firmly confiscated, leaving him to blink painfully through his contacts.

Mrs Lattimer-Stone met them at the door. She wore a brown silk dress, up and down which little snakes of shimmer appeared and disappeared as she walked. Her dark hair was tied back in a thick plait, and her mouth was neatly painted in the shape and colour of a plum.

'How lovely that you were able to come at such short notice. I'm so glad that you were free.' Mrs Lattimer-Stone did not sound particularly glad, or particularly anything. Her voice was pleasant and husky yet without any rises or falls. She never smiled. Sometimes she drew her mouth in and narrowed her eyes to show that she was *thinking* a smile.

The Lattimer-Stone house seemed to Ryan to be a lot of living rooms stuck together, full of glass and shiny chrome. Instead of pictures, some walls had huge sticking-out bits of board with two splotches of colour and nothing else on them.

Just for a moment Ryan wondered what the Lattimer-Stone household would look like upside down. He half smiled as he imagined inverting the whole vast room like a snow globe and watching all the guests shriek ceilingwards to the music of smashed decanters.

'Oh look,' said his mother in a faint, flat voice. 'The Coopers are here.'

Chelle's mother noticed Ryan's mother at the same

time, and bore down on her. Listening quietly by her side was an elderly woman whom Ryan recognized as Miss Gossamer.

Miss Gossamer always reminded Ryan of a mummified cat he had once seen in a museum. It had originally been left among the rafters of an old house to keep out evil spirits. The cat had looked half starved, but with a shocked, sleepy, supercilious look.

Ryan caught Chelle's eye and his smile faded. She looked sick with worry. He slipped over to her side.

'What's wrong?'

'Ryan . . . I pretended to be ill but they didn't hear me, so I had to come . . . and Donna's coming, she's coming here . . .'

It took a few moments before her meaning hit him, and then he gaped, astonished that he had failed to spot such an obvious problem amid the dizziness of events.

'It's all right, we'll . . . we'll go over here and sit down next to the peanuts.' He sank into one squashy chair, and Chelle dropped into another. 'And if Donna comes in and you start leaking her thoughts, you just stuff as many peanuts in your mouth as you can, and if that doesn't work I'll say it's your asthma and I'll help you outside.'

Chelle nodded.

'And . . . Josh will be here soon, and he'll think of something,' added Ryan. He saw a faint glimmer of hope in Chelle's eye as she nodded again. Just for a moment Ryan felt a pang that his own reassurances had not been enough. He cast a glance over his shoulder to scan the room for his friend.

He quickly spotted him, over by one of the fireplaces. He was without his sunglasses and wore a black shirt and beige trousers very different from his usual clothes. Something peculiar had happened to his hair. It was darkened, but its spikes curled and clung oddly. It looked rather as if it had been slicked flat by one hand, and then furiously ruffled by another. Ryan suspected that this was exactly what had occurred.

There was something peculiar about Josh's expression too. He was biting both his lips together and staring out through the crowd with a look of focused rage and dislike. Ryan followed the line of his gaze, expecting to catch sight of Mr Punzell's piratical shirt or Donna Leas' green-painted eyes. With a lurch of his stomach he realized that Josh was glaring at Ryan's own mum.

He had completely forgotten that Josh disliked her. In fact, he always tried not to think about it, because it made him feel as if something inside him was being slowly ripped in two like a piece of card. He had first become aware of it a year before when Josh had led Ryan out bat-spotting one dusk-time. They had been missed, and when they returned muddily to Ryan's house they found two sets of parents waiting outside. Josh's parents had said nothing and shown no sign of anger, but had simply held the car door open for him. Ryan's mother had swept forward to grab Ryan by the shoulders, turned him this way and that as if to check he had all his limbs, then shaken him hard and yelled at him. While he was letting the waves of angry relief break over him Ryan had looked past her to see Josh fixing her with a look very much like hatred.

On the far side of the reception room, oblivious to the hostile gaze, Ryan's mum was detaining his dad's sleeve and tugging at the handkerchief in his pocket to set it straight. Ryan's father was enduring this with an expression that hovered between amusement and impatience.

Ryan risked a wave, and the motion caught Josh's eye. For an instant or two Josh's gaze fixed on Ryan's face with the same look of blind enmity, but then he seemed to recognize Ryan and the expression faded. Beside him, Josh's father, a tall man with grey, immaculate hair and yellowish, fuzzy sideburns was explaining one of the big board pictures to a thin woman in a clingy wasp-striped dress. Neither of them noticed Josh slipping over to Ryan and Chelle.

'What are we going to do, Josh, do you have a plan?' Chelle's voice was pitiably hopeful.

'Course,' Josh answered, a little too firmly. 'Look – we've got to sort this wish out tonight or we'll never get another chance with all of us and both of them in the same place. So . . . we need to get each of them away from the party and . . . lock them up somewhere together. The east conservatory. So they have to talk and get to know each other.

'Chelle,' he continued, 'you can do Mr Punzell, he likes you. Ryan, you'd better lead Donna. Down that corridor, third left, other side of the book room, key's on the hook by the door.'

'But—'

'Just call her to the phone or something.' Josh had a fierce glitter about him that Ryan did not quite understand.

They paused to nibble peanuts with dry mouths. Amid their silence, Ryan became aware that his parents' tones were quite clearly audible above the hushed museum voices that all the other adults seemed to be using. Ryan winced and did not dare meet Josh's eye.

Ryan's mother and father, it seemed, wished to discuss something, and saw no obstacle in the fact that they were standing at opposite ends of the lounge. The other adults were so startled to hear them casually shouting across the room that it completely spoilt Jeremiah Punzell's entrance. The Soul Repair man walked with careful nonchalance in through the main door, only to find that nobody was looking in that direction at all. Ryan thought for a moment that he was going to slip out and enter again when more people were watching.

Mrs Lattimer-Stone slid her chocolate way towards Mr Punzell, narrowing her eyes in a cat-smile, and let him hold her fingertips for a moment. She then led him around, introducing him to people, while Josh's Aunts trailed after them, completing the parade. As Chelle struggled out of her chair Ryan could not help thinking that she would have little chance of reaching the 'psychic' through the wall of politely interested adults. But remembering his promise to rescue her if she lost control of her mouth, he nodded to Josh and followed.

'. . . I am also interested in curing the ills of the mind and mystical soul,' Mr Punzell was explaining to the wasp-striped woman as Ryan and Chelle approached, 'so I make use of hypnosis and, on rare occasions, a *psychic projection of will*.'

'So . . . you can project the power of your mind into somebody else's?' The wasp-striped woman sounded happily scared and completely fascinated.

Punzell nodded slowly and solemnly, as if admitting to a secret pain.

'Of course, I always take the greatest care not to harm the other person's mind. I take a simple thought, and while talking someone into a slight trance I transmit that thought into their head . . .'

'Excuse me . . .' squeaked Chelle, as she tried to find a gap in the wall of backs. 'Excuse me, but Mr Punzell said that he'd do a star chart for me . . . excuse me . . .'

Her voice had faded to a thin, whispery chirrup, and yet somehow Mr Punzell heard it. He gave her an indulgent smile and moved aside so that she could enter the group.

'Excuse me, Mr Punzell, you said that you could do me a star-chart thing, and I think I probably need one, because, um, my life is full of surprises . . . and isn't he handsome standing there with his Isis amulet, I wish he'd wear the suede waistcoat more often . . .' Chelle's eyes crossed slightly, then she gave a half-witted look around her, before fleeing towards the nearest door. A ripple of indulgent laughter followed her.

'You have an admirer, Jeremiah.'

Mr Punzell gave a small bow in acknowledgement. 'I should probably follow her and make sure she is all right,' he murmured.

Oh yes, yes, thought Ryan. *Go!* He had already glimpsed the figure of Donna Leas at the other door. She was wearing a shiny, silvery-green, mermaidy dress, which she kept tugging down at the hips to stop it creasing across her stomach. She looked quite despairing as she saw Mr Punzell leaving the room. Ryan turned his step towards her, remembering his allotted mission with dread.

'Donna Leas . . . oh, you don't mean that dreadful girl, do you?' With a shock, Ryan recognized his mother's voice. 'Good heavens, is that her? I nearly lodged an official complaint about her a couple of years ago. I would have done if Ryan hadn't asked me not to.'

With horror, Ryan saw his mum detach herself from her conversation with Mrs Cooper and bear down on Donna Leas.

On the other side of the room, Mrs Lattimer-Stone laid a gentle hand on the sleeve of Mr Punzell to stop her guest of honour escaping. Ryan heard the words 'palm reading for Joshua'. Next to her, Josh stood, totally, dangerously motionless.

'What nonsense! Ryan doesn't chase people round libraries!' Hearing his mother's exclamation, Ryan guessed that his father had not mentioned Donna's phone call to her. Despite her terrible timing, at that moment the sight of his mother, brandishing a vol au vent with one hand and firmly grasping the wrong end of the stick with the other, filled Ryan with a painful surge of love and pride.

There was something wrong with the air in the room, however. Ryan felt a tingle across his knuckles, and glanced down to find that his second eyes were back, clearly visible on his unbandaged hand, and a-flutter with motion. In panic, he looked across the room at Josh. Josh's face was mask-like as he raised his head to look directly back at Ryan.

Their eyes met, and then something in the light fittings above them tutted softly and glassily to itself. There was a brilliant flash and a tinkling rush of sound, then blackness swamped the room.

13

Enchantment

Darkness was the first shock, but close on its heels followed another greater jolt to Ryan's mind. The darkness was not absolute, Ryan saw, as the now-feverish tingling of his knuckles intensified.

A soft rain was falling from above, a dim, insistent trickle of light. Ryan stared, upwards, flexing his fingers without thinking so that the eyes on his hands blinked and focused. Every bulb in the ceiling was silently spitting gobs of faint luminescence, which fell slowly and silently as snow and winked out as they hit the floor. The slender watch on Mrs Lattimer-Stone's wrist was bleeding light like molten butter. At the same time, Ryan was occasionally aware of a faint, sinuous undulation in the fabric of the shadow, like the wavering of underwater weed.

The radiance seemed to ooze and drip and puddle. In particular, it oozed and dripped and puddled over Josh. He remained motionless, staring down at his own hand, which was still extended with the fingers spread. Ryan thought he was grinning, thought he could see the strange liquid light sliding over his teeth.

'Christ!' someone exclaimed.

Everybody's seen Josh glowing like a Christmas tree, thought Ryan.

'Joshua?' Mrs Lattimer-Stone was looking around her, paying no attention to her leaking watch. Ryan saw Josh turn his head a little at the sound of her voice, then deliberately drop into a squat and back away from her. 'Joshua – we need the matches . . .'

A dull blob of light fell on to Mrs Cooper's eyebrow, and she did not even blink.

Nobody's noticed, Ryan realized. *Nobody but me can see the light. Nobody but me can see anything at all.*

Something like a bomb of fizzy sherbet detonated in his stomach, and then he felt a grin spread helplessly across his face. He could see everybody, with the help of his secret hand-eyes, and nobody could see him. It was a strange and powerful knowledge.

A number of guests were clumsily trying to comfort Miss Gossamer. She was on her knees drawing deep, hoarse breaths – her nerves must have been devastated by the sudden darkness. Ryan slipped past the huddle of figures and stooped next to Josh to whisper in his ear.

'I'm going to get Donna to the east conservatory. You'll have to do Mr Punzell.' He saw Josh's eyes fix on nothingness as he cocked his head to listen. Even Josh could not see him in the blackness. The fact gave Ryan a twisted, excited feeling in his stomach.

Donna was twirling the stem of her wine glass

anxiously, and she jumped when Ryan spoke right next to her.

'Excuse me,' he whispered, 'you're needed . . . by Mr Punzell. He wants your help with something . . . something feng shui.'

Her large hands smoothed her dress again, and she looked a bit shy and frightened. Just for a moment Ryan almost felt sorry for her. *But we are trying to give her her heart's desire*, he told himself.

Down the corridor, third left, other side of the book room, Josh had said. Ryan reached out for Donna's hand, and she took a firm hold of his sleeve.

'Slow down!' she hissed as he led her across the room. 'You're pulling me into furniture!' He stopped feeling sorry for her. They left the main reception room, and Ryan led her down the corridor and through the third doorway.

'It's just along here.' The door to the conservatory was open. There were blinds hanging at all the great windows, letting in ribbons of faint blue light. Donna stepped into the conservatory, and the blind-light tiger-striped her. She hadn't let go of his sleeve.

'So where's Mr Punzell?' For the first time there was a touch of suspicion in her voice. He halted just outside the room, out of the light from the blinds, so that she could not read his expression.

'He said to wait here. He definitely said here.' Next to the door, Ryan could see a metal ornament in the shape of a dragon's head, with a hook jutting from the lower jaw. He stealthily extended his left hand towards it, but it was just out of reach. 'I think it's because you can see the garden from here and the lines of energy running up and down it . . .' Ryan took all his courage into his hands and snatched his sleeve free from Donna's grasp.

He slammed the door, leaned all his weight against it and scrabbled at the hook for the key. It was not there.

He put all his energy into holding the door handle straight against Donna's efforts to turn it. As he did so he became aware of some strange, muffled snorts and murmurs coming from behind him. Half turning, across the room he saw a bulge in the floor-length curtain, as if somebody was hiding behind it.

The draperies flurried aside, and Ryan glimpsed Chelle's face with its mouth full of handkerchief. The next moment the handle turned under his grip and the door wrenched open. Large hands found and gripped his shoulders, dragging him into the conservatory.

Ryan wriggled out of Donna's grip and dropped to a crouch, then shrank back into a darkened corner. Donna was breathing loudly, and he tried to match his breath to hers so that she wouldn't hear where he was.

The fall of silence made the slam of the door and the key turning in the lock all the louder. Of course, thought Ryan with a strange sort of calm, Chelle must have been hiding with the key, waiting to lock Mr Punzell in if he followed her. She doesn't know I got pulled in here as well as Donna.

In the safety of darkness, Donna's face crumpled. Even though she was so much larger than he was, suddenly Ryan could not quite remember how to be frightened of her.

She was just feeling for the strings of the blinds when approaching voices became audible.

'Donna?' There was candlelight quivering beneath the door. It was Mr Punzell, sounding rather harassed and not in too good a mood.

'I've been locked in.' Donna's tone was childish and petulant.

'The door sticks sometimes.' Josh's voice.

'No, I've been locked in! With a key!'

'So you have . . . look, Joshua, it's in the lock.'

The key was turned back again, and Donna pushed her way out. Ryan remained crouched in the shadows. Donna stared around her at the candlelit book room, then marched over to the long velvet curtains, from which a subdued whimpering sound was audible.

Oh Chelle, thought Ryan, *you didn't run back and hide there, tell me you didn't . . .*

The curtain was tweaked back by Donna's angry hand.

Oh Chelle, you did.

Donna reached out and snatched the handkerchief from Chelle's mouth.

'. . . it's that same girl, I'm sure of it,' babbled Chelle as soon as the plug was removed, 'the one I saw with the others in the street, and up in the reception room, she must have turned the key on me . . . and what's wrong with her, why is she talking like that, it sounds like she's saying . . . it sounds like she's saying everything in my, my . . .'

Donna had gone completely white and was staring at Chelle open-mouthed.

'. . . it must be a trick, some kind of joke they've put together but how would they be able to . . . oh no, and Mr Punzell's right there, I've got to think about . . . mustn't think about . . .'

'What's wrong with her?' Mr Punzell dropped on to his haunches and stared at Chelle, his ill temper forgotten.

Josh raised his eyebrows and opened his mouth slowly, but words did not come. He turned the motion into a stretch-yawn and brought his hands back behind his head.

As he did so, however, Ryan's thoughts were sliding coolly and cleanly into place. He stood up gingerly and moved to the door.

'A psychic projection of will,' he said, a bit more loudly than he'd intended. Everybody else in the room jumped slightly and turned to look at him.

'It's something we were practising with Donna . . . it was what you were talking about before, transmitting thoughts, and Donna was having a practice with Chelle because . . . we . . . asked her to. And Donna's very good at it. Even through a door. And now we don't know how to turn it off . . .'

Mr Punzell stared at Donna as if he had never properly seen her before. She looked a bit like a rabbit caught in headlights.

'. . . mustn't think about big blue eyes . . .' whispered Chelle. 'Books! I'll think about books, there are lots of books on the shelves . . .'

'Brilliant!' breathed Mr Punzell. 'Come here, Donna, look at the books I'm pointing at, and, Michelle, you just keep on talking, let the thoughts flow through you.' Gently he drew Donna to the nearest bookcase and held the candle up to the shelf.

'. . . *Great Landscape Gardeners of the Eighteenth Century*,' whispered Chelle, '*A History of the Avant-Garde*, *The Pioneers of the Bauhaus Movement* . . .' She must have been getting the book titles right, because Mr Punzell kept nodding and swallowing.

'So blind, I have been so impossibly blind . . . Donna – you were in the house the first time all the lights blew out, were you not? And now again. So much uncontrolled power . . .'

'. . . what?' murmured Chelle. 'Perhaps he's right, maybe I did, I don't know . . .'

Mr Punzell suddenly seemed to remember Chelle, and glanced around at Josh and Ryan.

'You had better take your friend away from here . . . no doubt she will start to recover when she is removed from the Focus of Power. She will probably be very drained, what with having been a channel for another's psychic energies. I suggest you find her something sugary. And milk, lots of milk.'

Milk was extremely useful, it seemed. Ryan wondered what else it could cure besides radioactivity and psychic strain.

Chelle took her handkerchief from Donna's unresisting hand and pushed it into her mouth. Then the three children walked from the room, leaving Donna with the face of a sleepwalker, and Mr Punzell resting his fingertips on her temples and looking at her as if she was the most interesting person he had ever met.

They were only halfway down the corridor when Chelle pulled the handkerchief out of her mouth again.

'Listen!' she whispered. They listened. They could hear nothing but Mr Punzell's distant voice.

'What?' asked Josh.

'Listen!' Chelle sounded as if she was grinning. 'It's me! I'm not saying anything!'

It was true. Despite Donna's proximity, Chelle was no longer spilling out her thoughts. And Ryan became aware that he could no longer make out the others' faces in the dark corridor. His knuckle-eyes had closed and dwindled once more.

'Do you think that means that . . .'

'I think so. I think we've done it.'

There was a stuttering brilliance overhead, and all the lights came on, leaving them blinking. Josh was grinning broadly.

'I think we've done it,' he said again. 'I think we're the bloody champions. I mean, Chelle, did you see Ryan? That was beautiful. Ryan, you just appeared out of the darkness, voice booming, with your eyes all big without the glasses and shining in the candlelight, and everybody was like, whooo, demon boy . . .'

'Oh yes, it was just like that!' Chelle hiccupped with laughter.

'And upstairs, did you see that? With the lights?' Josh extended his hand, and stared at it for a moment. 'Paff!' he whispered. 'Just like that. Did you see? I could get used to that.' He drew his hand back and spent a few moments staring into his own palm.

14

The Attack of the Harley

Naturally, Ryan's parents had hated the party, but this had at least put them in a good mood with one another. During the drive home, they laughed at Mr Punzell and were sure that he had arranged for the lights to go out himself.

Lying in bed that night, Ryan ran a finger over his warts. They had smoothed themselves flat against his skin. It always seemed like bad luck to assume the best, so he tried to tell himself that the nightmare of the Well Spirit almost certainly wasn't over, that granting Donna's wish couldn't have been enough. Despite himself though, he could not help hoping that the Magwhite curse had been lifted.

The next morning, having slept deeply and dreamed lightly, he went down and discovered a strange woman on the doorstep, painting faces on the milk bottles.

At first all he could see of her was rounded shoulders covered in mottled indigo velvet and a bush of frizzed black and purple hair. Then she pulled herself up into a squat and showed him a broad-cheeked, white-painted face.

He stood there in his socks and stared. She stared back. The paintbrush in her hand dripped.

'Oh God,' she said finally in a flat, hard voice. 'She has young.'

'Um . . .' Ryan's gaze flitted to the milk bottles, which had been decorated with the shapes of skulls and were wearing little painted collars of feathers and bones like tiny tribal warriors. 'Um . . . could we have the full cream for Weetabix, please? It's the one with the gold lid.'

Very carefully, the woman with the paintbrush lifted one bottle and handed it to him. He thanked her, closed the door and took it to the kitchen.

'Mum, I think Pipette Macintosh is on our doorstep.' He held up the milk bottle. A light entered his mother's eyes as she ran from the room. After a few minutes she returned.

'I missed her,' she explained. 'She flew past on her scooter just as I reached the gate. Jonathan, no!' Ryan's father paused with his thumb just indenting the foil lid. 'Nobody is to touch these bottles until I've had the chance to study them, and get Gerry to look at them – this looks like some kind of voodoo-curse motif . . .'

'A terrible curse,' muttered Ryan's father. 'She has doomed the whole household to the smell of bottled cheese.'

It was just after lunch, while Ryan's mother was

happily researching the history of voodoo, that the phone rang.

'Ryan? It's Josh. Look, you've got to get to the park this afternoon so we can talk. I'm going to phone Chelle in a moment.' He sounded excited, happy and businesslike. 'I've found out something really cool.' He wouldn't explain any further, and as Ryan hung up he could not crush a hope that Josh had noticed his own Well Spirit curse lifting. After all, the crackle on the line had been much fainter than before, and Josh's voice clearly audible.

The three of them met in the park.

Josh squatted beside the others and took his new digital watch out of his pocket. 'Watch this.' Josh held it by its straps and stared at it. His eyebrows twitched, and his breathing became audible. After a few moments the little display changed to 'alarm set' mode, and the alarm time counted up through eight o'clock, nine, ten. A beep sounded and it returned to time-display mode. Josh had not touched any of the buttons.

'I've been practising that all night. After I pulled off the light-bulb thing, I thought, I've got to see if I can control this. I mean, the well-thing must have given it to me for a reason, right? Ryan, you say that my power looks like great big drips of light oozing all over everything. Fine, whatever. But some of it seems to work like electromagnetism.' He stared down at his watch. 'You know I can . . . feel these little contacts under the buttons here, and if I concentrate I can just . . . *zap!* make something happen between them.' He laughed quietly and put the watch on his wrist, then looked up at the others. 'What the hell's wrong with you two?'

Chelle looked as if she was about to cry. 'I just thought it was going to be over, because we'd granted a wish, and I thought that was, that was, that was it . . .'

Ryan swallowed and looked at the nearby pond, where silver pearls of water welled in the throats of the lilies.

'Course it isn't,' Josh answered bluntly. 'We've got to grant all the wishes for the coins we took – any idiot can see that.'

'But we can't! There's too many of them, and some of them might have gone to live in Australia or died or something . . . we have to *tell* somebody, Josh.'

'Don't be stupid. There weren't that many coins. And we're not going to tell anybody. Look, it's not so bad. We've just been thinking about this wrong, that's all. We're not sick; it's not like we've got *chickenpox* or something. We've got . . . powers.'

'My powers look quite a lot like chickenpox,' Ryan murmured resentfully.

'It's all right for you,' Chelle chirruped hopelessly, 'controlling your powers and making bulbs go out, and Ryan can use his to see in the dark, but I can't control mine and my mum's already telling everybody what I said to Mr Punzell because she thinks I've got a crush on him and it's sweet and Mrs Gossamer keeps asking me about it, in lots of different ways so I won't notice . . .'

'Who says you can't control it? Maybe you just need

to practise like I did, and then you'll be, like, doing the whole mind-reading thing on anyone you like, but without saying it out loud. Have either of you tried doing anything cool, or have you just been ignoring the weird stuff and hoping it'd all go away?' He stared from one crestfallen face to the other. 'Well then, don't get grouchy just cos I've had the guts to try stuff out. C'mon – we need to think about the next wish.'

'The only other one we know about is Will,' Ryan pointed out. 'He's on the shortlist for the magazine prize – I checked – but they won't be picking a winner until the motorcycle show tomorrow.'

'We'll have to show up and make 'em pick him.' Josh spread out a battered copy of *Silverwing*. 'Look – here's a picture of last year's winner. See that lottery-ball-machine-thing next to him? That's how they picked the winner. And I bet I can make it drop the right ball so Will wins.'

'I don't think my parents will let me go to a bike show,' Ryan muttered, feeling stupid. 'They're already afraid I might go crazy and turn into a biker or some-thing.'

'Biker Ryan.' Josh collapsed into his silent shaking chuckles. 'But they'll let you go to a fête, won't they?' he said eventually. 'Just don't mention the bikes.'

The day of the motorcycle show was bright and sticky with heat.

They caught a cross-town bus, then followed the signs to the showground.

They heard the show before they saw it. The mosquito whines of motorcycle engines became great tearing grak-grak-grak roars that somehow made the summer sun weigh all the heavier. Revving engines answered one another across the field. The wind itself was warm, and there was a smell of oil, hot dogs and summer grass.

The Golden Oak showground was a broad, blank space of grass often used for funfairs, charity events and summer fêtes. Today the grass was rutted here and there with the thick stripes from tractor wheels and curving zipper-like tracks from motorcycle tyres. Dotted across the grounds were hundreds of motorbikes, with smiling owners who seemed to be enjoying themselves even if they did look very hot in their black or banana-yellow motorcycling jackets. There were some families, the younger children looking bored and miserable amid the heat and noise. A perspiring mime artist, wearing clown-paint, blue pantaloons and a sandwich board advertising the Ebstowe fair, occasionally presented lollipops to children, with a pained-looking smile.

'Miserable subhumans,' Chelle said in a low, lugubrious drawl. It didn't sound very Chelle-like.

'She's off again,' hissed Josh. 'OK, look about. Wet Will must be close if Chelle's picking up his thoughts.'

'You sure, Josh?' Ryan hesitated. 'Only . . . it didn't sound much like Will's way of talking.'

'Well, maybe he's even more depressed than usual today.' Scanning the crowd, however, they saw no sign of Will Wruthers.

'The best I can hope for is death by sunstroke,' said Chelle in a low, bitter, mournful tone. The others looked at her. She shrugged. 'Even if I fainted in the mud here,' she continued in the same un-Chelle-like tone, 'everybody would just trample over me.' Aware that she was drawing some funny looks, Ryan bought Chelle a toffee apple and she sank her teeth into it to stop herself saying anything else.

'Hang on,' said Ryan, 'I'll see if I can find him.'

As it turned out, pushing through the crowd involved headbutting a lot of leather-clad elbows. Ryan looked around in vain for Will's tremulous features and found his way blocked by the sandwich-board clown mime, who wanted to give him a leaflet and a lollipop.

The creamy paint of the mime's face was smudged with sweat. His eyes were windows into a world full of misery, loathing and despair.

'Come to Ebstowe Fair for a day of family fun,' the mime intoned joylessly. It was unmistakably the same voice that Chelle had been using shortly before.

Ryan found his way back to the others.

'We've found another wisher,' he muttered.

'Score! But we can't worry about that now. Look over there, *Silverwing* magazine's got its own stand.' Josh pointed across the field. 'Let's head that way and see if we can spot Will.'

As the threesome drew nearer the *Silverwing* stall Chelle again began whispering to herself anxiously.

'. . . what am I even doing here? What if Mum phones work and finds out I'm not there? And what if I win? No no I won't think like that, I won't win. But what if I do? But then again . . . oh . . . just look at it . . .'

At the front of the *Silverwing* platform stood the Harley-Davidson Ultra, in all its gleaming, metallic-blue glory. For the first time, Ryan almost understood Will's obsession. The metal of the Harley bulged and rippled as if it had muscles. This was a motorbike that would slice the horizons in two and find you new ones before you could breathe, all the while leaning easily back on itself as if it wasn't even trying.

Across the back of the platform ran a row of seats. Will Wruthers sat in the seat at one end, twisting his hands and looking at the Harley.

'. . . ten minutes until they announce the winner . . .' To judge from Chelle's whispers, Will seemed tied up in knots between hoping he won the Harley and hoping he didn't.

'There!'

Ryan winced as Josh's excited elbow caught him in the ribs. Following his friend's pointing finger, he saw a lottery machine full of balls up on the platform.

Over the next ten minutes the seats started to fill up as the other shortlisted people arrived. When a small crowd had gathered before the stand, a bald man in motorcycle leathers walked on to the platform and tapped the microphone, then started giving a brief intro.

'Josh . . . how do you know which ball to make pop out?' Ryan asked under his breath.

Josh bit his lips together and chewed at them.

'Probably got everybody on the shortlist numbered in alphabetical order. So . . . Wruthers is bound to be last, isn't it? Number twenty.'

Ryan could almost hear their plan creaking under his feet like a badly built bridge.

The bald man finished his speech, went over to the Harley and let its engine thrum, then returned to the microphone. 'Now, time for our own little lottery.' He turned to the machine.

'Oh please oh please oh please . . .' whispered Chelle, 'number sixteen, number sixteen . . .'

'It's sixteen, Josh!' hissed Ryan urgently.

Josh nodded. His mouth was twitching, and Ryan realized that he was mouthing the word 'sixteen' over and over again. The ball machine stopped stirring the balls and made a skreeking, grinding noise. The bald man winced then gave the audience a wry smile.

Behind him a video screen showing motorbikes curling around a racecourse fizzed with static.

'Josh . . .' whispered Ryan warningly. His friend did not answer. Looking up, Ryan found Josh's face fixed in a pale mask of focused rage, his eyes piercing the ball machine. The backs of Ryan's hands stung and tickled, and when he dropped his gaze he saw to his horror that his unbandaged warts were a grape-like cluster of bulges, and that their lashes were fluttering as if about to part. Chelle caught his expression and looked downwards too. Her eyes widened. Terrified, Ryan glanced back at Josh, a panicky word on his lips, but suddenly he was looking at his friend through a halo of pale gold, like a blot left on the eye after staring at the sun, and the whole scene seemed too bright.

Nobody else seemed to have noticed. A ball dropped out of the machine into a steel basin beneath, and the bald man stooped for it. The murmur of the crowd hushed expectantly, so everybody heard quite clearly when the comfortable growl of the Harley rose to a deafening roar. Suddenly it bucked its front wheel, and surged free from the grip of the man holding its handlebars.

Will Wruthers' eyes widened as the Harley bounced off the ball machine with a deafening crack and careered towards him. He pulled his knees to his chin and flung his arms around his head. A metallic clang, a chorus of screams, and the Harley roared over the back of the platform. Will's seat was no longer there. Will was no longer there.

'Josh,' Chelle breathed aghast, 'I think you've killed him . . .'

Josh said nothing. He was breathing heavily. His face held no expression at all. Ryan noticed that a ball had rolled to rest against the microphone on the platform. It had '16' printed on it. The ball that sat forgotten in the bald man's hand seemed to be number eleven.

The threesome let the surge of the crowd carry them

forward and then stood staring at the prone figure of Will Wruthers. The Harley had knocked him clean off the back of the platform. He was still tangled in his fallen chair, and displayed no signs of life.

15

Dangerous Driving

The St John Ambulance people were there very quickly.
To keep himself from panicking, Ryan silently ran
through a list of prime numbers, each as cool, smooth
and regular in his mind as a pearl on a string. He was
relieved to see that the ambulance men did not shake
their heads at each other or cover Will's face.

'I don't think he's dead,' Ryan whispered.

Josh said nothing. His jaw was clenched.

Ryan felt another tingle across his knuckles as Will
was moved very gently on to the stretcher. Sun bubbles
danced on Ryan's lashes, and for a moment there was a
streak of glisten on his vision, like the sort he would
sometimes see before a migraine. He took off his
glasses and blinked hard to clear the streak. Everything
instantly got much worse.

With his normal eyes open and his glasses off, he
was muzzy with double vision. During the second that
his eyes were closed, however, the scene before him
jumped into a new clarity. With only his secret eyes
open he could clearly see, extending from Will's chest,

a single translucent tentacle, softly snaking. As he watched, a non-existent wind tore it ragged and chased it into nothingness, like a smoke ring.

'Oh no.' He clutched his hands up against his chest. *Don't let that be his spirit leaving don't let that be his spirit leaving* . . . A terrible, horrible, unworthy thought sprang into his mind. *If he dies then we'll never grant his wish and we'll be like this forever* . . .

'Hold it in.' Josh had a hand on his shoulder and was glaring down the few concerned onlookers who had noticed Ryan's behaviour.

'I'm not going to be sick,' hissed Ryan with unusual fierceness, hoping that he was telling the truth. 'I'm just having a laugh a minute with my "power" right now, all right?' He squeezed his eyes shut reflexively, and again the air about him was thick with migraine-streaks, ghost snakes. When he opened his normal eyes the snakes were still faintly visible, pushing from the chests of the people around him, distorting the world behind them like wrinkles in a glass pane.

'Ryan? What's happening?' It didn't help to look at Chelle. Little ghost-snakes kept venturing questingly, fearfully, from her chest like eels from a hide-hole, then pulling back as if stung. Josh was no better, with a great, translucent python thrashing and whiplashing, seemingly trying to tear itself free from his breastbone. Ryan pushed his fists into his armpits and doubled up, closing his real eyes tight. He felt hands grab his elbows and start to lead him away. The voices of the crowd faded slightly, and the megaphone announcements became a smudge of sound.

'OK, we're clear.' He felt a grip on his sleeve. 'Ryan, look at me.' Ryan straightened and slowly opened his normal eyes to stare through Josh's yellow lenses at the pale-lashed eyes behind. They were wide, focused and sincere. 'You're OK, Ryan. Breathe.'

Ryan took a few deep breaths before letting his eyes stray from Josh's steadying gaze. The distorting snakes that had streaked his vision seemed to have gone.

'Everybody in the crowd had these . . .' Ryan swallowed, '. . . these *things*, like tentacles, coming out of them and waving around . . . except Will. He had one but when he was on the stretcher it . . . it . . . kind of melted away . . . Josh, maybe that was his soul, maybe we killed him . . .'

'Just look at me and listen, OK? He's not dead. It's OK. He tucked up his legs just before the bike hit, didn't he? You both saw that, didn't you? The bike didn't hit him, just the chair. It's not a big platform to fall off. He's OK. It's OK.'

Josh was right.

The next day, after a sleepless night, Ryan read in the local paper, to his intense relief, that 'Will Wruthers' injuries proved to be slight and he is recovering well in St Barnabas' Hospital.' *Silverwing* magazine had apologized for the incident, and to make amends had promised to pay for Will to go on a 'Direct Access' course to learn how to ride a motorcycle. They were also willing to make a payment towards any motorcycle of his choice.

I wonder if that'll be enough to help him buy a Harley-Davidson, thought Ryan. *And I wonder if he still wants one.*

'Ryan!'

Ryan jumped to hear his mother's voice just behind him.

'Let me see those.' She snatched hold of both of his hands, pulling the bandage back to expose his warts fully. 'Why didn't you tell me about this?'

Ryan dropped his gaze to his hands. His warts were pale and bulging like blisters, but there were no signs of eyelashes or eyeballs.

That afternoon she took him to a specialist. Dr Marston was a tall man with tired eyes. He prodded Ryan's warts gently, then a little more firmly, and Ryan had to grit his teeth to stop himself wincing.

'Well, there's no redness, but the swelling is tight – probably full of fluid. I could pierce the swellings with a sterilized needle, but you'd have to keep them very clean to stop them getting infected . . .'

'No!' Ryan's voice was squawky with panic. He hid his hands behind his back. It must have looked childish, but he was filled with terror at the thought of long steel points sliding into his hidden eyes.

'Oh . . . we'll try a tube of that cream you mentioned instead,' Ryan's mother declared impatiently, when at last she realized that for once Ryan would not give way. 'We'll come back if it doesn't work.'

On the drive home, to Ryan's dismay, she made it quite clear that he should leave his warts unbandaged from that point on, 'to let the air get to them'. Now Ryan couldn't even hide one hand.

Back at the house, Ryan discovered a message on the answering machine from Chelle, which took five minutes to ask him over for tea.

Josh and Chelle were already in the Cavern when he arrived. Josh had a new and darker pair of sunglasses.

'We've been to Ebstowe Fair, the one the sandwich board was all about, and found out all kinds of stuff,' began Chelle, 'and I don't like the new wisher; he's even worse than Donna only in a different way, and when I have his thoughts in my head it's like stirring really cold porridge round and round with your finger. It's horrible . . .'

'Yeah. Where were you?' Josh's new glasses had lenses shaped like slanting headlights. Evil beetle eyes. 'We phoned, but your dad said you'd gone out.'

'My mum took me to a doctor about my warts.' It was ridiculous, but Ryan felt hurt to think that the others had gone to the fair without him.

'Did you give anything away?' When Ryan shook his head, Josh nodded approval. 'Yeah, well, we couldn't hang around waiting for you to get back. We've only got two weeks until term starts, haven't we? Besides, I had to get out of the house. Donna and Punzell are driving me mad. My parents say they've got to stay and mend the feng shui so televisions don't explode, and sometimes they just do, right? So they're still in the house every day.'

'It's a bit like that with Miss Gossamer,' Chelle said, nodding vigorously, 'she's always about, watching . . .'

'And it makes me sick. I keep coming across them with Punzell rubbing her shoulders to "align her energies", and her making little "ooh" noises. And when he's not there, then she's following me around everywhere and pretending not to. I think she's scared I'll tell Punzell she's not really psychic. For God's sake, we granted her wish, didn't we? I hope Wet Will isn't going to be such a royal pain now he's got his wish.'

'Has he definitely got the Harley then?'

'Oh come on! They're helping him buy any bike he chooses. What's he going to get? Anyway, forget about him,' Josh said impatiently. 'Chelle, tell Ryan about the new wisher, and then I'll tell him what we're going to do.'

'Oooh, it's so sad, he's so miserable, and I want to like him but I don't because he hates everybody so much. And his brain's got this, like this . . . smell, it's like an old people's kitchen smell but he isn't really old enough for his kitchen to smell like that. And he's an actor, and his name is Jacob Karlborough, and he just keeps thinking about how he should have got this part in this play called *The Case of the Strangled Parrot*, then he had to work for the fair as a mime, playing Harlequin, and he hated it, but now they've made somebody younger Harlequin instead, and Jacob has to be just one of Harlequin's helpers, and he hates that even more. And he thinks about all the people in the fair, and how they don't realize he should be famous really. And he thinks about how some day he'll show them, and get a part in a West End play, then he starts from the beginning and thinks about it all over again.'

'So we need to make sure he shows 'em,' Josh butted in enthusiastically. 'Get him famous so he can get into a West End play and rub everyone's nose in it. Listen – there's going to be a "magic, mime and music show" on the last day of the fair, and he's going to be Harlequin in it one last time. So we need to make sure lots of people see him performing, so he gets famous.'

'Let's hope he isn't rubbish,' Ryan muttered. 'How do we make everyone see him?'

'Oh, I've got lots of ideas about that. I mean, what if all the rides and everything started going wrong? Everybody'll end up going to the Harlequin tent instead—'

'Josh, no, please, really, really, no . . .' Ryan had visions of Ferris wheels spinning away from their axles, roller coasters slingshotting their cars at the sky . . .

Josh looked sullen, but was brought round by concentrated begging from the other two. 'OK. Whatever. Anyway, Ryan – here's the really clever bit. Your dad's a theatre critic, isn't he? So you just make him come along, and then afterwards get him to write his column on this clown guy.'

'He's never going to do that!' Ryan exclaimed, horrified. 'He mostly reviews big London shows and touring plays . . .'

'Well, you can get him there, can't you? And afterwards just . . . keep going on about the best bits of the show, so he doesn't forget them. Look, we've only got a few days till the big show happens. This is all you've got to do, Ryan; we already scouted everything out and did all the planning.' When Josh put things like that, it was impossible to say no.

'I just hope I can get away without Miss Gossamer following me,' twittered Chelle faintly, 'and yesterday when I was going to the post office to get some stamps for Mum she kept saying, "Can't you send one of the older girls? Little Chelle and I were having such a lovely conversation" . . .' Chelle's words had a comforting patter, like gentle rain, but this did not console Ryan much. His father hated pantomimes and magic shows. He wasn't sure he could even make him sit through a whole 'mime and magic' show, let alone like it.

Chelle was still talking. 'And even though I knew it was a dream it was really scary because the legs of her chair kept moving and creeping her closer and closer to me and she was just sitting there pretending she wasn't moving, and the worst thing was I kept trying to tell everybody and make them see her following me all around the house, but it was like they couldn't hear me . . .'

Josh's eyes were still hidden behind the evil beetle glasses, but Ryan could tell that he was watching him.

'You'll do it, Ryan,' Josh said suddenly. 'You're

smart.' He said this as if it ended the matter, which of course it did.

They had to clear out of the Cavern a little before six because Miss Gossamer wanted Chelle's help with sorting through clothes for a jumble sale.

During dinner, Ryan's mother enthused about everything she had discovered concerning the voodoo symbols painted on the milk bottles. As far as she could tell, she had been cursed with death, childlessness and having her eyes eaten by the god Legbar. She was thoroughly delighted about all of this. And then, halfway through sawing at a block of cheese, she suddenly looked misty-eyed, and left the table to look for a better knife, rubbing sternly at one eye with the heel of her hand. Ryan's father sighed deeply without seeming at all surprised. It did not seem to be a good time to talk about funfairs.

Breakfast did not seem like a good time to bring it up either. His parents were in the throes of an icy post-argument lull.

He finally took the plunge the following morning, when his father was giving him a lift to collect the prescription cream from the chemist.

'Dad . . . I'd really like to go to the Ebstowe fair.' There. 'I just thought it would be nice . . . as a family . . . all together.'

His father glanced at him in the rear-view mirror, quite cautiously, as if he really was looking out for something dangerous incoming. 'Well . . . perhaps. We'll see, shall we?'

It was fortunate that Ryan's father also checked the wing mirror before pulling out. He slammed on his brakes as a motorcycle with a red L-plate sliced past the window, its rider garish in his neon-yellow over-jacket. The bike wobbled to a halt at the lights ahead, and the rider placed an unsteady foot down. Looking out through the back window, Ryan spotted two more motorcyclists wearing the same yellow jackets, one with the words 'instructor' emblazoned on it in black.

The lights changed, and the motorcyclist ahead looked over his shoulder, revved the engine, lifted his feet on to the rests and toppled over sideways with a crash. A bobbly bit broke off a lever that stuck out from the right handlebar. The queue of traffic had to wait while he crawled out from under the bike, lifted it with great effort, straddled it again and wobbled off down the road.

Ryan watched the luminous yellow figure until it was out of sight. The rider's face had mostly been hidden by the helmet, but the part visible through the visor had looked an awful lot like Will Wruthers.

16
Fair Punishment

That evening Ryan's father brought up the idea of visiting the fair 'as a family'. Ryan's mother, ever unpredictable, decided it was a wonderful idea. A wonderful idea, that is, until the day itself, when she had an early phone call from Saul Paladine's ex-wife, who wanted to tell Ryan's mother all about him and give her his letters. Ryan's mother got extremely excited and drove off to Nottinghamshire, leaving a note.

Ryan's father handed Ryan the note without saying anything. He drove Ryan to the Ebstowe fair without saying anything.

Ryan had not noticed on his last visit what a sad town Ebstowe was. Apparently it had been very popular about a hundred years before. The big sweeping promenade along the sea front looked a bit lost, as if it was wondering where the women with big hats and white parasols had gone. Now that the pocked, brightly coloured plastic towers of the funfair came into view, Ryan thought it seemed very strange next to the rest of Ebstowe, strange and wrong. It was as if somebody had found a gentle, dignified old lady whose friends were all dead, and forced her to wear a funny hat.

'I shall insist on you enjoying this,' muttered Ryan's father, unbuttoning the collar of his shirt as they approached the turnstile. 'I will want proof of glee.' He did not like heat or crowds, and Ryan felt at once guilty and pleased that his father had agreed to brave the fair for him.

It was worse than Ryan had expected. When he was eight, the fair had been a magical, sun-soaked place. He hadn't been back since, however, and time had done strange and terrible things.

He remembered riding a carousel with swings that swung out sideways when it spun, and feeling as if he was flying. That ride was gone, leaving only a stripped round hub with steps set in the sides. A row of inexplicable plastic camels lurched in a line, bug-eyed and grinning despite their missing noses and chipped knees. The sides of the crazy house were painted with clumsy rip-off Disney figures, Mickey and Donald's ugly cousins.

While he was staring about himself, trying to smile for the benefit of his father, Chelle ran up to him.

'Have you seen, you have to pay for the rides as well as to get in! It wasn't like that last year, oh hello, Mr Doyle.'

'Hello, Chelle.' Ryan's father was giving him a shrewd sideways look. 'Would I be right in thinking that Josh is somewhere here too?'

'Yes, but he's busy shooting things at the moment and

he's already won a dolphin but look he gave it to me.' Delighted, she waved a bright blue dolphin in their faces. Its pupils wobbled in its plastic eyes. Ryan's father recoiled slightly.

The threesome walked on in what would have been an uncomfortable silence if one of them had not been Chelle.

'. . . and the dodgems were too scary, not properly scary like the ghost train but nasty. I paid and tried to get into a car but all these boys got there first and nobody noticed I didn't have a car and so I just stood at the side . . .'

There was a look of quiet suffering on Ryan's father's face. Ryan had a feeling that before long it would get a lot less quiet. Chelle, on the other hand, seemed to be enjoying herself.

Ahead at the rifle range they saw Josh surrendering his gun and being handed a red cowboy hat by the stall-holder. He brought the hat over and dropped it on to Ryan's head.

'Good morning, Mr Doyle.' He was doing his talking-to-parents voice again. 'I'm very glad that you and Ryan were able to come.'

'I wish fewer people had had the same idea,' said Ryan's father. Indeed, there were long snaky queues in front of most of the rides, all already full of hot and impatient young children. Looking around, Ryan noticed that there seemed to be quite a crowd massing outside the entrance gates. Strangely, the crowd seemed to be chiefly made up of grown men and boys in their late teens.

Ryan's father had noticed this as well, and was frowning at it. There was a silence, and then Chelle gave a small squeak as if she had spotted something.

'Oh . . . look at that!' With rather unconvincing surprise, she pointed across the fairground towards a large blue tent. 'That poster says there's a show inside with mimes, magic and music . . . and it starts in five minutes. Let's . . . all go inside right now.'

'It is in the shade, I suppose,' assented Ryan's father.

'Perhaps you two could go in ahead and save a place,' Ryan said quickly. 'Josh and I can get some drinks.'

His father disappeared into the tent with Chelle. Ryan could not help noticing that there seemed to be quite a lot of people inside already.

'Have you seen the crowds outside?' Josh was grinning like a zip. 'And there's more coming. Hundreds. Betcha.'

'That's . . .' Ryan blinked as two annoyed-looking men pushed past, glaring around them, one holding a nearly empty beer bottle. 'Yes, that's really good. How . . . where did they come from?'

'Ebstowe football stadium.' Josh stretched. 'I was going to try to do something to stop the game but I thought, nah, even if I blow all the lights and set off the fire alarms that'll just hold things up. But then I remembered the Shuttlecock. It's the pub up by the stadium, where all the locals go after the game. Last night I went and leaned up against the windows and did all the lights and fridges. Broke 'em all. And I made some posters on Mr Lattimer-Stone's printer, with ads for the fair and saying it's got a cheap beer tent, and stuck 'em up near the pub. So all the locals'll come straight out of the game and over here looking for cheap beer, and they'll look for it in there because it's the only tent. Makes sense, doesn't it?'

'Ye-e-es,' said Ryan with feelings of deep unease. 'That . . . kind of . . . makes . . . sense . . .'

By the time they got back to the blue tent, there was standing room only. A lot of men were pushing through the crowd this way and that and calling loudly to one another.

By pushing along the tent wall he found his father, who was stooping slightly with the canvas pressed against his head. Chelle was sheltering behind him. Ryan's father did not look happy and seemed to be craning to gauge the crowd.

'Ryan,' he said with quiet seriousness, 'if things get too crowded here and we need to leave, we're going to duck under the tent canvas here, instead of using the main entrance, all right?' The canvas walls did not quite reach the ground, and Ryan could see sunlit tarmac through the gap.

A blue spotlight appeared on the stage, juddered and adjusted itself slightly to the left. From somewhere above, a square frame was lowered. It had been painted to look like a night window. A woman with a white doll face, tiny pursed red mouth and round pink cheeks ran on to the stage on tiptoe, then settled down on the boards, her hands pillowing her head to show that she was sleeping.

'Are you all right?' Ryan's father had noticed Chelle with both hands forced over her mouth, making little sounds as if she was about to throw up. 'Is it your asthma?' He could not know that she was stopping herself speaking someone else's thoughts. The canvas of the tent twanged slightly, and when Ryan looked down he saw his father holding its fabric up so that Chelle could crawl out into the daylight.

The lights dimmed further, and then the shining figure of a man seemed to leap through the window with magical grace, his boots hitting the stage with a slightly less magical thud.

The doll-faced woman woke and raised her hands either side of her face in a gesture of surprise and alarm. The figure in gold approached her and, plucking a rose from the air, offered it to her. With his other hand he reached into space and produced a gleaming goblet.

'Mine's a pint!' shouted somebody in the crowd. There was a roar of laughter, which made Ryan realize how many grown men there were in the tent.

The spotlight grew brighter, and the laughter became louder as the features of the Harlequin were more clearly illuminated. He was doing a good job of keeping a straight face despite sweating heavily in his pleated gold costume.

'Look at him!' shouted someone else from the audience. 'He's old enough to be her father!' After this, everybody decided that they were allowed to shout at the stage. When a parade of 'Harlequin's helpers' capered in from the wings, all in gold pantaloons and skirts, the laughter became deafening.

Something was happening over at the entrance, something that involved a lot of shouting.

The doll-faced woman was staring out across the audience with a spangled handkerchief in her hand, as if deciding whether to run. Harlequin, however, was keeping to the tinny cues of the music. She let him take her hand and patiently guide her through the steps of the dance, but her head kept looking towards the audience.

There was a thud, and Ryan knew that somebody had hit somebody. It didn't make a satisfying *pock!* noise like in films, but it had the sound of something real that would hurt. The crowd swayed and surged, losing any interest it had had in Harlequin's antics.

'Now,' Ryan's father said quietly, stooping to lift the canvas, but it was not needed. With a faint musical sound the guy ropes were giving, and the canvas flapped loose to reveal a gash of sky. Only then did they realize that the chaos was not limited to the tent. The doll-faced girl shrieked and ran as dozens of hands grabbed at the tent canvas and pulled it loose, leaving the Harlequin and his helpers open to the sky.

The visiting crowd had become an invading army. There was a loud smashing sound erupting from the grubby, spotted mirrors in the crazy house. A pelting match had broken out between groups of the marauders, with one team using plastic ducks as missiles, and the other, plush dolphins.

Harlequin's helpers scattered, shrieking hysterically. Only the Harlequin stood alone, staring about him at the carnage with a strange serenity. *Perhaps he's in shock*, thought Ryan. Ryan's father had pulled Ryan, Josh and Chelle to relative safety behind a tumbled ice-cream cart. Chelle's mouth was still full of fist, and Josh's wide eyes held a fierce, wild light, but Ryan's father did not notice. He was staring at the Harlequin with unsuppressed fascination.

As the cap of the helter-skelter broke off and crashed to earth, accompanied by a roar of triumph and screams of dismay, Harlequin looked about him with burning eyes. He raised both palms to his face and, as little plumes of blue smoke issued from jets hidden in his gloves, he blew them like a kiss towards the death of the fairground and smiled. Ryan's hand-eyes flicked open just in time to see a single ghost snake tethered to the clown's heart raise itself as if in salute, and then fade.

17

A Storm and a Sanctuary

The day after the fair, Ryan's father read them his latest column.

'This week I have been a martyr to my family,' it began. 'On Monday my wife compelled me to attend the opening performance of *The Coldrake Legacy* featuring Saul Paladine. On Wednesday I submitted to the entreaties of my small son and visited the theatricals of the Ebstowe fairground.

'The two performances gave me some interesting opportunities for comparison. Ebstowe's "mime, music and magic" extravaganza ended some half an hour before the advertised time, for reasons I will explain shortly. *The Coldrake Legacy*, on the other hand, started a full hour later than scheduled. It seems the air-conditioning in the theatre had been producing a curious smell, undetectable to anyone but the celebrated Saul Paladine, who refused to perform until he was sure that there were no fumes that might tickle his throat and endanger his famous voice. This sensitivity is no doubt a great burden to Mr Paladine and should not be mocked, but nonetheless I intend to do so at some length . . .'

Ryan's father went on to describe the anarchy at the fair in a very funny way. He had gone to the trouble of finding out the name of the mime artist, and described the way in which he had gone on with his performance even as the fair was destroyed around him.

'And so,' the article ended, 'I believe that Saul Paladine has a great deal to learn from Jacob Karlborough. The determination to maintain one's art in the face of overpowering odds seems to have died in the West End theatres, but it is good to find it alive and well amid the dingy spangles of our seaside resorts.'

Ryan was silently outraged. 'Small son' made him sound like a five-year-old, and 'entreaties', as if he had been bursting into tears and clinging to his father's leg. Ryan's mother was loudly outraged. She said that 'compelled' made her sound like a 'domineering harpy' and if the article was published there would be trouble. The article was published. There was trouble.

The resulting squabble simmered through breakfast and throughout the family's shopping trip. Outside the supermarket, it erupted into a blistering all-out row, hands clenched around the handles of carrier bags.

'Well, God forbid that my feelings should stand in the way of a turn of phrase!' Ryan's mother was screaming. Her features were almost unrecognizable.

Ryan's father's mouth barely moved. His sentences were curt and short, and his face bore a wild look of concentration as if it was taking all his effort to keep them that way.

Some ten yards away, Ryan stood there stupidly holding a carrier bag full of canned sweetcorn while he watched the continents of his world collide and the stars fall out of the sky. Almost involuntarily he started counting through the Fibonacci sequence in his head to keep himself sane. One, two, three, five, eight . . . Today the numbers failed him. The way they built up only seemed an echo of what was happening before him, where every bitter sentence added to the last to make something bigger and worse.

On the far side of the car park he noticed Mr and Mrs Lattimer-Stone watching from inside their estate and muttering mask-faced to one another. He felt worse than naked in front of them, as if something had torn out his middle and left him a ridiculous doughnut boy that everyone could look right through. As their car pulled away he wondered if they felt sorry for him, and then hated himself for even caring.

You're supposed to be clever, said a goading voice in his head, with much the same note of bitterness and contempt Donna Leas had once used. *If you're so clever, do something about it. Say something. Make it better.*

He looked about himself for inspiration, but all he saw was a supermarket trolley drifting slowly towards the wire fence, in thrall to the pull of the slope. It looked as helpless as he felt. Then he felt a sensation like that of a raindrop sliding across his knuckles, and he saw all four of the trolley's wheels swivel as one. It turned in time to avoid crashing into the wire, and began to glide towards him, against the slope of the tarmac.

Oh no . . . not now . . . not here . . .

Another trolley completed the same arc behind it. One trolley, two, three, five . . . Fibonacci trolleys.

Ryan pulled out one of the sweetcorn cans and hefted it to shoulder height, but the muscles in his arm seemed to have gone slack. What was he hoping to do, scare them away like stray dogs? The trolleys juddered their plastic child seats with a wet paddling sound and jangled their chains. Ryan was reminded of a snake's rattle. Feeling sick, he decided to come quietly.

Ryan's mother and father noticed nothing as their only son was taken into custody by a host of supermarket trolleys and herded to the far side of the car park.

He was not surprised when the trolleys corralled him to the fountain in the corner of the car park. An artificial 'waterfall' spilled from an upper shelf into a lower pool, the glossy curtain of water broken only by two abstract metal figures. The larger, apparently a smiling mother, seemed to be holding her baby son up into the flow. Both had limbs that tapered to points.

Somebody will see this, thought Ryan as the mother lowered her baby, tucked it under one arm and leaned forward to stare at him with the two oblique slashes she wore for eyes. A miserable shred of him wished somebody *would* see it, and that they'd storm over to bully the truth out of him and make the whole thing stop. But the world went on blind in sunlight, leaving Ryan staring into a noseless face bubbling with green water.

'Hhhwwehhlllumh pfhawrrrrthh . . .' It was worse than he remembered it.

The water that chuckled into the shallow basin had lights in it that almost made pictures. Taking a deep breath, Ryan held out both fists in front of him. He closed his eyes and . . . opened his eyes.

With his strange new vision he saw a gleam of a stream with a low bridge over it and a bank trailing honeysuckle into the water. It might have been a picture from a calendar, and it was utterly unfamiliar to him.

'Wwehllmp hffaawwwwwdthhh . . .'

Just stop, Ryan begged silently, as a dusting of tiny drops settled against his cheeks. All she wanted was an agreement to whatever she had said, and she would stop. He nodded, feeling as if his muscles were spaghetti. *Just stop.*

'Ryan!'

His mother's voice. Ryan opened his normal eyes, heart pounding. The metal mother and child had returned to their innocent, playful pose. He slumped. There were little stars of water on his spectacle lenses.

'Ryan.' His mother took him by the shoulder. 'Why did you slip off like that? It doesn't help to have you running off and sulking right now.'

He looked up at her in mute misery. She frowned back, and apparently saw something which stopped her being angry with him. Instead it seemed to make her more angry with his father when they walked back to join him, but Ryan felt too weak to care about that.

A frost settled on the house when they got home. Ryan did not want to talk to anybody. When Josh phoned to invite him to a cafe down the road, he said yes, without asking his parents first.

'Great, I'll get a car round to you stat.' Josh was hissing with laughter. 'You'll see what I mean in a mo.' Nowadays there was only a thin rustle of static when Josh called, another sign of him getting his 'powers' under control.

Ryan went up to the landing where the opera music from his father's room tangled and clashed with the Brahms from his mother's room, then changed his mind. He went back downstairs and left them a note on the kitchen table.

A horn sounded outside the front door, and Ryan opened it to find a small green Renault parked outside. Chelle waved through a back window. Josh got out of the passenger door, and Ryan could see that Donna Leas was in the driver's seat.

'Jump in,' called Josh, and Ryan climbed into the back next to Chelle, biting back his questions.

It was a short drive, one that they could have walked easily. The back of Donna's neck was red above her sleeveless summer top, and as she drove she kept jerking the steering wheel this way and that.

'Stop just here,' Josh said loftily. 'Wait for us; we'll be an hour or so.' He was clearly enjoying himself.

As they got out of the car, Ryan peered back at

Donna's set face. How had Josh managed to tame the library witch? Was this some new power that they had not discovered before?

'I'm buying the drinks,' Josh said when he got inside. 'And I feel like chips. We're all having chips. So, Ryan – ' he nudged him – 'what d'you think of my new chauffeur?'

'She drives a bit like she'd like to crush your side of the car,' was all Ryan could think of to say.

'It's cool, isn't it? All today I've been like, oh, Donna, I need a lift to the cafe, or, Donna, go buy me some cigarettes, will you? And she has to. It's great.'

'Why? Why does she have to?'

'Cos she's scared stiff of Punzell finding out she's not psychic. She doesn't know how we did the Chelle reading her mind thing, and she doesn't know why machines keep going weird, but she knows it's us. It's obvious. And we had this massive row yesterday – I told her if she wanted the bulbs to keep popping when she was in the room, and didn't want me to tell Punzell everything, then things had to be a bit different, that's all.'

Chelle tittered slightly. Josh grinned.

'Aw, look, Chelle, Ryan's trying not to smile but he can't help it, can he? Oh, *c'mon*, Ryan, you remember what she was like at school, right? Just cos they gave her power over us. Well, now we've got power over her – it's payback, that's all. Justice.' Josh glanced at Ryan, then abruptly lost patience and pushed back in his chair so the feet rocked. Behind him the radio spat static for a second. 'What are you looking so sick about? You like messing about with bus stops and not having money to buy things, do you?'

'No.' Ryan felt too weak to think of the right thing to say. 'Yeah. Whatever. I mean . . .' He roused himself. 'I mean, yeah, you're right, Josh. Sorry. I'm just a bit . . . things happened this morning.' He told them about the car-park fountain. He said nothing about his parents' argument.

'That's great!' Josh banged the edge of the table with his spoon, as if he was knocking his words like nails into the wood. 'We got another lead. Nice one.'

'Did we really finish the Harlequin's wish?' Ryan looked at Chelle, who nodded vigorously.

'Oh yes, he's all done. I was in his thoughts and then when the top came off the helter-skelter he was full of *ooh*, and happiness, and then it all sort of went *pop!* and I wasn't in there any more . . .'

'I think I saw the wish being granted.' Ryan frowned. 'This ghostly snake thing was rippling out of the Harlequin's chest and it suddenly melted into air – the same as happened with Will at the bike rally. I think the snake-thing *was* the wish, and it vanished because it was granted. But . . . at the rally when I looked around *everybody* had the same kind of snakes . . .'

'Well, everybody wants something, don't they?' answered Josh. 'Even people that don't drop coins down wells.'

'But then . . . why didn't I see them before?' Ryan cast his mind back to the dinner party, when his hand-eyes had been open full-stretch. Now that he thought about it, had there been a nebulous shifting in the darkness, an almost imperceptible writhing of the shadows?

'Practice.' Josh grinned. 'You're learning to see more, Ryan.'

'I wish we'd known what the Harlequin's wish really was from the start,' Chelle murmured. 'I mean, I knew he hated everybody at the fairground, but I thought all the time that he just wanted to be famous in a West End production and show them and really, really he—'

'He wanted to show them.' Josh grinned behind his beetle glasses. His spoon had started tapping out the beat to the song on the cafe's stereo. Ryan recognized it as 'Avenging Angels' by Space. 'Well, they got showed, all right.'

'But it's not really our fault, is it, Josh, we didn't mean to break the fair, it doesn't count, and we wouldn't have done his wish if we'd known that really he was wishing for the fairground to be trampled into little pieces . . .'

'I would,' said Josh. 'It was a crap fair. We're like vigilante justice. And it's not like anyone was badly hurt. Forget about it. Tell us more about the fountain-speak.'

After Ryan had reproduced the burbled words as best he could, Josh ran for Donna's road atlas and flicked to the index.

'Let's see if it's a place name, like last time. Sounds like it starts with a "w" anyway. Webb's Hill . . . Whelmford, that's the closest we've got. Here, look, it's not far away, it's only a few miles from Magwhite.'

Like Magwhite, Whelmford was a small village that

lurked on the northern edge of the great sprawl that was Guildley, where the town was just giving way to fields. The village took its name from the little tributary mead which ran through it, connected with the spider's web of canals round Magwhite and then joined the Eff, the great river which pierced the heart of Guildley, swung south and finally flared into an estuary near Ebstowe on the coast.

'Come on! My chauffeur'll take us there right now. Oh . . . wait a minute.' The man behind him had given up on the fruit machine. 'It wants to,' Josh muttered. He always said that about fruit machines that he thought were ready to pay out. He walked over, and Ryan watched as Josh's hand moved from coin slot to button to button. A thick chinking-chunking sound came from the innards of the machine, and coins started spilling out into the little tray.

'Magic,' Josh whispered. Ryan stared.

Before playing, Josh had put his hand up to the coin slot at the top. He just hadn't put a coin in.

Donna drove them to Whelmford in silence. Ryan noticed that on the parcel shelf was a bag belonging to Josh, which seemed to contain three library books on electromagnetism, an old circuit board and what looked like photocopied diagrams of the inner working of machines. Clearly Josh had been studying his power some more.

Electromagnetism. Yes, it was an appropriate power for Josh. Magnetism and electricity. Draw people in and spark things off. Not for the first time Ryan wondered if the Well Spirit had given each of them a power to suit their character. Ryan, with his 'upside-down' way of viewing the world, was given a new, strange sight. Chelle, unable to prevent anything falling into her brain or out of her mouth, became the mouthpiece for the wishes of others. And Josh of course was the action hero, the one who would make things happen.

At Whelmford Donna parked, yanking the handbrake so that it grated.

'I have to go back to the office,' she snapped. 'I work afternoons on Wednesdays.' Hearing her voice was shocking after her long silence. Ryan had almost started to think of the new, docile Donna as some kind of animatronic replica.

'You can be late.' Josh gave a grin like a mantrap, flipped a lever and eased his seat into recline. 'In fact . . . I kind of like it here. Maybe we'll sit in the car and digest our food for a bit first.'

'Josh . . .' Ryan saw Donna's hands forming fists around the steering wheel and wondered if his friend was pushing his luck. 'Um, I'm going to take a look for that bridge I saw in the um, you know . . . OK?'

'Catch you up,' Josh said lazily as Ryan scrambled out of the car followed by Chelle, who was watching Donna with a similar air of apprehension.

On either side of the little river were wide, tarmac-covered waterside footpaths. There were lots of cleanly painted benches, rubbish bins and signposts with red, yellow and blue spots on them to show where the footpaths went. There was a wire-mesh fence to stop you falling the two feet into the water.

'There it is,' he whispered suddenly. Before him was the calendar picture bridge the Well Spirit had shown him.

Chelle walked out on to the bridge. Behind her honeysuckle swayed softly, peach-coloured petals curling like hair. She rested her elbows on the curved iron rail and hunched her sun-freckled shoulders. And then she started to giggle. It was a pleasant, infectious, husky giggle, but it did not belong to her.

'Oh, it's hopeless,' she murmured. 'Just look at it, it's not moving. But I can't leave it in the hedge until the next delivery tomorrow – what if it rains?' The giggling began again and, despite himself, Ryan felt his spirits rising like lemonade bubbles in sympathy. He lifted his eyebrows in question, and Chelle nodded, grinning.

There was a gate on the far side of the bridge, set into the wall. The sign upon it read 'Mead Priory – Private'. Ryan joined Chelle on the bridge and peered across at the gate. It was hard to feel shy in the face of the golden giggle they had heard. And in any case, he felt the strangest sense that this place was *his*. The sun had been waiting and keeping it warm for him.

A fringe of honeysuckle and some other creeper overgrew the gate, but beyond Ryan glimpsed a gleam of grass and red brick. The creepers were shaking slightly, and a finger of brown paper jutted from the foliage.

'Hello?' he called out.

'Oh no!' whispered Chelle in a panicky undertone. 'Wait . . . oh, I see them on the bridge. Kids. That's OK then.'

The honeysuckle thrashed, and then a strong brown hand grabbed a fistful of tendrils and tugged them aside. Through the new gap Ryan glimpsed a pale blue T-shirt and a triangle of shadowed face.

'You'd better go,' he muttered to Chelle through smiling teeth. Obediently she scampered out of sight.

'Don't go!' It was a female voice. Ryan approached the gate slowly. 'Hi, um . . .' The curtain of creepers rustled again, and a face appeared. It was a woman, with her hair tied back bandanna-style by an Indian-looking yellow shawl studded with tiny mirrors. Her face was tanned darker than her lips so that they looked pale, but healthy pale. Freckles clustered on her upper forehead and cheekbones, and some of them had melted together. 'Sorry, but do you think you could just . . . work that antler free your side?' Ryan could see now that a weirdly shaped parcel was lodged halfway through the thick creeper and that a deer's antler had ruptured the brown paper.

'Sure.' He laid careful hands on the smooth, bony cool of the antler and set about trying to work it free. He supposed that it must be a stuffed and mounted deer's head, until an ill-timed tug pulled the paper around the head loose and he found himself staring into the tiny, peevish features of a rabbit. 'What . . . ?'

'Oh, sorry!' The husky giggling began again. 'It's a jackalope. It's all right, it's not real – people a hundred years ago used to glue horns on to stuffed rabbits so that travelling fairs could take them round the country and people would pay to see them. Collectors like them.'

'So you're a collector?' What would a collector wish for? A suit of armour? A Fabergé egg? Ryan squinted through the greenery. 'Try pulling again.'

'OK.' Tug. 'No, I'm not really. I buy collectors' items online and then sell them on again. And usually,' tug, 'they leave things in that mail box there,' tug, 'but I guess this didn't fit so they left it on the step and I couldn't pull it through the . . . woah! Here he comes!' With a rustle the jackalope disappeared. 'Thanks!'

'Why didn't you get them to deliver it at the front door?'

There was silence and for a moment Ryan thought the woman had gone. When she reappeared at the gap her features were slightly defiant.

'I don't have one,' she said simply. 'I had it bricked up five years ago. And I had the Russian creeper here planted so that people wouldn't spot the gate unless they knew to look for it. Nobody can find me unless I decide I want them to.'

Ryan thought of car-park diatribes and painted milk bottles and schoolyard scorn and spluttering billboards.

'That sounds brilliant,' he said with feeling.

'Well,' she sighed, 'Mr Jackalope's shown me something I knew already. I'm going to have to cut all of this back . . . so I can get out if there's a fire or something.'

'Um . . .' *Think! Think like Josh.* 'Well . . . I'm trying

to make some money by . . . helping people with gardening. I mean, it's been so hot and lots of plants need watering . . . I thought I'd go door to door just to ask.'

'Really? Wow, it'd be great to have some help with this . . .' Again there was a peculiar, slightly defiant hesitation as she sucked at a briar scratch on her arm. 'Look, I'm getting some new secateurs delivered in a couple of days – if you really wouldn't mind dropping in after that, we could attack this beast together. What's your name?'

'Ryan.'

'I'm Carrie. See you soon, Ryan.'

She waved goodbye with two fingers made fat by her gardening gloves.

'Slick,' was all Josh said when Ryan got back, but he kept grinning at Ryan until Ryan felt he could fly.

As they drove back Chelle recounted the few scraps of Carrie's thoughts she'd heard – most of them related to the jackalope or gardening. Meanwhile Donna clenched and unclenched her jaw as Josh played with the tuning on her car radio without touching it and turned the volume up loud.

Ryan got home to find that his note was still on the table. He crumpled it and put it in the bin. At dinner his suspicions were confirmed. Nobody had noticed his absence. But it was all right. He munched cauliflower cheese and thought himself to a moated tower hidden by briars.

It was several hours after dinner, just as everybody was getting ready for bed, that the phone rang. When

Ryan answered the phone he scarcely recognized Chelle's voice. She was almost hysterical.

'Ryan! I don't know what to do! It was on the local news! It's Will Wruthers – he's had a horrible accident on his motorbike, and he's in hospital, and he's really badly hurt . . .'

'Where are you, Chelle?' Ryan could hear traffic in the background.

'I . . . I snuck out and was walking to the hospital to see if they'd let me see him . . . but she followed me, so I hid in the phone behind Basement Bargains and now I don't dare go out in case she's there waiting for me . . .'

'Who? Who's out there?'

'Oh no – she's coming in, Ryan, she's—' There was a squeak from Chelle and some thick wet clicks as if the receiver was being manhandled at the other end. Then he heard a dry, crackling voice and knew that Miss Gossamer had snatched the phone.

'Is that the Lattimer-Stone boy or the Doyle boy?'

Ryan held his breath. In the background he could hear Chelle's high, asthmatic yelps for air.

'I know it's one of you, anyway. I want you to know that I've been watching you for a week. I've seen the three of you, stealing people's private thoughts and spitting them out, putting curses on everything around you and wearing the evil eyes your filthy master gave you. Everybody else may think you're children, but you don't fool me. You're nothing but foulness, all three of you, and before you poison another innocent life I shall send you back to the hell that owns you.' The line went dead with a bang.

His hands unsteady, Ryan dialled Josh's number, but there was no response. He sat shaking, the receiver cool against his hot cheek.

She knows. Miss Gossamer knows everything. Oh, Chelle, why didn't you tell us?

Oh. Oh, Chelle. You probably did, didn't you?

'I'm coming, Chelle,' Ryan said into the dead receiver and slammed it down.

18

Dead Leaves

Ryan did not care whether his parents heard the door bang. The evening air was cool enough that he huffed out small ghost breaths as he broke into a jog. He felt nothing but lightness and clearness, as if someone had rinsed him out with very cold water. His hands were shaking, and he did not know what he was planning, but somewhere Chelle was gasping for breath.

He ran four streets before he saw the lights of the hospital with a throb of relief. But, like many big buildings, the hospital pretended to be closer than it was. By the time he saw the gaudy blue and yellow sign above Basement Bargains, there was a stitch like a tear in his side.

He was not quite sure what he expected – perhaps to find Miss Gossamer had completed her transformation into the mummified cat, slinking off down the street with a squeaking Chelle in her jaws. Instead, on a bench beneath a street lamp he saw Miss Gossamer and Chelle seated side by side. Chelle was stooped over her inhaler, and the old woman's hand rested gently, reassuringly, upon her shoulder.

Ryan came to a halt. He had never felt so idiotic. Miss Gossamer wasn't a monster, and no adult could stay angry when confronted by a timid twelve-year-old going into paroxysms of asthmatic terror. They'd talked, both of them had calmed down, he was as useless as ever.

'. . . and if I'd had a daughter, she'd have been about your mother's age,' Miss Gossamer was saying, her words falling light and dry as dead leaves. Ryan didn't move. He felt that if he stirred he would spoil the tenderness of the moment and crush her sentences beneath his trainers.

'Do you know,' continued Miss Gossamer, 'I can sometimes see the granddaughter I should have had. Just about your age. Reddish gold hair, as mine once was, and a turn-up nose like my mother's. And big grey eyes. Everybody in my family has grey eyes. She's wearing green satin shoes with a strap. My old party shoes. I'd have bought a pair just like them for her. Freckles on her forehead and hands, because she plays out in the sun all day. She's a sunbeam.

'And I know if I open my eyes she'll be there next to me, swinging her legs and smiling up at me. But then I do, and she's not there.' The old woman's voice changed and became a strange leaden bleat. 'No, *you're* there. Instead of my beautiful girl, *you*. You who have no right to exist. *And you're in her seat.*'

Chelle's eyes were wide, and her hands shook as she

tried to work her inhaler. High, strained hiccups emerged from her throat, along with another sound, a horrible impersonal wheeze. Nothing was over. Nobody was calm.

'The worst of it is, your parents are such good people, and they have no idea what you are. Sooner or later I shall have to tell them of course. I can't leave good people in a house with something like you. They shouldn't have to breathe your air. Can you imagine how I dread seeing their faces once I've told them everything? Looking at you with fear in their eyes?'

'Chelle . . .' Ryan's voice was a feeble rasp. 'Chelle . . . can't breathe, Miss Gossamer.'

Miss Gossamer became very still, and then her hand gently pat-pat-patted at Chelle's shoulder, as if comforting her.

'The air doesn't want to be breathed by you, does it? That should tell you something. It's good air. It knows.' Her voice still had a hard and horrible tremble in it.

'Miss Gossamer, she's having an attack!' Ryan was recovering his own breath now. 'Please, please, look at her, she – it's an asthma attack, a bad one, she's had them before . . .'

Miss Gossamer looked slowly around at him, and the street light ambered her mummified features. Nothing seemed alive in her face.

'Ryan Doyle. I thought it was you on the line. Your friend Josh would at least have had the courage to say something. You're the slyest one of the three, though, aren't you? Nobody suspects poor little Ryan with his ugly glasses . . . and those painful warts of his.'

She tipped back her head a little, and her eyes were alive after all. Ryan felt his stomach plummet as if he'd trusted his foot to a rotten plank and was now watching the splintered timber tumbling over and over itself as it fell towards black and distant water. And he suddenly knew that Donna Leas had never hated him, and the children at school had never hated him, and that in all the silly violence of rage and spite his parents had never hated each other, because this was different, and *this* was hate. This had brewed itself to a blackness like ink.

'Only innocents have the right to be treated as real children,' she said. 'It's no good crumpling up as if you're going to cry. I don't believe in your tears any more than I believe in Chelle's asthma.'

'Well, you'd better,' shouted Ryan, 'before she starts turning blue and I start yelling for an ambulance.' His voice sounded deeper and hoarser than he had ever heard it. He had never, never talked that way to someone older than him. But it was as if Miss Gossamer had torn up a contract between them. If she would not treat them as children, why should they treat her like an adult?

'The hospital is just there, Ryan. If you were really concerned, you'd agree to have all three of us go together. We can have somebody look at your warts while we're there.'

Her implied threats set his blood banging in his ears. He held out his fists, knuckles forward, and for once felt a fierce satisfaction as, with a soft rending sensation, his hand-eyes opened.

'These warts?' He no longer cared if she thought he was some kind of demon child. 'You don't know all the things I can do with these, do you?' Between the stubby lashes that sprouted from his knuckles glimmered the gluey moonstones that were his new eyes. 'You'd better leave her alone, or you'll find out.'

'Perhaps I shall call for an ambulance for us all,' suggested Miss Gossamer, still in a tone of quiet menace. In that instant Ryan's sneaking hope that some adult would discover the threesome's predicament and solve it for them died a cold, miserable death. There was nothing at the hospital for them but psychiatry and long wart-eye-lancing needles . . .

So why was Miss Gossamer keeping her own tone so low? Why wasn't she calling for an ambulance?

'Yes, why don't you?' Ryan said slowly. He could feel his mouth becoming small and rigid, the way his father's had in the car-park argument. 'Do it now. I'll help you. Let's all have a good yell.'

Miss Gossamer's hand slid from Chelle's shoulder. Deep furrows sank either side of her mouth and trembled, but Ryan didn't know what they meant. And then she took a deep and bitter breath, stood and walked stiffly away down the street. He had never known how victory felt, this sensation of liquid metal through the marrow of all his bones. His mind was still buzzing with unneeded energy. But he let darkness swallow her and retrieved the inhaler that Chelle had dropped.

'It's OK, Chelle, c'mon, breathe, she's gone.' Chelle's mouth was a loose, downward crescent, and at every heave of her chest there was a high, fluting squeak. 'C'mon, it's not a bad attack this time – I said that to scare her . . .' Ryan had no idea if this was true, but instinctively he knew that he had to convince Chelle that it was. 'You don't have to breathe like that . . . it's OK, it's OK . . .'

For a while Ryan thought he'd have to get her to the hospital after all, but eventually she started to breathe without the awful squeak.

'Thanks,' she whispered, as Ryan helped her to her feet. 'Sorrysorrysorrysorry . . .'

'Don't be silly. Come on, you're going to stay at mine for a bit till you're OK. You're not going home yet.' They walked in silence for a while.

'She'll tell my mum and dad, she'll tell . . . they're going to look at me with fear . . .'

'No they're not. If she tells them you're a demon mind-reading child, they're going to look at *her* like she's gone senile. Just now we called her bluff about getting an ambulance, and she *bottled out*. She can't tell any more than we can.'

'She . . .' Chelle paused to jerk another hiccup of breath into her lungs. 'She's right about me, I've always felt it, I'm just like this hollow thing where a proper person ought to be . . . that's why I've got the thought-speaking power, isn't it? People's thoughts run right through me and out the other side because . . . because . . . because there's not enough *real* person inside to get in the way . . .'

'No! She's an old cow, Chelle. A stupid, mad old cow.' Ryan heard his own voice sounding ugly and angular, as if he was about to cry or throw up.

'She'll pay in blood,' said Chelle with sudden viciousness. Ryan's heart and feet both stopped dead. He turned to see Chelle's face contorted in what looked a great deal like pain, her eyebrows working in a way that should have been comic but wasn't. Her tone was flat, but far from emotionless. She was almost singing the words, all on the same low note. 'She has to, I can't bear it, knowing that she's just walking around thinking nothing can touch her. Smiling. I know right now she's smiling. Perhaps she's thinking about me and smiling. She needs to choke on her Chardonnay, she needs to strangle in her shawl, I need to take that smile off her face forever . . .' Chelle's features grimaced and then crumpled into a more familiar misery.

'Chelle, tell me that wasn't you!'

'No, of course it wasn't, I don't know who it was, another wisher, somebody passing, I don't know who, and oh, it felt like I just put my hand in a drawer full of knives without meaning to, but they've gone now . . .'

'It wasn't Miss Goss?'

'No, I'd know if she was a wisher, wouldn't I?' whispered Chelle.

Ryan had to admit that logic was on her side, and yet there had been something strangely familiar about the tone of the voice in this last outburst. He mentally compared it to the 'voices' of the other wishers whose thoughts Chelle had spoken, but none of them seemed to match.

'Ryan, I don't care what she wished, I don't want to make anybody pay in blood, I don't like this, I don't like *doing* this any more . . .'

'No, I know.' Ryan was also shaken by the sheer venom in the unknown wisher's tone. 'We can't go on like this. Chelle . . . I'm going to have a talk with her.'

Chelle looked at him with awe and fear.

'You're going to talk to Miss Gossamer?'

'No, I don't mean her, I mean . . . Her.'

When they reached Ryan's house his parents had gone to bed, and it was clear that his absence had not been noticed again. Chelle's asthma attack seemed to have tired her out, and she fell asleep on the sofa with startling promptness under a couple of coats. Ryan called her mum and lied that Chelle had popped over to see him, then fallen asleep watching TV. Chelle's mum wasn't happy, but she agreed to let Chelle stay and speak to her in the morning. Ryan didn't know what else he could do. He left her to sleep.

While he brushed his teeth Ryan ran the shower for a while to fill the landing and bathroom with steam. Despite himself, he felt a steady, seeping panic, even as he saw his face disappear from the mirror and the towel rails grow fainter. He wondered if after this the ice-white peppermint of the toothpaste would always taste of apprehensive fear.

He padded back along the darkened landing to his room, got into bed and took his glasses off. As an afterthought, he slid a cold glass over the skin of his forehead and the now pallid, innocuous-looking warts on his knuckles.

'Glass House,' he thought as he lowered himself to the pillow. 'Glass House.'

For a long time he lay in an oppressive darkness in which his mind jogged against half-imagined anxieties, hearing the tick of the radiator and the buzz of distant cars. Whenever he tried to focus on the Glass House his heart beat in his ears and he hardly dared to keep his eyes shut. Eventually, however, his fears dimmed and lost detail, and sleep crept upon him gently like a valley filling with mist.

After a long while he found that his eyes were open, and looked around.

Glass House.

He pulled on his socks before lowering his feet to the cold, clouded floor. Was it a trick of the steam or were there fine cracks running across the walls now?

On the landing he paused and peered through each bedroom wall. His father was lying on his translucent bed, awake and staring at the ceiling. Glistening ghost snakes of the sort Ryan had seen before curled from his chest, seemingly active and alert. His mother lay asleep in the next room, floating upon her colourless bed. She was surrounded and cradled by her transparent tendrils, making her look a bit like a sea anemone.

The stairs chilled him through his socks. Beyond the living-room wall he saw Chelle sleeping in her cocoon of coats and was surprised by how tiny and timorous were the 'snakes' that quivered with her dreams.

He looked down at his own chest and squinted at the almost imperceptible tentacles that arced gracefully from it. *If they're wishes*, he thought to himself, *I wonder what mine are. Why don't I know?*

He opened the back door. Outside, as before, was a plain of tarmac beneath a sky like brown paper. Once again, in the distance he glimpsed a long chain of supermarket trolleys, and this time he was quite certain that there were a couple of human figures among them, thrashing slowly as if under water, their heads lolling this way and that.

Trying to ignore them, he strode towards the wall that divided the tarmac from the sky. He found footholds between the bricks and clambered on to the wall, feeling the rough moss prickle through his socks, and a damp wind rush up to meet him. Below him Magwhite yawned, a thousand yellow leaves whirling in its throat. He crouched, preparing to climb down the wall as he had with Chelle and Josh in the real Magwhite. It was not necessary however. The Trolley in the Tree was waiting for him.

Like startled birds, the parchment-coloured leaves in the nearest tree took to the air, revealing the trolley nestling among the twigs, its wire-lattice skeleton tarnished greenish-silver. As the leaves whirled and circled around the tree, the nearest bough unfurled gracefully so that its tip touched the wall beside Ryan's feet. Taking the hint, he crawled out on to the bough, occasionally gripping fistfuls of stems to prevent himself falling.

Ryan had always thought that trolleys had far too much body language for objects with no heads or limbs. This one was clearly waiting. As he stared at it, its seat flapped down. From the trunk of the tree jutted three horizontal slabs of soggy-looking fungus, softly rounded and brown as toast. The lowest did not crumble when he tested it with his foot, so he scaled them like rungs and climbed into the trolley.

There was a cracking sound beneath him, as if the branches were breaking under the strain of his weight. Ryan clutched at the wire sides as the trolley dropped and lurched forward as if to throw him out. But it was caught by another branch which swung and hurled the trolley on and forward. He and the trolley were falling sideways through a storm of thorn and crackle, explosions of twigs against metal, and clods of saffron-coloured moss torn from the trees.

Then the trolley stilled, tilted and dropped five gut-hugging feet into a huddle of mottled puffballs the size of melons. Clouds of floury spores huffed into the air and floated like smoke. Only as they cleared did Ryan see where he had fallen.

All around him, lime-green and smoky-yellow moss seethed and bubbled, pockmarked like coral. A few feet away, almost ludicrous in its familiarity, was the Magwhite well, looking just as it always had, the folded crisp packets still jutting from its grille. Somehow now, however, he could hardly bear to look at it. He could not fight the feeling that there was something seeping slowly from the well and hanging in the air above it. It was almost a smell that was almost a darkness that was almost an echo that was almost a bitter taste in the air.

And then he tightened his stockinged toes in the moss to give himself courage, clenched fistfuls of his coat pockets and tried to look at the Spirit of the Well.

She sat enthroned amid the fanned roots of an enormous overturned tree. The roots knobbed and knuckled, and among them were wedged weird trophies. A child's pink wellington boot choked with ivy, a hiking stick that had sprouted and given bud, the skull of a cat. A hundred bent cigarette butts smoked gently like incense sticks in a church shrine. A bent bicycle wheel spun slowly and unevenly behind her head, a halo for a strange saint. Her gown was studded with fragments of gold foil, punctured in crude patterns, and there was a tarnished, twisted collar of copper wire round her neck.

It was easiest to look at her hands. They were thick and strange, with lichen-green knuckles and heavy nails that might have been chipped out of dun-yellow quartz. They drew their fingers over and through the wild strawberry plant that trembled in her lap as if it was a pet.

He dared not look at her face, even though only her

profile was towards him. In his peripheral vision he could see her head turning slowly this way and that, as if trying to shake off some unbearable thought or torpor. Around it swayed long wreaths of darkness that seemed to bloom and fade in the air like streaks of ink dripped into water. It was hair, it was not hair.

Remembering Josh, Ryan made a small martial-arts bow, his hands folded in front of his waist.

'Um . . . Great Lady . . .' He was uncomfortably aware that the moss was slowly giving beneath him and that icy water was bubbling up around his feet like champagne. 'I had to come and talk to you. There's a . . . there's a problem.'

He felt, rather than heard, the answer.

Make the problem not be. Make the wishes be.

'That's . . . the problem, the problem is the wishes. There's a wish we only granted because we didn't realize it was all about destruction. And now we've got another wisher who keeps going on about revenge and someone paying in blood. And . . . that's a wish we can't grant. You must understand that.'

You must understand. Understand and make the wishes be.

'But we can't this time! And . . . there are some wishes that might need to be, um, un-granted a bit, because people are getting badly hurt and miserable . . .'

The Well Spirit's roar of displeasure was less a sound than a change in the flavour of the air. Burning tyres and a rasp of bitter-stale. Darkness clotting in Ryan's veins like treacle.

No un-granted. Wished hurt. Wanted miserable. Happy now.

'But . . . can't we just bring you lots more coins to replace the ones we took instead?' The air was darkening still, and the leaves were livid yellow as they settled around the throne to listen to the Well Spirit.

Nobody drinks, water is sour. Everyone drinks, more water rises. Let the mouths drink. Make the wishes be.

Bewildered, Ryan wanted to ask more, but his vision was misting. He waved his hand through the air to bat away a stray wreath of puffball powder, only to find that it was one of the faint ghost snakes arcing from his chest. All of his snakes were stretched out as if in a current towards the figure in the throne. With shock, he realized that at their extremity each dim tentacle had a faint, gaping, beakish mouth.

He gave a squawk and flailed at his own chest as if he could uproot them and found himself in darkness, struggling against a softness that proved to be his sheet. He was soaked with perspiration, and it was a moment before he could convince himself that he had not tumbled backwards into the damp embrace of the Magwhite moss.

19

The Shattering

'Your mother will not be joining us for breakfast . . .'
Ryan's father paused as he noticed Chelle seated at the
breakfast table, nibbling at a piece of toast, both feet
tucked nervously behind one chair leg.

'Chelle stayed here last night,' said Ryan, 'She had an
asthma attack in the street . . . so I brought her here –
it was nearer.'

'With her parents' permission, I assume?'

Ryan's 'yes' and Chelle's 'no' collided over the breakfast table and both subsided into confusion.

'Wonderful.'

Ryan's father slapped absently at his pocket a few
times with his newspaper. 'I expect that will turn out to
be my fault as well,' he muttered, and strode out.

'Did I . . . ?'

'No, Chelle,' said Ryan, reaching for a bread knife.
'It's not your fault. It's mine.'

After breakfast they phoned Josh and arranged to
meet in the park. Then, with an expression of great
apprehension, Chelle phoned her own house. Ryan

listened to the bubble of distant voices with sympathy and watched Chelle's eyebrows disappear behind her fringe as she attempted broken sentence after sentence. Chelle had once said that she didn't know how to be in trouble. From the sound of it, she would have to learn pretty fast. He wanted to say something comforting when she put the phone down, but he was short on comfort himself. At least all the yelling sounded like *ordinary* trouble. He had an idea that the Coopers might have sounded rather different if Miss Gossamer had told them that Chelle was a telepathic demon child.

'Josh'll have some ideas,' Chelle whispered faintly as they set off for the park. Ryan said nothing. He was bracing himself for something that felt harder than confronting Miss Gossamer, harder even than braving an interview with the Well Spirit.

It was a dazzling day, a honeyed hay-fever day. Bees swayed drugged through the park and fumbled in the throats of pansies. They found Josh sprawling on the grass with his hands behind his head.

'You both look like you've come to pay your last respects,' he remarked conversationally.

'Josh, we've got something to tell you, I was going to the hospital last night because, did you see, Will's been in a horrible accident . . .'

'Oh, so that's why you both look like that. Yeah, I saw the news story. Relax, he's not dead. Bet you he'll be wobbling around on his Harley again in a week.' As Ryan and Chelle sat down on either side of him, Josh rummaged in a carrier. 'OK, smile, or you don't get one of these.' He handed each of them a cellophane-wrapped package containing a square of folded black cloth.

Ryan pulled the cellophane from his and unfolded a large black T-shirt. On the front of it was a crude design a bit like a cartoon wishing well, and below that the white words 'Well's Angels'. Josh was husking laughter into his fist.

'Go on, put them on,' he said, grinning. 'C'mon, nobody else is going to know what "well's angels" means, are they?'

Chelle pulled her T-shirt over her head. Her fine fringe fluffed as she did so, so that some of it clung to her forehead and some shot straight upwards.

'It's really nice, Josh,' she murmured.

'Now look,' continued Josh, 'I've got today planned out. We're not going back to Carrie's for a couple of days, right? Well, we can't just sit about waiting for the Well Spirit to throw more trolleys at Ryan. I've been thinking – we know all the wishers ended up in Magwhite, or they couldn't have dropped coins down the well. So maybe some of them were there visiting, but probably some of them live there. So today we'll head out to Magwhite and just drive up and down until Chelle picks up something . . . put your T-shirt on, Ryan.'

Ryan had spread the T-shirt out across his lap and was running a finger over the rubbery surface of the letters and the well picture. He wondered if Josh had used fruit-machine money to buy them or just forced Donna to pay.

'You don't get your say if you're not wearing the uniform,' insisted Josh. 'This is a Well's Angels-only meeting.'

'I'm not putting this on.' *I just can't wear this*, is what Ryan had meant to say, but something had come down in his mind like a portcullis. He thought he saw Josh swallow with annoyance.

'You know, Chelle,' Josh maintained a relaxed, playful tone, 'it almost feels like there's somebody else here, but we'd be able to see and hear him if there was, wouldn't we?' Chelle looked utterly miserable. She gave Ryan a fearful look as if pleading for him to put on the T-shirt.

'I'm not wearing this,' Ryan said again.

'Why not, for crying out loud?'

'Because . . .' Ryan swallowed and stared down at his hands, lining them up to straighten his thoughts. 'Because I'm not doing this any more, Josh.'

'Not doing this? Not doing what? Not granting wishes? Well, that's funny because the thing is, you *are*, Ryan. We all are. Probably you don't remember, but we don't have any choice about it. We're not doing this for fun.'

Ryan sneaked a look at Josh, who was now leaning forward, propping his weight on his fists. *Aren't you, Josh? Isn't this fun for you?*

'Ryan didn't mean it like . . .' Chelle was twisting one thumb in the hem of her T-shirt. '. . . it's just some things that happened, some things, yesterday evening . . .' Ryan and Chelle tag-teamed the telling of the encounter with Miss Gossamer and the brief glimpse into the new mystery wisher's vengeful mind.

'You two haven't got a clue, have you?' interrupted Josh towards the end. 'You should've phoned Chelle's parents and got your version of the story in before Miss Gossamer could talk to them. You could've shown them Chelle while she was still blue and told them Miss Gossamer tried to kill her.' He frowned and inserted one finger behind his sunglasses to rub at his eye. 'That way, if she tried to tell anyone about us she'd sound like *even more* of a nutter.'

'Well,' Ryan continued carefully, 'after that I . . . went back to Magwhite . . . in my dream . . . to talk to the Well Spirit.'

'What?' He could feel Josh staring at him. 'You went and talked to her again without asking us?' Ryan's cheeks were tingling, as if Josh's anger was heat from an open oven door. 'Did you tell her we weren't working for her any more? Is that what you're saying? That had better not be what you're saying.'

'No . . . I didn't exactly. I just . . .' Ryan swallowed, hearing the defensiveness in his voice and feeling his carefully prepared arguments crumbling into apologies. 'I just told her about the latest revenge wisher, and told her that we . . . we couldn't do anything for that one. I mean, I only went to talk to her because it seemed like an emergency.' He looked quickly to Chelle for support. *Say something Chelle say something . . .* 'You didn't hear this new wisher the way we did . . . It was all about wanting blood, and it wasn't just a joke or a turn of phrase . . . it was about real, to-the-death revenge. So if that's their wish, we're screwed, aren't we? I mean, the fair was an accident, we didn't know we were meant to destroy it. That's not the same as hunting somebody for revenge in cold blood. I told the Well Spirit we couldn't do that, because, well, we can't, can we?'

Josh leaned back on to his elbows. There was a pale flicker of his eyelids behind his glasses.

'Why not?' he asked.

Ryan could almost hear his own mind snap like a blob of bubble wrap.

'Because . . . we can't,' he bleated helplessly, unable to think of anything else to say. He glanced at Chelle in desperation. He had expected her to back him up. But Chelle seemed to have chosen this of all moments to learn the art of silence and was watching him round-eyed over a fence of her own fingers.

'Why not? Has it crossed your mind that maybe whoever it is might deserve it? Anyone who gets them-selves hated that much probably asked for it.' Josh picked up Ryan's T-shirt by the sleeves and danced it to and fro before him. 'Angels, right? Angels don't just go around giving soup to the poor or singing over dead people. Angels avenge. Flaming swords. You know, mercy and justice.' Josh grinned again suddenly and rumpled the T-shirt up around the neck-hole, then leaned forward and pulled it over Ryan's head so that it sat round his shoulders. 'It's not going to be a big deal,

Ryan. Get a grip – we've got transport and money now, we've got a plan, we're getting the hang of our powers. Everything's on the up.'

'No,' said Ryan, feeling ridiculous with the T-shirt around his neck. 'No, it's not. It's really not. Nothing – *nothing* is on the up, Josh. Everything's getting worse.' He stared down at his hands and found them tensed and half-curled, as if trying to control his struggling thoughts. 'It's all wrong. Everything . . . just . . . tastes . . . wrong.'

Chelle gave a sick little hiccup of a panicky giggle, then choked it by pushing her fingers in her own mouth.

'To begin with,' Ryan was still staring at his hands, 'I think there's something wrong with what we're doing. I mean . . . yesterday Miss Gossamer was talking like we were some kind of evil force destroying people's lives, and the worst thing is . . . she's kind of right, isn't she? Will's in hospital, we broke the fair so lots of people got hurt and lost their jobs, and—' he took a deep breath – 'Donna's got her Mr Punzell but she's having to lie to him because she's . . . being black-mailed . . .'

'OK, Ryan.' Josh leaned forward again. 'Big fat news of the world: people are stupid. And they want stupid things. And it's not our fault.'

'Another thing,' Ryan continued doggedly, 'our plans don't . . . work, do they? I mean, each time they turn out all right, but not the way we expect. Something is making things happen, kind of helping us along in a twisted way, and I think it's the Well Spirit. I think, I think there's something really wrong with her that we haven't worked out.'

'Something wrong with her? What, aside from her not being human, and visiting your dreams, and puking water out of her mouth and eyes, and changing us to give us powers?'

'They're not powers,' Ryan added firmly. 'You say we're getting the hang of them. But that's not "getting better", Josh, that's getting worse. I think we're still changing.'

'And so?' erupted Josh. 'So you're going to do what? Tap your heels together three times and say, "I don't like it, make it all go away, I don't want to play any more?" What are you – five? You were the one that promised her we'd grant the wishes in the first place. Do you remember that? So no, Ryan, you don't get to back out because it isn't fun and leave us to do your dirty work. You get to stick at it with the rest of us.'

Ryan felt as if Josh had him pinned against the portcullis in his head and was trying to push him through it. He felt as if he had two wills. His everyday conscious will squirmed to and fro, trying to find a way to agree with Josh and calm him down. But the second will was the portcullis, and it would not budge. *No, this doesn't happen, we don't do this.*

'I didn't just mean me,' he said, very quietly. 'None of us should be doing this.' He reached up, knowing that he was going to push well beyond Josh's patience, and pulled the T-shirt off himself. 'And I'm not saying I know what'll happen if we stop obeying the Well Spirit. But anything's got to be better than this. We're snooping into people's lives and messing them up.'

'Yeah, well, how come it's not a problem when your mum does that?' Josh glared back into Ryan's shocked face. The tearing sensation that Ryan had felt when he watched Josh staring with hate at his mother was more intense than ever. 'I mean, that's why your parents are splitting up, isn't it?'

There was a rushing sensation, like the flood of wind at the wall above the dream Magwhite, and then somebody hit Josh. They didn't do it very well. Josh was up on his knees in a second and Ryan felt his nose sting and his eyes fill with water as Josh's arm knocked him across the face. *It wasn't* . . . he tried to say, and *I didn't* . . . But, he realized, it was, and he had, and indeed he was still trying to hit Josh, though more feebly now that the bigger boy was kneeling on his chest. His glasses were somewhere in the grass. He wanted to give in, curl up, but somehow he was still kneeing Josh in the back as hard as he could, while occasional blows struck his head above his shielding arm.

'I'm telling you for your own good,' Josh was saying over and over, through clenched teeth. Ryan's left ear turned to fire as a stray blow struck home. 'They won't warn you, will they? You know what they'll do? They'll take you out some day and buy you a computer game and take you to McDonald's and when you're happy and think everything's OK then they'll tell you. You got to prepare yourself. *They* won't prepare you.'

'Josh . . .' Chelle's voice was a monotonous squeak in the background, 'Josh . . . Josh . . . Josh . . .'

Josh rolled off abruptly, and Ryan sat slowly, then stood, shaky and humiliated, his arm still covering his face. He felt as if the anguish of every fight he had ever lost had been combined into a single instant, because this time it had been Josh humiliating him.

'Let him go,' said Josh as he staggered away. Ryan hoped that Chelle would follow him anyway, so that he could tell her to her pale, timid face that she was hopeless. He'd mainly gone to see the Well Spirit because she had said she couldn't face granting wishes any more, so why hadn't she said a word to back him up? But she didn't follow him, and Ryan didn't seem to have the energy for anger at that, just a tired, leaden sense of betrayal.

He unshielded his face and the world was a blur, but he couldn't go back for his glasses, and he couldn't bear to use his hand-eyes. He stumbled back to his own house with one hand feeling along the wall, and kerbs playing tricks upon him. When he opened the back door, his parents were waiting for him.

They took turns to speak in a way that was designed to make Ryan realize that he was in serious trouble. Miss Gossamer had spoken to Chelle's parents after all. She'd told them that she had seen Chelle and Ryan loitering with a gang of much older children up by the hospital, late at night.

'Miss Gossamer tried to kill Chelle,' said Ryan flatly.

'Ryan,' said his father without a hint of twinkle in his voice.

'Chelle had a really bad asthma attack, and Miss Gossamer kept on and on trying to frighten her, to make it worse. I brought her here because she was too scared to go home.' Perhaps it would have sounded more convincing if he could have put some outrage into his voice, but he was too tired.

'Miss Gossamer mentioned that she'd tried to persuade Chelle to go home with her, but that the other children had teased her out of it,' replied Ryan's mother.

'There weren't any other children.' Ryan sat down on one of the kitchen chairs and touched the tender places above his eyebrows. Unreasonably, he felt that all the years of obeying the rules should mean something, give him a 'Get Out of Jail Free' card just this once. But he had to stop talking the way he was. He had to be reasonable, so that the conversation would be over. He reached deep into his store of mental energy and patience . . . and there was nothing there. Nothing at all.

'What's wrong with your nose?' Ryan's mother asked suddenly. The mum-shaped blur came closer, and he felt his chin being cupped and his head tipped back. 'Who did this? Was it the older children?'

'Look, there weren't any!' Something in Ryan's head burst, and his voice came out impossibly shrill. 'She's lying, OK?' There was a shocked silence.

'Ryan. I don't ever want to hear you using that tone again, do you hear me?' Ryan's father.

'Why the hell not? You two use it all the time! Do you think I'm deaf or blind or stupid? Do you think you're protecting me when you don't tell me what's going on? Well, you're not.'

'That's perfect, that's just perfect. Now I have to deal with you changing on top of everything else. You choose this time to turn into a teenager.' Ryan's mother's voice was shaking.

'Well, I have to deal with . . .' *with more than you'd understand* . . . 'with mad women on the doorstep painting the milk bottles and voodoo curses and . . . and everybody talking about how my mum goes through people's bins and messes up their lives. You . . . you can't do that – picking into people's most private moments and taking them apart, and making them yours and . . .'

He turned and bolted blindly for the stairs. Behind him the now-familiar sound of argument erupted. The continents of his world were colliding again with world-crushing force, throwing shards of rock as high as the moon. He felt as if every time his foot struck a step, white fractures were spreading from the impact, shivering the very walls of the Glass House, frosting its floors and showering everyone within with gleaming, deadly dust. He had to force his secret eyes open to prevent himself rebounding off the frame as he reached his bedroom door.

20

True Crime

Ryan surprised himself much later that day by waking up on his bed in his clothes. It seemed impossible that after so many terrible things had happened he could have simply lain back and fallen asleep.

After painfully inserting his contact lenses, he made his way down the stairs. He felt cold, as if he really had shattered the Glass House that lurked beneath the familiar, leaving jagged unseen holes for the draughts to seep through. He was vaguely surprised to find that the living room was not a mess of wrecked furniture.

Discovering the house empty left him relieved but a little at a loss. After all he had said, he hadn't known whether his mother would be dangerously direct, or hurt, or stony, or volatile, but he had at least thought that she would be *there*.

On the kitchen table was a little parcel of bubble wrap and sellotape, on top of a note:

'This posted through door at lunchtime, Mum xx.'

The two crosses were in a different ink. Ryan imagined his mother stopping halfway out through the door, her laptop case in her hand, then nipping back to the kitchen to add the two kisses. Or perhaps her first pen had run out. He unwrapped the package. It held his spectacles, a little smudged but unbroken. He hoped that they had been posted by Josh because that meant on some level they were still friends. Chelle posting them would be just a pathetic apology.

He fetched himself a bowl and some cereal. It was weird to find that cornflakes existed after the end of the world. Weird, but comforting.

'I'm right and they're wrong,' Ryan told the flabby flakes in his spoon. That had a weird sound as well. 'I'm right and they're wrong.' Weird, but empowering.

'I hear that is a popular refrain for those your age.' Ryan had not noticed his father come into the room.

'You were my age too once,' was all that Ryan could think of to say.

'Rumours abound to that effect, but have never been proven.' Ryan's father hesitated in the doorway. He appeared to be eyeing Ryan as if he was an unexploded bomb. 'Ryan, do you want to discuss what hap—'

'No . . . maybe. Maybe when Mum gets back?'

Ryan's mother would have charged into the conversation, lance held high, but she was not there.

Where is Mum? Ryan wanted to ask. *Has she gone away forever? Is she angry with me? Are you angry with me? Did Miss Gossamer say anything else?*

'Can I go to the library?' he asked instead.

'Yes.' Ryan's father stroked back his own hair with an expression of relief mixed with disappointment.

Walking through the heavy swing door of the Eastgate Library, Ryan felt a sense of reassurance as if coming home. If he was to be able to think clearly anywhere, it would be here. The library had never turned to glass. Hurricane arguments had never swept through its aisles, throwing Ancient History on to the floor with Crime and Religion.

Only as he passed the reception desk did he remember that last time he had left the library it had been in disgrace. He gave Mrs Corbett the librarian a timorous look, but to his surprise she gave him her usual reassuring smile. Perhaps none of his recent great crimes and outbursts meant anything to anybody else.

He winced when he saw that the Local Interest section was packed with leaflets for the Crook's Baddock Festival. The festival was always the last flare of summer before the end of the holidays. It reminded him that the autumn term would start in just over a week.

Running his fingers over the peeling sticker on the walnut-wood shelves, he remembered Josh asking if there was a 'psychic-holistic-dippy-hippy' section. And yes, if he was to find out what was wrong with Magwhite, that would be exactly what he needed.

Most of the Folklore section was too general, with books on Irish fairy legends, vampires and ghost stories. Some books had indexes, however, so he flicked to the back, looking for 'well' and 'water spirit' just in case.

A lot of water demons and monsters seemed to be giant sea-snakes or 'monstrous wyrms' who lived in lakes, but one book also had stories of creatures that lived in wells or springs. Beings with nicknames like Jenny Green-teeth, Meg-of-the-Brook or Lady of the Rushes, who spent their time lurking beneath the surface of the water, waiting to drag in venturesome children or young men who approached in answer to the whisper in the windswept reeds. The book said that these stories were probably made up by parents who didn't want their children playing too near the water. Ryan was less sure.

Another book with a section on wells was dedicated to Anglo-Saxon and medieval saint legends. There was a long list of wells that had been dedicated to saints, the names of which were mostly strange to Ryan.

He glanced through the list without much interest, before noticing that one well, sacred to St Bridget, was in a Cornish village with a familiar-sounding name. Checking back to the first book on well legends, he found the village name mentioned again, as the site of a well haunted by a notorious female demon, Mother Leathertongue. He turned the two accounts over in his mind like Lego bricks, trying to work out how to fix them together. Could there be two wells in the same village? If not, how had Mother Leathertongue turned into St Bridget?

Ryan took the two most useful folklore books to the counter with a feeling of frustration. But what had he been expecting? A volume marked *When Well Spirits Attack: A Detailed History of Everything Wrong with Magwhite?*

'Mrs Corbett, what's wrong with Magwhite?' Ryan

asked impulsively. Mrs Corbett looked somewhat jarred at this break from their ritual conversation. 'It's just, our parents never like us going there, so I wondered if there was something wrong with it.'

'Well, a lot of people lost their lives there in some very nasty floods many centuries ago,' she said after a moment's thought, 'but I doubt it's that worrying your parents. Oh now, there was that old business with the well cult . . .' A pocket of air caught in Ryan's throat and bobbed with excitement as Mrs Corbett wrote the title of a book on a scrap of paper. 'Try this – it might have something on it.'

'Is it in the Religion section?'

Mrs Corbett shook her head.

'True Crime,' she said, and pointed.

It was a thin, crinkly little paperback called *Real Life Bogeymen*, and was broken up into ten short chapters, each on a different notorious criminal or group who had, in their time, caught the fearful imagination of the county. There was a nineteenth-century cobbler who lurked in lonely lanes dressed as an old pedlar woman so that he could waylay errand girls. There was a gang of young men who killed a postman in the 1940s for his Christmas sack. And then, in the 1950s, there was the story of the Magwhite well cult.

It was very nearly the story of a tragic miscarriage of justice. The body of a tiny baby girl had been found in one of the Magwhite canals, and various witnesses remembered seeing a girl in her late teens running along the towpath with a look of distress, late the previous evening. When the girl was identified, she reluctantly admitted that the baby was hers, and that she and her aunt had been hiding it from the world because she was unmarried. Everybody suspected the girl and her aunt of killing the baby to save the family name, but the girl insisted that she had been hounded for days by a group of 'witchy' men, who had eventually stolen her baby, and that she had been running up and down the canal side looking for them.

Her tales of these 'witchy' men did not improve her case. She described one of them as 'reading her mind and throwing her own thoughts at her in mockery' and another as 'using boils to spy on her'. She had actually been arrested, when a houseboat owner came forward to say that on the day the murder took place he had seen and recognized three men hurrying along the towpath with a baby. The three men were found to have many photos of the poor young mother and child. When interrogated, one of them confessed but insisted that they were forced to commit the murder by the well of St Margaret the White. The police finally concluded that the three had formed a strange sort of religious cult and that the baby had been a sacrifice. All three men were found guilty but insane. After their arrest their madness became more and more apparent, and within two years of being sent to a mental institution each of them had found a way to commit suicide.

Ryan felt sick. At the back of his mind he had wondered why nobody else had ever stolen coins from the well. Now he knew that they had. There had been other 'well's angels'. Maybe they had started off giving people bikes or boyfriends, and ended up killing a baby girl, telling themselves that they had no choice. Maybe there *had* been no choice. After all, what had happened to the men when they were imprisoned and unable to fulfil the Well Spirit's demands? If they hadn't been insane when they went into the mental hospital, Ryan could easily imagine them being gradually driven mad as the angry Well Spirit appeared to them again and again, snarling from their porridge or glaring from the steamed tiles of the shower, demanding that they carry out missions that were now impossible.

At the end of the chapter was a reference to another book, which apparently covered the story in more detail.

'Mrs Corbett? Do you have *Poachers, Prowlers and Psychopaths: The Dark Side of Guildley*? I can't find it in True Crime.'

'Yes, we do, though I think that's a rather more adult . . . ah.' Mrs Corbett peered at the screen, then at Ryan. 'It looks as if your mother has it. In fact, it looks like she's had it for . . . four years.'

'Oh . . . um, she probably doesn't remember that it's not hers,' muttered Ryan.

'Well, could you be a good boy and remind her?' Mrs Corbett sighed in annoyance, then gave Ryan a quick smile to show that she wasn't angry with him.

'Um . . .' Ryan paused at the doorway. 'Mrs Corbett, I don't suppose you remember how thick the book was, do you?'

Needless to say, when he got home, *Poachers, Prowlers and Psychopaths* was not prominent on any of the shelves. Mrs Corbett had told him that it was about four inches thick and a foot high. He knew that it had left the library wearing a tan and black dust jacket, but this didn't help since he was pretty sure that it now wouldn't be. There was nothing for it but to drag a chair from room to room, pulling all the books of the right size from the shelves, piling them on the kitchen table and stripping them of their jackets.

At one point Ryan's father walked through the kitchen, watched him with raised eyebrows for a bit and then passed on without comment. After a couple of hours Ryan gave up. The book was nowhere to be found.

All afternoon he toyed with the idea of calling Josh and Chelle to tell them what he had found out, but his imagination kept playing out conversations in which he broke his nose against the barricade of Josh's sneering hostility. Perhaps if he found out something useful, some alternative to serving the Well Spirit that didn't involve descending into dribbling insanity . . .

Late that evening, while Ryan was in his room, the phone rang. Ryan guessed it might be his mum and listened from the top of the stairs.

'Still rampaging about?' His father's voice. 'Well, yes, one could say so. This afternoon he "rampaged" over to the library for some vengeful homework research. This evening in a fit of unbridled rage and rebellion he flung himself into tidying our bookshelves and putting jackets on the right books.'

Pause.

'I hope Mr Paladine appreciates his place in your priorities.' Pause. 'Well, if not, then . . . what was that?' Pause. 'No, he doesn't want to, not until you get back. Do you know when that will be?' Pause. 'I have to be in London tomorrow evening so yes . . . Well, please try.'

Ryan waited for his father to put down the receiver before scampering back to his room to hug his pillow. His mother hadn't left forever, anyway. She was coming back.

The next morning, a little more sure of his ground, Ryan got another lift to the library with his father. However, after half an hour in the Folklore section, he walked out and found a bus to Whelmford. He had made a promise to Carrie.

As he walked along the edge of the river, again he felt a sense of peace settle over him despite the ominous greyness of the sky and a new sense of hanging heat. Had he returned here to help Carrie or to enjoy her refuge from the world for a little while?

To his surprise, when he reached the gate, a lot of the creeper had already been cut back, and he could clearly see the path that wound through a long narrow garden to the red-brick bungalow beyond.

'Ryan!' Carrie seemed just as surprised to see him there. She was gathering severed tendrils and stuffing them into a big dustbin bag. 'I didn't think you were coming! Your friend said you couldn't make it – we've done most of the work . . . but come in! We're making tea.'

Ryan's spirits sank. The Mead Priory was a sanctuary no more. The defensive wall of briars had been breached and there was an intruder inside the walls. He followed Carrie down a little crazy-paving path newly scraped of moss, and in through some mould-tinted French windows.

Josh stood over a rickety-looking tea trolley with his sleeves rolled up, pouring tea into two chipped mugs, one of which had clearly been used to mix paint at some point in its history. When he looked up, Ryan saw that he was wearing his sunglasses even in the darkened room.

The living room seemed to be a refugee camp for furniture, some expensive, some cheap, some pieces clumsily mended with gaffer tape. Most available surfaces were piled with boxes, clocks, vases, plaster busts, 1950s jukeboxes and picture frames. It was rather as if someone's attic had rebelled and taken over their house.

'Look who made it after all!' Carrie gave a smile which suddenly became thin and watery, as if something had made her unhappy. Seeing both of them together seemed in some way to make her nervous. 'I'll get another mug and those lemon sponges . . . it's just as well I made too many of them.'

There was an awkward pause after she'd left the room. Josh stared down into his mug and kept adding more sugar with the tiny ceramic-handled teaspoon, until Ryan thought he had decided to pretend he was alone in the room.

'She's kind of funny, isn't she?' Josh murmured at last, as if talking to himself.

'It's like she's not used to people and keeps suddenly remembering something about them that frightens her,' agreed Ryan, and then brought himself up short. It was no longer safe to discuss wishers with Josh. 'How . . . how are things going?' he asked instead.

'Good.' Josh stirred his tea slowly. 'We drove around Magwhite yesterday, picked up the thoughts of a couple of new wishers. One of them wants his girlfriend to be promoted to chief shoe-sales-person, and the other's about seven and has a thing for jiving robot toys. I've sent Donna to buy him one. Then we hung around near yours, and got another flash of that revenge wisher. Only I think she was buying groceries for a recipe, thinking about milk and stuff. And something about "easily with teaspoons".'

Perhaps, thought Ryan, Josh and Chelle had never really needed him. Perhaps he had even been slowing them down.

'Chelle's been winding me up a bit, actually,' Josh said, as if answering his thought. He raised his head to look at Ryan. 'When there's three of us . . .' He shrugged, wrinkled his nose and kept stirring in the long-dissolved sugar. 'It's like . . . you know coleslaw? It's OK, it's not got much taste, it's stuff that turns up as extra when you've ordered what you actually want. And you can eat a bit of it, or squersh it over on to the side of your plate. But you don't ever, like, sit down and think, "Mmm, I know, I'll order a big plate of just coleslaw." Chelle's coleslaw.'

Despite himself, Ryan felt a proud, simmering warmth in his stomach. He suddenly realized that, somewhere in the back of his mind, he had always hoped that it was his company that Josh really sought out, and that Chelle was more tolerated. However, now that Josh had voiced the idea aloud, he could also see the true ugliness of that hope. The glow of joy faded.

Ryan had been hoping that his hero would find the magic thing to say that would heal the rift between them. But this wasn't it.

'OK, truce.' Josh sniffed hard and spoke as if his words were costing him some effort. 'I'm declaring this table a no-sulk zone. Look, I've got this T-shirt in your size. We're driving right past your house tonight. If you've stopped sulking, we can pick you up.'

'I can't,' lied Ryan. 'My dad's got us tickets for the theatre this evening.'

Josh bit his lips, then slipped a fingertip behind a lens of his glasses to rub at one of his eyes. Ryan thought he heard a couple of the nearby clocks falter, as if they had held their breath for a moment.

'Here we are.' Carrie returned, bearing a tray. 'I've made custard as well.'

The custard had been poured so as to hide the burnt places on the sponges. Ryan took a spoonful, but as the custard slid from his spoon he was reminded of the weird liquid moss in the dream Magwhite. Suddenly he felt as if the three of them were huddled in a shadowed forest of telescope tripods, stag antlers, walking sticks and hat stands, as if in that instant the Magwhite woods had somehow surged softly into the house like smoke. He looked up and found Josh was smiling at him.

We're playing a game, and she doesn't know, said the smile. *That's fun, isn't it?*

'You never finished the story you were telling me while we were cutting back the creeper,' said Josh.

'Oh, that!' Carrie laughed, then gave the unhappy thin smile again. She glanced at Ryan apologetically. 'Josh was telling me that he once had to climb down the Magwhite well to get the bus fare. And I just asked if he'd found a ring while he was in the well.'

'She's told me that she threw one down there once, on purpose,' Josh explained, 'but she hasn't told me what she wished. C'mon, there must have been a wish.'

'The ring was . . . well, it was an engagement ring.' Absently Carrie scraped back the peel of custard to show the singed pudding underneath. 'And when the other person didn't . . . want to be engaged any more, I threw the ring down the well.'

'Then there wasn't a wish at all!' Ryan felt a flood of relief.

'Oh, there was.' Carrie gave a small, regretful grimace.

'It must have been a biggie,' Josh murmured, encouragingly.

'Don't say anything,' Ryan snapped quickly, and felt himself redden. 'If you do . . . it won't come true.'

'That's OK, I don't want it to be true any more.' Carrie pinched the base of her ring finger as if to see whether the ring had grown back. 'Maybe you won't understand this, but . . . I can't bear open spaces. I started to get that way when my parents died, and it got worse and worse until I could hardly bear going outdoors.

'Then I met someone who seemed to like me, and it made me feel safe. For the first time in years I was able to go out without feeling as if buildings were going to crash down on me, or like I was going to fall upwards into the sky. Knowing him was like having a little invisible roof I could carry around with me. I got a job and met lots of people. We got engaged. And then he changed his mind and moved to Arizona. The biggest, flattest, brightest place in the world, as if he'd picked somewhere he knew I couldn't follow him.

'Anyway, the bad stuff all came back, but much, much worse. Everything around me was terrifying and hurt. I couldn't bear people, not even the kind ones. I couldn't bear voices, or the smell and sound of cars, or the shapes of buildings. There didn't seem to be anything in the world worth the pain of stepping outside my door, so I decided I wouldn't any more. And then I got rid of my door, so the world wouldn't know where to come knocking.'

Ryan felt as if she was opening a wary hand to show

them her soul, soft and vulnerable as a baby chick. It was awful to watch.

'You don't have to tell us any more,' he said, unable to keep the plea out of his voice.

'Unless it makes you feel better to talk,' Josh added quickly.

'I wished that the world out there would just *go away and leave me alone*. Well, it did. The world couldn't get in, and I couldn't bear to go out. But it's been years now and I'm going to put in a new door. I've picked it out of a catalogue – it's red. And look! Here I am with people in my house, for the first time in two years!' She grinned suddenly. 'I think I'm allowed to take back my own wish, aren't I?'

Ryan opened his mouth, but his store of answers seemed to be empty.

Josh was still smiling. His knuckles gripping the mug handle were garden-greened, and Ryan remembered the tarnished fingers of the throned figure in his dream of Magwhite.

21

Spiders' Feet

Ryan turned down Josh's offer of a lift in Donna's car. As he walked away from the Mead Priory he realized that he was shaking. He had just met up with his best friend, but he felt as if he'd just been challenged to a duel.

What ring, Josh? What bloody ring?

Chelle picked up the thoughts of wishers whose wish-coins they had stolen. She was picking up Carrie loud and clear, there was no doubt about that. But there had been no ring in the blackened mess of coins Josh had shown them after climbing out of the well.

Ryan caught a bus back to Guildley and had to run from the bus stop to get back to the library before his father did. As his father drove him home, the streets appeared to be full of renegade trolleys and rubbish. A pair of boots, linked by their laces, drooped over a telephone wire, and Ryan fleetingly imagined them pulling themselves up the pole by their own laces so that they could spy out the land.

'Ryan . . . I have to leave for London tonight at about

seven. Your mother says she will be back no later than nine. Will you be all right until she gets home?'

Ryan imagined a future in which his parents organized their comings and goings so as to miss one another, always enquiring in the same careful, unemotional tone to find out whether he minded. He answered with a shrug.

Over dinner, Ryan's father stared out of the window as Ryan stirred his gravy. Outside, the sky was slowly turning to yellow paper, a Glass House sky, and nobody seemed to have noticed.

There's going to be rain. Rain'll spoil the blackberries. He was not even sure where the thought had come from.

Just as suddenly, he remembered collecting blackberries with Josh and Chelle on a day when the rain had left all the berries swollen and tasteless. A spider had run over Chelle's share, and Josh had waited until she'd eaten most of them before letting her know.

'Why didn't you *tell* me?' she had wailed, looking sick and miserable. Indeed, Josh had finally tired of her anguish.

'Look, you pillock, it's OK, it's . . . Ryan, tell her why it's OK.'

Ryan had racked his brain. 'Because . . . spiders have really clean feet. They . . . they clean them on their webs.' It was enough. Chelle had looked into his face with complete trust and relief and had eaten the rest of her berries.

Thinking back, Ryan was suddenly quite certain that if Chelle had been the only person to see the spider run across her berries, she would have eaten them without qualms. It was Josh talking as if they were dirty that had poisoned them for her. Poor Chelle, always waiting to find out what she was allowed to think or feel. No wonder she had been so quiet when Ryan and Josh were arguing.

Ryan could not imagine her having a stand-up row with Josh, but if she ever had, would he have taken her side?

No, said his conscience.

I'm just as bad as Chelle, he thought.

Worse, said his conscience. *You're just as bad as Josh. You talk like her friend and then treat her like coleslaw.*

When Ryan's father finally packed his overnight case and left, the house felt dark and empty. Ryan turned on the stereo in the kitchen, but that made him uncomfortable too. The sound was too naked and obvious. Something or someone would hear it and know where to find him. Something or someone would come, and he would not hear it coming. He turned off the music.

One foot high and four inches thick. Ryan began sorting through books again in search of *Poachers, Prowlers and Psychopaths*, but it was hard to concentrate. The thick yellow paper of the sky tore in thunder, and outside the window the grass flattened itself in a downdraught. When the rain began, it fell with too much force to gloss the leaves. The hedge and grass twitched and quivered as if under a pelting of dry peas.

He kept remembering Carrie's fragile but determined

smile as she talked about taking back her own wish. Would the Well Spirit allow that?

No un-granted. Wished hurt. Wanted miserable.

No un-granted.

The Well Spirit did not care whether people's wishes were stupid or regretted. *I wished that the world out there would just go away and leave me alone.*

Perhaps there were ways to 'make somebody's world go away', but none of them were good.

Rain, rain. Dripping billboards and glistening trolleys and blackberries swelling up like balloons. Rain with a tidal-wave roar. And then a sound behind the rain, a sharp little tap-tap-tap.

He looked up towards the noise, and with a strange sense of inevitability saw a pallid face peering in at the living-room window through a darkening draggle of hair. Ryan ran to the front door and heaved it open.

Chelle was sucking at her inhaler to recover her breath, and wore no coat. Her skirt and top were splashed up one side as if a passing car had doused her. Her calves were tiger-striped with mud. Ryan pulled a towel off the nearest radiator and handed it to her. She wrapped it around herself, then levered off her trainers. She eyed her damp feet, then stared, daunted, at the smooth and gleaming parquet floor of the hall.

'It's OK,' said Ryan gently. 'Just slide.' They half slid into the living room, Chelle's wet feet a little rubbery and stumbling against the tiles.

'They think we're playing board games in the Cavern,' Chelle said at last, 'but that was just a story he made up so he'd have an alibi. He went out my window, and Donna's driving him and he's going to get her to phone me on her mobile later, but when he went I waited five minutes and I was going to phone you but phones are machines and machines like him, so I went out my window instead and came here . . .'

'He was at Carrie's today, Chelle.' It was such a wonderful relief to let his anxieties fall out through his mouth. 'Carrie, the lady with the jackalope, made him tea, she trusts him and she's told him her wish and it's a really bad one, and if he's going back there to grant it . . .'

'I don't think so. I think it's the other wisher, the mystery revenge wisher, he's after. He keeps driving me around so I can pick her up, and we tracked her to this warehouse, and he said he was heading down there when he left today, and I don't like her in my mind, it's a her, I know it is . . .'

Despite himself, Ryan felt a throb of relief. Carrie would be safe that evening anyway. Josh might be inflicting terrible revenge on someone that night, but at least it wasn't somebody Ryan knew.

'And he wears his sunglasses all the time now, even indoors and at night . . .' continued Chelle.

'And he keeps dabbing at his eyes but really carefully so you can't see them behind the sunglasses . . .'

'And after you went he made me put a bucket in the Cavern because it's underground like the well and said it was a sort of a shrine, and he wrote letters and yes and no round the outside and he floats things in it like a

Ouija board so he can try to talk to the Well Spirit now you're not around, and I have to *sleep* in there . . .'

'And Carrie says she threw a ring in the well when she made her wish, Chelle, and Josh didn't show us any kind of a ring; he didn't tell us he'd pulled a ring out of the well . . .'

'And he's really enjoying the machine stuff and I think he's making cashpoints give him money and I know Donna's really scared of him now . . .'

'He likes it, he likes people being scared, and knowing what's in their heads, and changing their lives . . .' Everything was pouring out of Ryan as if he was a second Chelle, the unacknowledged thoughts sliding out of the shadows of his mind. 'He likes the power . . .'

'He really wants to do the revenge wish; he talks like the person who the wisher hates had done something bad to *him*, even though he doesn't know who it is . . . and none of this is *like* Josh . . .'

But in a way it was like Josh, all of it. Ryan suddenly thought of the tricksters in stories who made you laugh because they did funny things you didn't dare do, and then did more wicked things that were still amusing, and then turned your stomach over by doing horrible, diabolical things that were only funny to them. It didn't mean they'd changed; it just meant they'd slid off the far end of their own scale, an end you hadn't seen before.

Only . . . sliding that far off the end of the scale meant . . .

'He's going mad.' Ryan completed his thought aloud.

'I mean, maybe he found the ring in the well the first time and just hid it. But I think he went *back* to the well to look for the Well Spirit and to get more coins, so we'd have to keep doing this and he'd keep his "powers", and I think that's when he found Carrie's ring. And if so, he's not just wrong, he's losing it. He's not playing on our side any more.' They stared at each other round-eyed, feeling like revolutionaries.

'Why?' whispered Chelle. 'Is it because he was the one that went down the well – did the Well Spirit do something to him then? I mean, you said yourself that she was making all the wishes come out twisty and horrible – so is she . . . is she just . . . *evil* or something?'

Ryan gnawed his lip in silence as he thought. 'No,' he said at last. 'I don't think so exactly. I think she's kind of . . . confused. I mean, imagine this: you've got this really old god, and people worship her because they need the water from her well, and they hope it'll rain so the crops will grow, so they plop offerings into the water, copper amulets and that kind of thing. And so she gets used to granting wishes, nice simple wishes like, "Please don't let our village starve." Ryan could feel himself using his words to sculpt the storm clouds of the suspicions he had started to form in the library, giving them shape at long last. He looked down at his hands, tensed to wrestle his unruly thoughts into place.

'And then maybe after a while people forget the old god name, but they call her something like Mother Leathertongue or Maggie-of-the-Well, and she's suddenly a bogeywoman to scare children away from the well. And then the Christians take everything over, and they start calling her St Margaret the White, but people still remember that she would grant wishes in exchange for offerings. When I saw her in my dream her robe was covered in bits that looked like gold foil, but I found this medieval saint book in the library, with pictures of gold offerings that looked just the same – I think that's what they were.

'And then people start to forget about her. There were some big floods some centuries ago – maybe that was her getting angry, but she couldn't keep it up. Canals got built and everybody had running water and nobody needed her. Then they ran a road through Magwhite, and lots of people had to stop there to change buses, and suddenly people were dropping coins into the well again, not because they worshipped it, but because nowadays people make wishes like that in any well or fountain without really thinking about it. So all of a sudden she's choking on hundreds of these little bits of metal with weird new wishes. She doesn't know why or what's going on. I mean, she's got a throne made out of rubbish because people left it in her woods and I think she thinks it's offerings.'

'So she's just doing bad things to the wishers because she doesn't really understand what the wishes are?'

'Kind of, only . . .' Ryan screwed up his face, trying to find words for the shadowy idea in his head. 'It's not just her, it's the wishes themselves. I don't think *anybody* knows what wishes are. Because I think they're . . . I think they're sort of like conkers.'

'How?'

'I mean, there's the green prickly bit outside, and there's the real solid conker inside. I think wishes are a bit like that. There's an outer bit which is what the wish seems to be, but there's another bit inside which is kind of the real wish. And . . .' This was the hard bit. 'And I don't think when most people wish, they really know what they're wishing. It's like they only see the green spiky outer bit.'

Chelle looked confused, and Ryan talked more quickly to stop his ideas escaping him.

'OK, look. The shell bit of the wish might be, "I wish I had a Harley-Davidson." And Will really thought he wanted a Harley-Davidson, but he didn't, only in a way. I mean . . . that was just the green, spiky bit of the wish. Inside there was this shiny nut bit of wish. Which was, "I wish I was the kind of person who had a Harley-Davidson."'

'That's the same, isn't it?' asked Chelle.

'Sort of, but not really. I mean, he wanted to be somebody that everybody saw driving by on a Harley-Davidson, so they would think, Wow, look at that guy on the Harley, I bet he's really cool and interesting and exciting. And he wanted them to be right. Only this really cool person wasn't there, and Will Wruthers was instead. I mean, I mean, I think the shiny nut bit of the wish was . . . "I don't like this Will Wruthers, I wish he wasn't there."'

Outside, the thunder cleared its throat. Chelle stared at Ryan, her towel-covered knees drawn to her chest.

'Problem is,' continued Ryan, 'I mean, I *think* the problem is – she isn't very good at people. Not nowadays people, anyhow. She doesn't really get the green spiky bits of their wishes. She's been down a well for hundreds of years, right? So then she gets asked to do all this weird stuff about West End shows and bikes and dancing robots – how's she supposed to understand all that? That's where we come in, because she knows we'll understand the green prickly bit, and granting it is much easier and quicker with our help. But the shiny nut bit of wishes, she gets that, kind of. She can help with that. Because those are the great big, painful, simple wishes, you see. Life. Death. Love. Revenge. She gets that.

'Like she understands that Will Wruthers hates Will Wruthers as he is, and wishes he didn't exist.'

'Oh no, oh no, does that mean that now we've done the bike bit we're meant to go back and make him all different and cool and interesting? I don't think we can Ryan, he's so floppy and helpless . . .'

'No.' Ryan hesitated, watching Chelle's nervous beak of an upper lip pull down over her lower lip. 'I think it means we're meant to make him dead.'

Chelle met Ryan's gaze and her eyes widened as if she could see the images scrolling past his mind's eye. *Wet skid marks against dull tarmac. A fractured wing mirror jewelling the roadway. And tumbling in slow motion, like a piece of rubbish in the Magwhite dream, a figure in a leather biker jacket . . .*

'We can't!' wailed Chelle. She pressed her hands

against the sides of her head as if trying to push out the image.

'No, but Josh can. We've got to stop him. We've got to stop all of this.'

'I liked being an angel,' Chelle whispered huskily. 'Back before everything got ugly. I really liked it. I . . . I helped. Or I thought I did. And people listened to me, nobody usually listens to me . . . not even you, Ryan.' It was true, and Ryan couldn't deny it in the face of Chelle's sad, unreproachful gaze.

'I know,' he said helplessly, 'I'm sorry, and if I'd listened to you properly from the start I'd have realized lots of things a lot sooner.'

'Can't we still be angels, but fix people properly? At least the ones we broke by fixing them the first time?'

'I don't know. I don't think so. I mean, even if the Well Spirit didn't stop us, I don't think people are at their best when they're wishing sometimes. There's what people want, and there's what they think they want, and there's what they really need, and there's what they deserve, and if those things are all going to be different . . . what do we do?'

'Perhaps we should just try to get them to want something better. Ryan, I really liked being an angel.'

Ryan did not answer. There was an unusual hint of stubbornness in Chelle's low tones.

Chelle glanced at her watch. 'Oh – I'd better run back now. My parents have got Miss Gossamer to dinner, but I'm scared she'll sneak off to listen at my door, and Josh and Donna will phone soon and if Mum comes and knocks everyone will find out I'm not there again.' She scampered into the hall and wriggled her feet back into her trainers. 'When he calls I'll try to get him to tell me whether he knows who he's avenging against, and if he does maybe we can call the police or, oh, something . . .'

'Chelle, will you . . .' *Will you be all right?* Yes, he could ask that, but then Chelle would start to think that maybe she shouldn't be all right, and couldn't cope, and she'd lose this new, bright readiness. *Spiders' feet.* 'Will you . . . phone me right after he phones you? Only use a payphone, just in case your home phone is working for him.' Ryan had no real reason to think that Josh *could* make phones spy for him, but there was no point in taking chances.

Chelle nodded.

'Brilliant, Chelle,' Ryan said quietly.

Chelle suddenly gave him her brightest I-caught-the-cricket-ball smile, and before Ryan had time to offer her a coat or umbrella she had the door open and was running off into the rain. Chelle, a soggy angel in pink-trimmed trainers and no coat.

Ryan suddenly recalled that Josh was chasing after the revenge wisher, and the wisher's thoughts had last been picked up in his own neighbourhood. He had told Josh that he was out on a family trip to the theatre, so it would look odd if Josh and Donna drove past and saw all the house's lights on. He found the family's 'power cut' torch and scampered quickly around the house, turning off lights.

However, it was nerve-racking waiting in the dark. Ryan started sorting through the books again by torch-light, to take his mind off things. He knew that he did not need the torch, but he was reluctant to use his hidden eyes and see his own wish snakes curling from his chest.

He was just starting to wonder if maybe his mother had given the book away or returned it to the wrong library when he remembered the set of 'mother and baby' books on one of her bedroom shelves. Her bedroom window faced on to the garden, not the street, so Ryan closed the door and risked turning on the light.

There was a row of pink and pale blue volumes . . . and at the end a book with a black and tan dust jacket, and the title *Poachers, Prowlers and Psychopaths*. Ryan seized it triumphantly from the shelf and tweaked it open, then subsided with a small groan of frustration and disappointment. Once again, he had made the mistake of judging a book by its cover. This was yet another book in a borrowed jacket.

As he was preparing to throw it aside, the phone rang. He snatched the receiver of his mother's extension.

'Ryan?' Chelle's high, chirruping phone voice. 'Josh phoned, he called quarter of an hour ago, only it's taken me ages to find a phone box that's working and I've not got much money because one of them ate my fifty . . . Josh was laughing when he called, he sounded really excited, he says he knows who the revenge wisher is, and he kept laughing and saying, "easily with tea-spoons" over and over again . . .'

Ryan did not answer. He was staring down at the front page of the book in his lap. A glossy black and white plate showed an elaborate structure in the shape of a crude female form, fashioned entirely out of welded spoons. Underneath it, slanting words read 'The Voodoo Loa Ezuli, with Teaspoons'. Ryan snatched off the dust jacket. He was holding *Urban Shriek: The Sculptures of Pipette Macintosh*.

His mouth went dry. The mystery wisher had been noticed near his house. So had Pipette Macintosh. The wisher's thoughts had only ever been caught fleetingly. Pipette Macintosh rode a scooter. The wisher wanted revenge. So did Pipette Macintosh.

'Ryan? Can you hear me?' Chelle's voice sounded faint, then was swallowed by a hush of static, threaded through with a piercing feedback note. Ryan jerked the phone away from his ear.

He's close by. But close to her or close to me? Holding his breath, Ryan reached out and very care-fully parted two slats of the Venetian blind.

Josh was standing in the back garden by Ryan's favourite bench. His hands were slightly raised in front of him as if he was about to start conducting an orchestra. He was still wearing his slanted, beetle-eye sunglasses. The rain had plastered his hair to his head, but from the shape of the shadows in his cheeks Ryan could tell he was smiling.

Ryan let the blind fall. Before he could turn and run

for the light switch, the air of the room bristled against his skin like cat's fur. With a faint scratching noise, a pile of paper clips on his mother's desk leaped into a huddle. Nothing else moved, yet in the room's very stillness Ryan seemed to feel something tense. Then there was a faint tick above him, and the bulb went out, plunging the room into darkness.

22

The Dragon Behind the Wall

The roar of rain. Movements in the room, creaks, hums, a tick from the window latch. The lazily menacing *tinngg . . . tinngg* of coat hangers swinging in darkness. Ryan's skin prickled all over, as if he was feeling the breath of something big in the same room.

His hands tensed, and he felt a ripple of sensation as his secret eyes sprang open.

And this was worse than the impenetrable, restless darkness. Now, amid the shadows, he could make out objects haloed by a dim, primrose glow. The phone in his hand was a tangled mat of shadowy golden gossamer.

The air bristled again, and a pulse of gold washed through the room as if the headlights of a passing car had painted it for an instant. Suddenly his surroundings were alive with softly luminous objects, each stirring with jerky, furtive purpose.

The phone seemed to breathe in. A blush of gold in the air, sucked next instant into the handset. Without warning, a blue spark snapped from the aerial to his thumb. He dropped the phone even before he felt the tingling sting. It hit the floor with a crack.

It was the first shot of the ambush. Something beside him squeaked. A rounded head raised itself on a crane-like neck, black against the blind. A single pale eye met his stupefied gaze. Then there was pain as the angle-poise lamp lunged for him and its metal rim bit into his shoulder. At the same time, the right side of his jaw suddenly went cold. He tasted bruising on his gum. Something had hit him in the cheek.

Ryan crouched, shielding his face. Next to his head, his mother's computer was a hazy maze of light. Suddenly it oozed clots of gold and blots of blackness. A flash, a gunshot crack, the smell of burning plastic. Ryan sprawled backwards. His head struck the footboard of the bed.

Noises on all sides. A tinny wrangling from the wardrobe, a duck-paddle flap from the desk, a grinding roar. Ryan was scuffling a retreat along the floor when an invisible claw suddenly raked his face. He threw his arms up wildly and found himself wrestling a flock of coat hangers, fending off the hooks which sought his neck and eyes. Feeling his shoulder nudge against the bedroom door, he flailed for the handle.

His fingers were inches from it when again the texture of the room glistened and changed. A soap bubble of glow formed in the air around the door, then shrank inwards until it vanished into the handle. It happened so quickly that Ryan almost missed it.

He flinched away from the innocent-looking handle,

then snatched up a corner of the bed's coverlet and folded it over his hand. An unseen hanger claw scraped his temple as his muffled fingers fumbled at the handle. It turned, and he hurled himself against the door, propelling himself out of the room.

Outside was darkness, pure darkness. He flung himself sideways and flattened himself against the wall beside the door.

There was a soft wash of gold over the landing, bathing the area in which he stood. When it faded, the metal banister had taken on a sultry glimmer. With a tremulous squeak, screws in the nearby plug socket started unscrewing themselves. One by one they tumbled to the floor and rolled gently to and fro.

There was a pause, during which Ryan held his breath and his position. Then all at once the air seemed to snatch up the screws and fling them. Sharp pains stung Ryan's neck and face.

How does Josh know where I am?

A flying screw scratched the back of Ryan's hand, only just missing his new eyes. He glanced down, and was almost dazzled by the yellow haloes that wrapped his watch like overlapping sunbeams . . .

Stupid! Stupid! Stupid!

Hunched over to protect himself from the screws, Ryan struggled desperately with his wrist strap, and tore the watch off. *Anything else metal?* He thrust both hands into his pockets and drew out coins and his house key, all gently radiant. He threw them aside and searched himself desperately. No zips on his shorts or his sweater . . .

On hands and knees he scuttled along the landing towards the stairs, only to have one lens of his glasses frosted by a piece of angry shrapnel.

Idiot!

He tore off his spectacles, stared at the gleaming metal in the frames and threw them away from him, slightly sickened by the crunch as they landed. Now that his real eyes could not focus, he had to keep them closed so that his twin vision did not make him sick.

He reached the head of the stairs and half scrambled, half tumbled down them. There were fizzing and smashing sounds coming from the kitchen and the landing above, as if his attackers were now flinging themselves about at random, looking for him.

The hallway was gently stroked by a wash of false light, and Ryan saw to his despair that concentric golden globes were forming around the front door and rushing inwards to be absorbed by the handle and lock. At the same instant he heard the jangle of keys outside. It must be his mother returning.

'Don't touch it!' It was like trying to make one's voice rise above a whisper in a dream. 'Don't touch the door!'

Jingle, jangle. His mother sorting through her keys to find the right one.

Thinking fast, Ryan grabbed one of his mother's flower vases and hurled it at the door. It shocked apart just above the handle, shedding gardenias and splattering greenish water all over the door. There was a *spac!*

sound as a spark jumped from the handle. In the same heartbeat, or so it seemed, a key rattled in the lock and the door swung open.

'Mum—'

Run, was what Ryan wanted to shout. He had hardly time to see his mother's astonished face before something heavy hit him in the side of the head and knocked him against the living-room door. He steadied himself on the door handle reflexively, and heard a snap of static.

Oh no. That was his last lucid thought before a big midnight-coloured hand seemed to yank him inside out like a sock puppet.

Suddenly he was lying on the floor. There was a stinging tingle in his hand. Everything was dark and for a moment he couldn't remember why.

Smash. The mirror by the door. *Pic-pac-pac.* Wall cables tearing free from their ties. They snapped, splaying wires and spitting sparks. His cheek against the floor, Ryan stared hypnotized as each spark danced over its reflection in the parquet floor.

And beyond the sparks, framed in a lopsided doorway, he saw his mother as she ducked something, stared about her, then grabbed a coat from one of the hooks and a stick from the umbrella stand. One with a metal handle, he noted with a weak despair.

Run run run you can't understand any of this and he can see your handbag zip and car keys and loose change . . .

But Ryan's mother never ran from anything.

It was a dance of sorts, and somehow it seemed to

float towards him as if through water. A woman dancing through darkness in a dress suit, leaping the sparks that fizzed around her ankles and somehow just missing the radiator suffused with treacherous gold. Her flailing stick caught a flying candleholder out of the air and then swung back wildly and shocked the last shards out of the shattered mirror.

She flung the coat over Ryan, cloaking all his eyes in darkness, and then he felt her scooping him up bodily. There was a gasp of pain and a clatter, and he guessed that she had dropped the stick. He lolled against her as she dragged him down the hallway, his feet slithering against the polished floor. There was a rattle of the door handle, and the thunder of the rain grew louder. There was a breeze against his calves and a crunch of gravel beneath his feet.

When she pulled the coat from his head they had reached the pavement. Both of them with one accord sank to sit, the rain hammering and blinding them.

'I'm getting you to the hospital,' his mother was saying over and over, sounding as if she might cry. 'I'm getting you to the hospital, love . . .'

'Not in the car!' Ryan's voice sounded high and hysterical, and he didn't care.

The street seemed to be full of people. The Doyles' neighbours had come out to find out what had caused the screaming and smashing, and it turned out that many of them had already called the police. Ryan only calmed down when he saw his mother take out her mobile phone and use it to call an ambulance.

'Please . . . I just want to . . . hold it . . .' She let him hold the phone to his ear, and he heard the familiar dialling tone, with no trace of static or high electronic whine. Josh had gone.

When the ambulance arrived, they let Ryan and his mother hug each other tightly all the way to the hospital.

'I think someone broke in,' Ryan heard his mother saying. 'I just got back, I think they were still there, they'd torn up the house and ripped the wires out of the walls. I think he got a shock from one of the wires . . .' He met his mother's eye and she gave him a meaningful look. Although his mind was having as much trouble focusing as his eyes, he understood it. *This is going to be our story*, said the look. *This is what we'll tell them when they ask.*

He unfolded her hand and touched her palm with his fingertip. *Your name is Anne*, he thought. *That's so funny. You've always been Mum. Mum and Dad, the two pillars that hold up opposite ends of the sky. But you're Anne, and you're not a pillar and things can happen to you. Josh tried to kill my mum. Josh tried to kill Anne.*

When they reached the hospital Ryan's mother helped him out of the ambulance. Casualty had harsh low lights with a yellow glare like refrigerator bulbs. A young doctor hurried over immediately to look at Ryan, and asked him questions. But the questions were fuzzy and so was the doctor. *Josh tried to kill Anne*, thought Ryan and he started to cry. He couldn't help himself.

'Here, Ryan.' Why were they helping him into a wheelchair?

Ryan was wheeled down a couple of corridors into a large open room where there were a number of cubicles walled in by big curtains. It must be bad, they must be about to operate.

They helped him up on to one of the cubicle beds. One of the nurses kept talking to him calmingly, in sentences that didn't seem to have full stops. Sometimes she would say, 'OK, Ryan? Do you understand?' and he nodded, because he guessed it didn't matter if he understood or not.

'All right, Ryan, dragons.' His mother's voice, very quietly. She had invented the 'dragon game' when he had been very young indeed and facing a series of injections. There was a dragon trying to push through the wall, and the only way to scare him off was to face him down. And although it was a childish game, Ryan held tight to his mother's middle finger and together they stared intently at the opposite wall.

There was a pain in the inside of his elbow. Ryan's eyes filled with tears, but he didn't let the dragon through. The dragon was no match for Ryan and Anne.

At last he dared to glance back at his arm, and felt pins and needles in all his joints when he saw that there was still something sticking into his flesh, a little clear plastic something with a pink cap. Somebody clipped a thing like a clothes peg to one of his fingers. One of the doctors turned Ryan's hand over and examined his knuckles before Ryan could do anything about it.

'Just molluscum,' he muttered in an undertone to the nurse beside him, who jotted something on a clipboard. 'Ordinary warts.'

'The dragon's gone, Ryan,' said Anne. 'We scared him off.'

Ryan slept fitfully in his cubicle bed and kept waking to see his mother curled up nearby on a chair. At last he slept more deeply and when he woke his mother was gone and his father was seated beside him, quietly reading with a pocket torch. Hearing the rustle of Ryan's starched sheet, he looked up and smiled.

'It was your mother's turn to sleep,' his father murmured in an undertone. 'How are you feeling?'

'Are they going to operate on me?'

'Probably not. Do you remember getting an electric shock?'

Ryan nodded, hoping his father wouldn't ask him to describe the circumstances.

'Your mother tells me you blacked out for a moment, and you seemed confused afterwards, so the hospital has to keep you in for a while just to make sure you're all right.'

'I'm all right,' Ryan said quickly. 'I'm a lot better. Is Mum OK?'

'She's fine. Concerned about you, that's all. Ryan – do you know who broke into the house . . . ?'

'I didn't see them. It was just a lot of bangs and crashes in the dark. I was sneaking down to the front door when Mum got home.' Ryan waited for his father's nod and felt a flood of relief. 'She . . . she was really great, Dad.' He wished he could show his father the picture of his mum dancing through death and mayhem to rescue him. 'If you'd seen her . . . you'd never want to be angry with her again.'

'Ryan, you don't have to say things like that.'

But I do, because, because . . .

'You're splitting up with Mum, aren't you?' It came out in a breathy, tremulous, five-year-old's voice.

Ryan's father raised his eyebrows and scrutinized his book as if waiting to see what it had to say for itself. Then he took a deep breath and released it.

'All right.' His voice sounded deeper than usual, and he spoke carefully as if to an adult acquaintance. 'I know that your mother and I have been quarrelling recently, and I remember what you said the other day.' Ryan suddenly felt that perhaps he did not want to hear what his father had to say. 'Sometimes a couple goes through a phase of arguing a lot, but that does *not* necessarily mean that they are going to break up. It doesn't absolutely mean they won't, but in our case . . . we almost certainly won't. The truth is, things have actually been getting a lot better between us.'

'But . . .' Ryan tailed off. It seemed so obviously untrue.

'If we had decided to end our marriage, it would probably have been the summer we moved to Guildley four years ago. We spent months stepping on eggshells for fear of breaking everything. I knew things were getting better when we dared to raise our voices or say what we thought again.'

Ryan's eyes filled with tears of relief.

'Josh said . . .' he began.

'Ah. Things become clearer. So Josh made you think we were breaking up.' Ryan's father sighed. 'I did not plan to tell you this, but now I think it may be useful to you to know it. Josh's parents are undergoing divorce proceedings – it's an open secret. They've been living almost separate lives for quite some time.'

'Dad . . . I really wish you'd told me all this before.'

His father studied his own shoe for a few moments and then nodded slowly.

'Dad? Can visitors come in and see me?'

'Yes, though not right now. Visiting hours are nine a.m. until nine p.m., I believe. Who did you want to see?'

'I don't really mind. Only not Josh. Just . . . please not Josh.'

'We always find it difficult to forgive our heroes for being human. I think Josh may have been taking some complicated feelings out on you. Try not to take it personally. But you don't have to see him if you'd rather not.' Ryan's father rose and peered down at Ryan with a troubled, tender smile. It was, Ryan realized, very much like the smile he occasionally gave Ryan's mum. 'You look tired. Get some more sleep, Ryan.'

Ryan lay for a long time with his eyes closed but his mind busy. At long last he understood the hatred he had seen in Josh's face on the night of the bat-spotting, as he had stared at Ryan's mum. Anne shaking her son, in a rage of concern and love, while the Lattimer-Stones waited dispassionately by their car. Anne, bossy and windswept, bullying and steamrollering her loved ones, and willing to fight like a she-wolf in their defence.

The Lattimer-Stones would fill in their divorce papers as if they were crosswords and then decide in cool, civilized tones which of them would take the cars, the house, the adopted son. Ryan's mum was everything The Haven lacked, everything that Josh lacked. *That* was why Josh hated her. *That* was the real reason Josh had set out to destroy her. The revenge wish had simply lit his touchpaper.

Anne was sleeping now and the ward was silent, but there was still a dragon behind the wall.

23

Soul Repair

'Ryan! My mum and dad brought me over and I was worried because all I knew was you'd had an electric shock and my sisters said if they were keeping you in that probably meant it had fried your brain . . .'

Chelle squeaked the visitor chair over to Ryan's bed.

'I think I'll leave you to judge how thoroughly Ryan's brain has been cooked.' Ryan's father stood and stretched. When he was tired there were always faint grey smudges like ash down his cheeks. 'I'll be back in an hour. Ryan, your contact lenses are on the side table.' Nice, non-metallic contact lenses. Ryan had never imagined that he would regard them with such affection.

Chelle clenched little fists of excitement on top of her bare knees until Ryan's father had gone.

'Ryan, what happened? The phone screamed then went dead when we were talking last night, and this morning your mum phoned my dad and she was saying someone broke in and tried to kill you, then she wanted to know if my parents knew where Miss Gossamer had been when it happened and they said yes, she'd been at dinner all evening, and then there was the most incredible row and I could hear your mother even though she was on the other end of the line.'

'She thinks it was Miss Gossamer?' Ryan was assaulted by a weird mental image of a demented Miss Gossamer rending her way through the house, ripping out cables and flinging toasters.

'Well, I heard them talking about it afterwards when they forgot I was there and it sounds like she told my dad all about my asthma attack and said that Miss Gossamer was trying to kill me by making it worse. And then she said she'd been spending two days finding out all about Miss Gossamer—'

'What?'

'Yes! Looking up records and everything, and my dad said he thought probably doing some things that could get her in trouble, and she said that Miss Gossamer had a history of instability and she shouldn't be allowed anywhere near children . . .'

Ryan felt himself flushing. After their argument his mother had not run off to shadow Saul Paladine. She had charged into battle against Miss Gossamer, armed only with a fragment of the truth and a host of misconceptions. She was on his side, beautifully, madly and possibly illegally.

'. . . and she'd lost a baby and then had a breakdown and started trying to steal other people's babies or toddlers from outside shops and she was found taking one of them for a walk near the canal . . .'

'Stop! Chelle, did you say she lost a baby? Do you know how she lost it?'

Chelle's face furrowed.

'It died. No! It drowned. Because after your mum phoned, my mum and dad were wondering if she might have drowned it herself because of being all disturbed . . . and they don't trust her any more, Ryan, and they won't leave her alone with me, and I so love your mum, I love her, and when it's Christmas I'm going to buy her books as presents for everyone, even you, I hope you don't mind . . .'

'Chelle!' Ryan stared at her open-mouthed, as the facts slid together like cog-teeth. 'I know what happened to Miss Gossamer's baby! She didn't kill it. The Well's Angels did – an early version of us, fifty years ago. That's why she got so worked up at the Lattimer-Stones' dinner party when she heard you speaking Donna's thoughts, and saw what Josh did to that bulb. The men who murdered her baby probably had the same powers as us, and she recognized them. That's why she's been spying on us ever since, trying to catch us out. And that's why she hates us so much.'

'But it can't have been her trying to kill you yesterday, Ryan, she was with us all night . . .'

'Course it wasn't. That was Josh.'

'*Josh?*' Ryan watched Chelle's face collapse as she listened to his account of the night before. 'Maybe . . . maybe he wasn't really trying to kill your mum. Maybe . . . it was just meant to scare her?'

'It was meant to scare her all right. I mean, you'd be

scared if the lights went out and everything in the room started exploding and attacking you, wouldn't you? So you'd run to the door and grab the handle, and, *kzap!* Josh did something special to the door handles, something he didn't do to anything else. I think he was stuffing them full of static electricity, enough to kill anybody who touched them. Maybe the only reason I survived was he didn't have time to do all the handles properly, so he didn't bother so much with the living-room one – the one I touched. If I hadn't got to the front door in time . . .' There was a sombre silence.

'Is your mum OK?'

'She's not hurt. Mum and Dad are allowed to sleep at the hospital till I'm better. She's probably safe while we're all here. But every time she nips off to the shops for something I keep thinking, what if Josh is waiting for her on a street corner, so he can make something go wrong with the engine, or the brakes . . .'

'Can't we warn her?'

'And say what? What do I tell her? Not to go near anything metal? Everybody already thinks I'm concussed.' There was a cold, white pause.

'It's the well making Josh do it, isn't it?' Chelle said in a small voice.

'It's the well *letting* him do it, that's for sure,' Ryan muttered grimly. 'And he's getting more powerful, so that probably means she is too. Maybe every wish we granted just made her stronger.'

'Then . . . then we have to ungrant them and make her weaker, don't we?'

Ryan opened his mouth to say that they had no reason to believe that would work, and then realized that he had no reason to believe that it wouldn't.

'You mean . . . try to fix the wishers, like you were saying before?'

'Yes! And then when Josh isn't so much in her power we can talk to him and get him to be less mad, and besides we have to fix Will quickly anyway, because of what you said about the Well Spirit wanting him to kill himself on his motorbike. And he's right here – he's in this hospital.'

'Chelle, he's never really met us before. If we show up and start trying to tell him what to do with his life, he'll think we're nutters.'

'No, he won't.' Chelle went pink. 'Actually . . . he's really nice.'

Chelle had been making good use of her morning. After arriving at nine and discovering that Ryan was still asleep, she had found out about the nurses' coffee room, where a big board showed which patients were in which wards, and had sneaked off to visit Will.

Chelle beamed as she told the story. Perhaps finally getting into serious trouble had made her less worried about the prospect. Ryan had learned that cornflakes still existed after the apocalypse. Perhaps Chelle had discovered that there was still life after Trouble.

'Nice work, Chelle.' He sat up carefully, pulled back the covers and reached for his contact lenses. 'Let's see if we can sneak over there and talk to him before my dad gets back.'

Will was in a little ward with six beds. One of the other beds was occupied, but the man in it seemed to be asleep. When Will saw Chelle his face lit up. Ryan noticed that there were dark shadows round his eyes, however, as if he hadn't been getting much sleep.

'Chelle! And is this your sick friend?' Will glanced at Ryan and a slight look of perplexity crossed his face. Perhaps he had recognized Ryan from the tea shop. Ryan perched on the edge of the bed, feeling his stomach cramp with stage fright. He'd got used to seeing Will Wruthers from a distance, and having all Will's thoughts helplessly spooling out in front of him. Up close, Will seemed much bigger, more adult and more real.

'Yes, and it's all right, his brain isn't fried. How's your spleen?'

'They still don't know,' Will grimaced. 'Apparently the specialist won't be around again until this afternoon.'

'Will has to stay here for when his spleen explodes,' Chelle added in a stage whisper.

'*If* it explodes, not *when*.' Will grinned. 'It probably won't. I'm just under observation. They've said I can probably go today.'

'Ooh, you've been doing some already, that's so great, can I read it?' Chelle snatched up some scribbled pages that lay across his bed.

'Of course you can.' Will glanced at Ryan. 'Chelle's been setting me homework so I don't go stir crazy.'

'Well, he was telling me about having two accidents, both with Harleys, and how he thinks they've got a grudge against him and he made it ever so funny and I said he had to write it down and send it in somewhere as an article or something . . .' Chelle retreated to the far end of the room to read. Her thin pale lips moved slightly as she skimmed the pages, giggling occasion-ally.

Will watched her with a kindly expression that some-how took the limp thinness out of his face.

'Chelle's got such an original way of seeing the world – I could listen to her for hours. I was just about ready to go mad when she dropped in, saying she'd read about my accident in the paper. I'd been here two days with-out any visitors, or books, or sleep.'

Ryan remembered Will worrying about his mother and wondered why she hadn't been to visit. Perhaps she really hadn't forgiven her son for getting a motorbike.

'I'm sorry about your accident,' he murmured.

'Yeah, came to grief on my Harley.' The mention of the Harley was a little too nonchalant, and there was a frightened light in Will's smile as if he was unsure whether something was going to hurt or not. 'You like bikes?'

'Yeah. Kind of.' Ryan remembered his unreasoning envy of Josh straddling the motorbike. 'Only . . . I don't think I really want one. I'd just be getting it so I could be, y'know, "Biker Ryan".' During the following silence, Ryan did not dare look at Will.

'You know what's funny?' Will said at last, and Ryan was glad to hear his voice still sounding natural and friendly. 'They don't tell you about the runny nose you get when you're biking. I mean, in films you never get these guys in leather jackets getting off their bikes and going pfneeuh, pfneeuh, and wiping their noses on their sleeves.'

'Sounds gross.'

'Yeah.' Will gave a rueful little sideways tilt of his head and stretched his arms and legs carefully. 'Yeah,' he muttered again, more quietly, as if talking to himself. 'Ha. Biker Will . . .' He sighed and pushed the heels of his hands into his eyes. 'I can't afford to keep the Harley anyway. I've been missing so much work, I can't manage payments on the bike and the new flat. It was tough enough already. Better sell the bike and move back in with Mum. That'll make her happy at least.'

'No no no no!' Chelle scooted over from the far side of the room and broke into a dance of smiling rage at the end of the bed. 'Don't! Well yes OK, you should sell the bike, but you can't move in with your mum again. Because I've got your article now, and I'm not giving it back if you do, haha.'

'Chelle, the whole reason I got a flat was because my mum wouldn't have a bike in the house . . .'

'But maybe the whole reason you got a bike was so you'd have to move out? And she hasn't come to see you in hospital, and that's horrible. And anyway your article's really, really good, and I'm going to send it to *Silverwing* and you can't stop me, haha.'

This was a new Chelle. A Chelle with a strange, impish, capering confidence. Will was smiling tolerantly, Will was laughing and relenting. He was not going to talk to his mother just yet, he promised, if only Chelle would let him look over the article and improve it before she sent it anywhere.

'Oh! And when you get out, can you please deliver this note for us?' Chelle added as they prepared to leave. 'It's for Whelmford, it's not *all* that far from Crook's Baddock.' Chelle tore out a sheet from Will's notepad and scrawled on it. 'It's a nice lady Ryan knows who can't leave her house, and Ryan does gardening for her, and we're going to hers for tea on Wednesday only she doesn't know it yet, and you should come too! And she's got jackalopes.' She made it sound like a disease. Laughing, Will promised he would.

'Chelle,' Ryan whispered as they scampered back to the children's ward, 'you made it sound like Carrie was an old lady or something.'

'Yes!' Chelle beamed at him. 'And when he finds out she's young and pretty he'll go all nervous and shy and then she won't be frightened of him.' Chelle seemed to have given her angelic duties worrying amounts of thought.

What do we do about Carrie? wondered Ryan. Once upon a time, Carrie had granted her own wish, locking herself away from the world, but now she had set out to 'ungrant' it again, by ordering her door. She must have partly succeeded by the time Josh took her ring out of the well, since Chelle was able to pick up her thoughts – the Well Spirit clearly considered hers an ungranted wish. Now Josh would want to re-grant her wish in some horribly permanent way. How could he be stopped? And would giving Carrie a new friend in the shape of Will really do anything to help?

Ryan was discharged at four, but his parents told him that they wouldn't be taking him straight home.

'The police are still taking photos of all the rooms,' Anne explained as they gathered their belongings. Ryan's stomach lurched. What if the police looked through the house and found no sign of a break-in? Would they decide that he'd gone mad and torn everything up himself?

'Mum . . .' Ryan fumbled for words. 'Did you give a report? About . . . what you saw?' What had she seen anyway?

'Yes.' His mum's perennially direct gaze clouded and she dropped her eyes. 'I told them that I saw things being thrown at you through the door by somebody in the kitchen.' She raised her eyes again and smiled, calmly and levelly. 'You may have to talk to them, but don't you worry. It'll be OK.'

'We're going to head back and talk to them ourselves now,' Ryan's father explained. 'The Coopers have said that we can drop you off at theirs to spend the afternoon with Chelle. Are you all right with that, Ryan?' Seeing Ryan pale slightly, he added reassuringly, 'I believe that as of this morning the Coopers are minus one house guest.'

So the quarrel between his mum and the Coopers had reached some kind of truce, and Miss Gossamer was no longer welcome in the Coopers' house. However, it hadn't been the prospect of meeting Miss Gossamer that had caused Ryan's sudden pallor.

'Dad,' he murmured when he caught a moment alone with his father, 'you'll . . . stay close to Mum, won't you?' He halted, uncertain how to continue. His father smiled slightly and pushed a lock of hair back from Ryan's forehead.

'I had better,' he whispered back, 'for the sake of the police. If she stays in this mood she may try to wrestle their investigation away from them.' They both looked across to where Ryan's mum was frowning at Ryan's medical chart and interrogating some poor nurse. Glancing up at his father's face, Ryan recognized for the first time the glint of pride that had perhaps always lurked amid the exasperation and amusement.

Chelle and Ryan were dropped off at the Coopers', Chelle nervous at the thought of finding a message from Josh waiting for her. But there had been no word from Josh, and half an hour later a Cavern Conference was in session. On Ryan's suggestion Josh's Well Shrine, a blue plastic bucket which had been Ouija-labelled in green marker pen, was relocated to the wardrobe. When a rug had been carefully draped over it, and the wardrobe door shut, they felt safe enough to speak above a whisper.

'You sure it's OK to use the phone?' Ryan couldn't help asking.

'I think so, I've . . . borrowed my dad's work mobile and Josh doesn't know about that.' Chelle tucked her hair behind one ear and started to dial.

'Is that Mr Punzell? This is Chelle Cooper, you remember, your friend Donna psychically projected into my brain.' Pause. 'Oh, but no! I'm not calling for her, I'm calling for you! You're my only hope!' A pause, during which Chelle began to smile in anticipation. 'It's my friend Ryan, everything in his house exploded and attacked him and he was taken away in an ambulance, and nobody believes us and they say it was just a gang breaking in but we know it was . . . no, I don't think it was bad feng shui, Mr Punzell . . . it was this lady artist who's been putting voodoo curses on Ryan's mother and we think they bounced and hit him. And can you pleasepleaseplease talk to her, because we don't think she knows what she's done and . . . and could you please . . . oh yes, she's called Pipette Macintosh, and she's in the directory. Oh thank you, Mr Punzell, I knew you'd help us.'

She pressed a button to hang up, and smiled her eyebrows way up into her fringe. Chelle's personality seemed to be bulging out in unexpected ways, to fill the gap left by Josh, and Mr Punzell had agreed to help. He was certainly vain, but evidently vanity sometimes made people do unpredictable and generous things.

'What about the mime-actor Jacob Karlborough?' Ryan asked. 'How do we ungrant his wish?'

Chelle wrinkled her nose. 'I don't know if we can. We can't really unbreak the fairground. And as for the green spiky bit of the wish . . . well, supposing your dad's article *did* help him, and he got parts in plays, and he's started to be famous and happy . . . I just *couldn't* undo it and spoil it all for him. I couldn't. I don't want to take away that little boy's robot toy either.'

'No. You're right,' agreed Ryan after a moment. 'OK, we'll leave them alone. So I guess . . . now we wait.' A phone call, a motorbike article, a tea-party invitation . . . perhaps these would do nothing . . . but perhaps . . .

'Eeuw!' Chelle jumped up, wiping her knee, and ran to the window. Ryan realized that there was a dribble of water running from the wall to the place on the floor where she'd been kneeling. 'It's shut!' she exclaimed in a surprised tone. 'I can't see where the rain's getting in.'

'Chelle . . .' Following the dark snail's trail of the water, Ryan had realized that it did not start at the window. He followed it back along the line of the wall, to a spreading puddle around the wardrobe . . .

There was a thick sound, like a horse's hoof lifting out of sticky mud, and a surge of greenish water spewed through the crack under the wardrobe door. From within came a glassy, echoing sound, like droplets falling in some vast cavern.

They both jumped. The colour seemed to drain out of everything, and Ryan's knuckles stung. He was back in the world of nightmares, but this time Chelle was there with him.

'Ryan, we've got to pile things against the door, you've got to help me move the bed—'

'The door won't hold her, we've got to open it and destroy the shrine—'

'Oh no . . . no . . .' Chelle's voice climbed in pitch as the wardrobe door pushed itself open. A tide of murky water rushed out, carrying weed-draped plimsolls and a frisbee. The rug over the bucket was shrugging oddly and had nearly bucked itself off. Water was dripping from the clothes rail and sounding against the base with a weird, cavernous clarity.

'Grab boxes! Anything!' The rug slipped off the bucket. The water within was spilling over the edge, and seemed to be boiling without steam. Ryan seized three board-game boxes from Chelle and slammed them down over the top. It was all he could do to make himself kneel and grapple the bucket.

'Open the bedroom door!' Chelle flung the door wide and ran ahead of him as he staggered down the hall, feeling the boxes buck against his chin as something pushed from below.

A shrill, laughing conversation upstairs, a television-crowd roar in the living room, and nobody with enough attention spare to notice as two children scrambled past, struggling to prevent a god escaping from a bucket.

The bathroom door was open, and he hurled himself in, half falling against the toilet. He released his grip on the boxes and the water sluiced out into the waiting bowl, accompanied by a deluge of pieces from the tearing Monopoly box. When the bucket was empty he tumbled back and Chelle slammed down the lid. Both lunged for the flush handle, then waited while the cistern roared, gurgled and faded. When they started to hear the same cavernous dripping from beneath the closed lid, they flushed again, and again, and again. At last all was quiet, and they raised the lid to find only clear water with a few floating plastic hotels in it.

'We've done it now,' murmured Ryan.

24

Gathering the Fragments

Something was wrong.

Ryan was sitting at the breakfast table as usual, spreading jam across his toast with great care, listening to the rustle of his father's newspaper and the chime of his mother tapping her teaspoon dry against her mug rim. When Ryan reached across for the jam jar, though, it seemed to recede from him along the table top.

He looked up. Where his father and mother had been sitting a moment before there were only softly swaying nests of translucent tentacles.

I'm asleep. Ryan stood up, looked about him at the steamed and splintered wreckage of the Glass House, then stepped through a jagged hole in the front wall.

Now the sky was dark copper, kettle-belly. Little spasms of violet lightning flickered like scratches in an old film. Beyond the car park's edge he felt, rather than saw, the decline towards the Magwhite well. There the dark air was fighting itself, and Ryan thought he glimpsed rent boughs, pushchairs, streamers of cordon tape, yellowed bones, all twisting in slow motion among the leaf swarms, as if tossed to and fro by some vast autumnal tantrum. He sensed the wordless summons in the roar, knew that the darkness demanded him.

But he did not obey. Doubled against the thrust of the wind, he stumbled towards the snaking chain of trolleys along the side wall. The wind blew leaves into his face, and when they touched his skin he thought he heard fragments of words spoken, or wordless gasps.

'She's calling you,' whispered the Man in the trolley chain gang.

While the trolleys ahead of him and behind slid to and fro as if on a boat deck, the Man moved more naturally from one foot to another, as if he was trying to keep warm. His face was hunched down to his chest, his eyes hidden beneath a sodden curtain of earth-coloured hair. His hands were tucked into his armpits, again as if he was cold.

'I wanted to talk to you,' said Ryan.

'Be my guest. Pull up a trolley.' Ryan took cautious hold of the nearest trolley and swung himself into it. Now he could see chains trailing from the Man's wrists and ankles, linking him into the line of trolleys.

'I wanted to talk to you. Well's Angel to Well's Angel.'

'That's nice, I like that. Well's Angels.' The Man laughed suddenly, and sounded far more human. There was something soothing in the sway of the trolley, though Ryan had to keep bracing to keep his balance.

'Are you . . . alive?'

'I don't know.' The Man sounded interested, as if he'd never wondered about it before. 'Not very. I never paid my debts . . .' Left foot, right foot, left foot, right foot . . .

'Why doesn't she just let us pay her back in coins?' Ryan clenched his teeth against the cold and leaned forward to whisper, fearful that the leaves would pick up his words piecemeal and carry them back to the well.

'Oh, that wouldn't do for Her. Her power's all about flow, all about give and take, isn't it? It's not enough getting offerings; She has to be able to pay for them by granting wishes, or She gets choked by Her debts. Now look, you'll fall, you can't resist the motion, just sit down and let yourself go with it.'

Ryan sat down, for his legs were indeed getting shaky.

'What if a granted wish gets ungranted again?' he asked.

'She wouldn't be pleased with that,' the Man said grimly. 'It takes power from Her. Not as much power as it would if She ungranted a wish Herself though – that's a pact She can't break without crippling Herself.'

'And . . . what happens when you stop doing what she says?' Ryan asked.

'She gets Her penny's worth out of you. You're made to pay with everything you have and it's still not enough and you end up here.' The Man looked furtively over his shoulder towards the dark maelstrom of leaf and litter. 'Look, I understand Her better than I did. You and I can help each other. I think I can deal with Her if I can just get out of here.' The Man's breath smelt of canals and wet toadstools. 'If you could take my place here, just for a little while . . .'

'I've got a friend waiting for me—' croaked Ryan, pulling backwards away from him.

'You can't resist Her without me!' the Man snarled suddenly, lurching against Ryan's trolley. 'She'll make you see things Her way!' The Man's right hand lunged out to grab Ryan's wrist. On each knuckle was a full-size, perfectly proportioned human eye, baby blue and bloodshot. 'You'll see! You'll see things Her way too!' As his attacker's face drew close, Ryan stared up through matted hair into deep sockets where in place of eyes were two tiny, shrivelled warts.

Ryan yelled with terror and beat with his free fist on the eyes of the hand that gripped him. He did not stop until he felt the vice on his wrist slacken, until the trolley overturned and tipped him into ink.

Lying on the floor in an unfamiliar and dim room, Ryan blinked hard three times to convince himself that he was awake. Memories surfaced, and he pieced together the mystery of his whereabouts. Instead of returning to their poor fractured home, the family had decided to spend the night in the local hotel, which stood on the edge of the park.

I'm awake. His tumble to the floor had not woken his parents, who still breathed softly in the double bed opposite.

Ryan padded quietly to the window and tugged a

crack in the blind. His knuckles had started to burn and itch again and he could not resist resting them against the soothing cool of the window pane. Even without his lenses he could make out the low ceiling of cloud. As his eye fell on the blurred green pool of the park he squinted . . . and then tiptoed off to the bathroom.

Coming back with his lenses in made nothing any better. He really was awake, and there really were two shopping trolleys in the trees on the edge of the park.

Returning to their house later that morning was more difficult than Ryan had expected. The most horrible thing was the carelessness with which things he used daily had been thrown about and broken. Ryan thought grimly of the times he had sat on his favourite bench, 'turning the house upside down'. Josh had turned the house upside down with a vengeance, and no amount of looking at it inverted would set it straight again.

The ladles and fish slices had run rampant in the kitchen, and all the tall jars along the top shelf had smashed, cascading Ryan's mother's colour-coded pasta on to the floor and sideboards. Wires had pulled themselves loose from the speakers, the sockets and the video player.

'They're things,' Ryan's mother declared after silently regarding the sole surviving coffee percolator for a few moments. 'Just things.'

Her philosophical stance was tested, however, when she visited her bedroom and found that her computer's innards had been fried, and that even the back-up disks on which she had saved her half-written book on Saul Paladine were completely blank. Seeing her standing by her computer as if by a grave, Ryan tactfully tiptoed away to help tidy. The front path was strewn with the fragments of the burglar alarm, which had apparently exploded like a Roman candle. Ryan knelt down to pick up the pieces.

While he was crouched on the ground, he noticed something pink appearing furtively round the corner of the hedge. It was palm-sized, studded with sequins and feathers, heart-shaped and flat as a cookie. As Ryan watched, it became clear that it was dangling from the tip of a bamboo cane. More and more of the cane emerged unsteadily from behind the hedge until the heart thunked against the letter box, swayed, jiggled and thunked again.

Ryan tiptoed over and peeped around the hedge.

'Um . . . Miss Macintosh? Our letter box doesn't push inwards like that, you have to kind of flip up the lid first and then push things through . . .'

Hundreds of raindrops nestled like fish eggs in Pipette Macintosh's thick, frizzed hair, which was starting to droop and draggle. The water had also humbug-striped her cheeks with mascara. Ryan wondered how long she'd been there, trying to poke the little heart through the letterbox.

'The curse was never meant for you,' she said in her usual flat, pebbley voice. She raised the cane so that the heart rattled down its length and came to a halt against her fist. Her gaze flitted over the plasters on his forehead and inside his elbow, the bruises that Josh's fist had left on his cheek. 'It was misdirected. I should never have let you pick up that milk bottle.'

Ryan knelt down next to her so that they could talk properly.

'Miss Macintosh . . . do you think you could take off the curse, please? Because it . . . really hurts. And please don't curse my mum; I don't want her to be dead. You've already killed her computer with her next book in it.'

'Did I?' A marbly gleam of glee entered Pipette's eyes for a brief moment. 'Please believe me, I never knew my own powers. I am spending time now with someone . . . rather special . . . who can help me understand them.' Mr Punzell, no doubt. Ryan guessed that someone who could make houses attack people would interest him much more than poor Donna's 'psychic projection of will'.

Pipette unhooked the pink heart with some difficulty and pressed it into Ryan's hand, her broad mouth working with emotion.

'Take this,' she said. 'Your life may depend upon it until I have had a chance to remove the curse. And rest easy about your family. I Shall Do Nothing More.' She straightened. 'A childlessness curse,' she muttered under her breath. 'I should have guessed what might happen.'

As Ryan entered the house again, his father's eye fell

upon the pink talisman in his hand and all the muscles in his face tensed instantly.

'This is harassment,' he muttered under his breath. 'You'd think at a time like this that woman would have the decency to stop her campaign of—'

'It's all right!' Ryan called out hurriedly. 'Look, it's got "protection" written across it in – eeugh – cake icing. Dad, Miss Macintosh just meant it as a . . .'

'. . . peace offering,' finished Ryan's mum, who had appeared in the doorway. Whereas Ryan's father's face had hardened at the sight of the 'voodoo artefact', hers had softened. Ryan placed it in her waiting palm. She stared at it for a while, then gave a defiant and slightly belligerent sniff. 'Hmph! I'll be more impressed when she drops the lawsuit.' However, as she left the room she was still gazing at the heart with an almost youthful smile, the sort she wore when she looked over pictures Ryan had painted at the age of five.

'Why's Mum looking so . . . ?' In her face Ryan had seen the pleased hope he had felt himself when he had imagined Josh posting his glasses back through the letter box. 'It's not like they're friends making up! She's never cared what Pipette thinks! I mean, if she does, *why does she write those books*?' And that of course was the question he had been wanting to ask all along.

'We all have different ways of dealing with our heroes,' Ryan's father said sotto voce.

'The people she writes about aren't her heroes! She writes horrible things about them!'

'She writes the truth, or as near to the truth as she

can find. What better way of celebrating someone? To find out everything you can about them? It certainly gets their attention.'

'But they . . . hate her.'

'Yes,' sighed his father, turning to go. 'Every time.'

Ryan moved over to the window and looked out into the garden, where his mum was sitting on his favourite bench, looking at the heart.

'Oh, for God's sake,' Ryan's father suddenly muttered under his breath. The book in his hand had the words *Typhoons, Tornadoes and Toddlers: DIY for Every Disaster* down its spine. 'Is nothing in this house what it seems?' He stripped off the dust jacket, sighed and dropped the offending book on the table.

'I think I know where the cover to that one is,' Ryan said gingerly, picking it up. The spine now read *Poachers, Prowlers and Psychopaths: The Dark Side of Guildley*. He scurried away to read it.

The chapter on the Well Cult in the book told Ryan little more than he had already suspected, but it did give the name of the girl whose baby had been murdered – Madeleine Gossamer. There was a bleary black and white photo of a young woman, her face a frozen, shell-shocked mask. He stared at it and wondered what she had wished. Perhaps when she had been 'expecting' and terrified of somebody noticing, she had just wished for the baby to go away. And then after the baby had been born, the 'witchy' men had appeared and taken the little girl away forever.

Pipette was right. Wishing for childlessness was very dangerous indeed.

In the late morning the Coopers turned up at Ryan's house with a box of odds and ends, including a walk-about phone.

'Just till you get your broken things replaced,' beamed Chelle. 'Look! It's fluffy!' She rubbed at the phone's nylon tiger-striped fur.

Chelle reacted eagerly when Ryan told her about Pipette's visit. 'It's working then! Oh, wouldn't it be nice if she really did have voodoo powers? She could summon one of those big voodoo spirits, and maybe we could get it to tell the Well Spirit to leave us alone. It would be so nice if we could play them off against each other like, you know, parents or teachers or some-thing . . .'

Ryan went on to tell her about his nightmare. 'And this morning . . .' he hesitated, wondering if he was going to sound idiotic, 'there were two trolleys in a tree . . . watching our hotel.'

Chelle nodded. 'Same with us – only one of them was wedged in our hedge and the other one was up on the post-office roof, *peering* . . . so that means that the Well Spirit really knows we've both . . .'

'. . . gone rogue,' finished Ryan.

'I don't suppose that means she'll take away our powers, does it?' Chelle asked with a strange mixture of anxiety and hope in her voice.

'Doubt it.' Ryan grimaced. 'She's more likely to try to force us back into obeying her. The question is, if she knows that we're working together, does that means Josh knows too? Have you heard from him?'

'No.' Chelle's forehead creased. 'Mum says Mrs Lattimer-Stone phoned this morning to find out if he was at ours. He's barely been home since you went into hospital.'

Chelle had more news. While she and her family were out, an envelope with her name on it had been pushed through the door. Within was a letter from Will letting her know that the motorcycle magazine *Silverwing* had said they were provisionally interested in a follow-up article from him. He was now typing up the rest of the notes he had handwritten in hospital.

'But he said he couldn't deliver the note to Carrie. He couldn't find the gate.'

'Ryan grimaced. 'He went round the front of the house, didn't he?'

'No, that's just it, he didn't. He says he searched up and down the river bank for ages, and he couldn't see it. He says it wasn't there.'

Carrie had given her phone number to both Ryan and Josh while they were visiting. Chelle shut the bedroom door carefully, then watched as Ryan dialled on the furry phone, trying to ignore its musty smell.

The phone rang about fifteen times before an answering machine cut in. There was something horribly wrong with the voice on the message. It started off sounding like Carrie, and then the words started to break into chunks, as if something kept catching in her throat, or as if she was laughing in fierce guttural gasps. Then it slowed right down and sank in pitch until it was a throaty grating surrounded by static. A beep followed.

'Carrie?' A rattle on the other end of the line.

'Stop it! Stop it! Stop it!' The phone slammed down. Had that been Carrie? Ryan had hardly been able to identify the words, let alone the voice. It wasn't somebody answering the phone; it was the wail of somebody being attacked. Chelle's eyes were bright, questioning pennies. His hands shaking, Ryan phoned again and waited dry-mouthed through the macabre machine message.

'Carrie, please, it's Ryan, please answer.' A slow click and another rattle.

'Ryan, please stop calling now.' It was Carrie's voice, but there was a terrible desolation and weariness in it. 'You've all had your fun with "the mad lady".' Ryan thought of Carrie's fragile smile trembling and shattering.

'Oh, Carrie, what's he done, I'll *kill* him. What's he done?'

'It just doesn't work. I thought I could build up my courage and get out of here, but it just doesn't work.' There was now no shrillness in her voice, just a flat, drab certainty, which was much worse. 'I told myself the world wasn't as bad as I remembered, but it is. I can hear your friends, every night, and sometimes during the day, smashing things against my walls, laughing, scraping stones down the windows. And all the phone calls – the ones where they just hang up when I answer, and the ones leaving messages for "the nutter"—'

'Listen . . . you've got to get out of there! Somewhere he doesn't know where you are!'

'I couldn't open the gate.' Her voice sounded crumpled as if with tears of frustration. 'All those hours of clearing creeper and it seems like it all grew back overnight. Maybe it's a sign that I'm never meant to get out . . . or maybe I just thought it was only a day since I cut it back, maybe it's been weeks. I don't know, the sky's so dark with all this rain there's no real day or night any more. But if it has been weeks, where's my door? Why haven't they brought me my door? My door's just a dream, isn't it? It's not coming.'

Ryan swallowed the hard lump forming in his throat and tweaked the aerial.

'Carrie . . . who's there with you?'

'Nobody!' There were deserts and dark empty seas in that wail, and the phone at the other end was slammed down. Ryan stared into Chelle's expectant gaze.

'There were other voices on the line,' he said as steadily as he could. 'There was this rushing sound like wind, and when it was strong I could hear someone breathing out pieces of words, like the ones I heard when the leaves brushed me in my Magwhite dream last night. And Carrie couldn't hear them.

'She's trapped in her house, and somehow there's a bit of Magwhite in there with her.'

25

The Hijack

The Coopers stayed for a sandwich lunch, then helped the Doyles in trying to force life into a tiny black and white television that they'd brought with them. All the while, Ryan remained miserably mute, his head full of Carrie in a darkness where whispers whirled like leaves.

The TV buzzed and flashed, then showed a parallelogram world with slanted cars and toppling people.

'. . . inches of rain in the last two days . . .' The bored tone of a news reporter cut in. 'Organizers insist that the Crook's Baddock Festival will continue in spite of the weather and flooded roads. In the meantime, these early arrivals hoping to attend the festival can expect a long, wet wait before they reach Crook's Baddock . . .' A crooked image of miserable-looking families seen through the rain-streaked window of a coach, followed by a shot with a 'diversion' sign in the foreground and a long traffic jam snaking off into the distance.

The idea burst a latch in Ryan's brain and swirled through his thoughts, blowing everything askew.

Her power's all about flow, the man in his dream had told him. *All about give and take.* So if you could dam up the flow, just for a little while . . . Ryan's eye fell again upon the file of gridlocked cars.

'Mum? Dad?' he said slowly. 'Is it OK if Chelle and me go to the library this afternoon? We're thinking of doing a school project on the Crook's Baddock Festival, and we'd like to photocopy some stuff there.' Ryan received a look from Chelle that wasn't even questioning, just expectant.

'Of course, but you'll need a lift . . .' Ryan's mother ran upstairs, and came down with a sheaf of clear plastic 'envelopes'. 'And you'll need these to stop the photocopies getting soggy.'

It was not until Chelle and Ryan were safely ensconced in the library that Ryan tried to explain his idea.

'It was the thing that kept bothering me from the start. Why wouldn't the Well Spirit let us pay back our debt by giving her more coins, or some really valuable offerings? I tried to ask her in one of my dreams, and she said something about if nobody drinks, water goes sour, but if everyone drinks, more water rises. I didn't understand it until the other night, when the Well's Angel in my dream explained it better. She needs the offerings, but that's because her power comes from *granting* the wishes. If she doesn't then the wishes, her

269

water or well, go all stagnant and green and yick. She doesn't want more wishes. She's already got too many that she can't grant, so they're like a traffic jam, or a blockage in a pipe, or a dam in a river. There's so many of them they're weakening her.'

'So . . .'

'So we need to weaken her some more. We need her knocked silly by a hail of new wishes she doesn't understand. Even if it just stuns her, it might give us enough time to rescue Carrie.'

'Oh yes! And then when we're at Carrie's house we can try to find Josh too, can't we? Ryan, I'm really worried about him. We've got to talk to him and . . . save him.'

Could Josh be saved? Ryan's feelings about Josh seemed to be in a little box that he dared not open. He stayed mute as Chelle continued.

'But, Ryan, if we go back to the well and put down lots and lots of coins, won't she know it's us and do horrible things to us? I mean, even if we tried to make them difficult, complicated wishes that didn't sound like us, wouldn't the inside, "conker" bit of the wish give us away? Because underneath we'd be wishing something like, "Leave us alone!" or, "Die, Well Spirit, die!" over and over again, and she'd notice, wouldn't she?'

'I agree, I don't think it'll work if it's us wishing,' answered Ryan. 'She'd know it was us after we chucked in the first coin, and then we'd have trolleys jumping on us from the trees before we could throw the rest down.

We need an army of wishers. It's risky, because we don't know what they'll wish. But right now I'm afraid to go to sleep, and you're afraid to use your loo, and both of us are afraid to go near water, metal or electrics in case something attacks us. This is stupid. We've got to do something.

'We're going back to Magwhite, Chelle. We're just not going there alone.'

When Ryan and Chelle abandoned the library, each of them was clutching a collection of printed sheets under their coats. Both looked with some resignation at the dented carcass of a supermarket trolley that lay in the road outside. To judge from its posture, it had been gliding across the street towards the library when something had hit it.

'You know,' said Ryan as they turned their steps towards the bus stop, 'I'm almost getting used to this.' He was getting used to a lot of things, he realized, not just trolley persecution. Mere weeks ago, simply visiting Magwhite had filled him with an almost unbearable thrill of the forbidden. Now here he was, a veteran of disobedience, heading out to perform what was almost certainly a criminal act.

Gutters spewed water instead of draining it away, and cars slowed to churn through the brown flood in every dip. Ryan did not have to swing upside down to turn the world on its head now, for reflections were everywhere. He winced each time he had to cross a puddle. Perhaps the inverted reflection below him was really their enemy in disguise . . .

When the bus arrived, it was nearly empty. The pair climbed aboard and fidgeted in the back, Ryan continually wondering where Josh was and imagining strange sounds in the bus's engine. They were a few stops short of Magwhite itself when the bus ground to a halt behind a queue of traffic, with a slushing of wheels through water. Most of the vehicles ahead were coaches, some of them labelled down the side in French or Spanish.

'This'll have to do,' hissed Ryan. 'We're not far from the place I saw on TV this morning.' They got up, and the driver looked at them quizzically but opened the doors.

'You don't want to be walking far in this,' he said, jerking a head at the coffee-coloured current along the edges of the road, its surface still leaping with heavy drops.

'It's all right,' Chelle assured him sunnily. As soon as they dismounted, however, they found the roadside streams soaking through their trainers. They scrambled up on to the verge and struggled on.

'There it is!' The diversion sign was where Ryan remembered. It stood in full view of the halted traffic, so they had to lurk until the jam melted and the traffic eased into motion. As the last vehicle took the turning, they ran out and grappled with the sign until its metal tripod closed, Ryan grabbing the frame and Chelle the legs.

'Let's get behind the hedge!' There was a little gap that let them squeeze through into a dripping cornfield. They manhandled the sign along the edge of the field, the plastic envelopes inside their coats slithering against each other. Getting the sign over a stile back to the road was a clumsy business that left Chelle with pinched fingers and Ryan with a bruised temple.

'OK, here.' They set up the diversion sign, then with all their combined force twizzled the little signpost that stood at the junction so that its arms poked into the hedge. As another coach approached, they huddled under the trees and watched as it slowed and then obe-diently took a right turn to follow their new 'diversion'. After scraping the worst of the mud from their legs, Chelle and Ryan scampered in the same direction, along the road to Magwhite.

Ryan had forgotten about the sign at the edge of the village with 'Magwhite' written on it, but the hedge had half-swallowed it already, so it was easy enough to pull branches down from an overhanging tree to conceal it.

By the time they reached the damp and deserted centre of Magwhite, they had been overtaken by three cars and another coach.

'OK, Chelle, I'll hold and you tape.' The water had got into some of the plastic envelopes, smudging the print, and the masking tape peeled a bit in the wet, but nonetheless soon there were little plastic-coated posters stuck to walls, windows and trees.

'CROOK'S BADDOCK FESTIVAL HERE TODAY'

read some. 'WELCOME TO CROOK'S BADDOCK' read others.

'Hey!' Both of them started guiltily. A man was crossing the road towards them, holding a road atlas above his head to shield him from the rain. 'Excuse me – can you please the way to Crook's Baddock?' Ryan thought his accent might be Spanish or Italian.

'Yes!' Chelle bounced cheerfully. 'Here! Crook's Baddock here!' She pointed downwards for emphasis.

'And where is the festival, please?' He had a gentle face, a moustache, and currently a diagonal crease of anxiety above one brow. Looking past him, Ryan saw a big coach with 'Arriba' in swirly letters along the side.

'Well, the festival's only just started because of all the rain, so nothing's really open, but there are lots of lovely sites of interest . . .' As Chelle's rate of speech accelerated, the man's diagonal worry line deepened.

She exchanged a glance with Ryan, then handed him the remaining plastic envelopes. 'Guide!' she exclaimed, pointing at herself with both hands. 'I show you arooouuuund.' She drew a big helicopter rotary circle about herself to indicate the whole of Magwhite. 'OK?'

Ryan took the hint and slipped off towards the car park. Earlier that day they'd found a leaflet that showed a footpath winding down to the towpath. If Chelle did manage to install herself as makeshift guide, she would be leading her group this long way round, down the path, along the bank of the canal and then up the steps to the well. The job of creating 'lovely sites of interest' from scratch before she got there was left to him.

Despite himself, he felt queasy as he entered the car park. This was the first time he had been back to the real Magwhite since the theft of the coins. His hands shook as he scrambled up on to the clammy wall, and he felt a violent shock as he saw a trolley lurking in a nearby tree. It was a second before he recognized it as the one that he had wedged there with Chelle and Josh on that first rainy evening. The wind stirred the bough on which it rested, and it gave a thin, metallic mewl as if in sleep. He slithered down the wall, his feet scrambling clumsily for footholds.

Leaves glued themselves to his trainers as he stumbled down the slope. A stump by the waterside became the remains of the Farthingmoor Gallows. The graffiti-stained bridge became the Bridge of Oaths. Then, feeling a little sick, he scrambled towards the well itself. He taped up a sign that read 'Well of St Margaret the White' and ran for it.

'. . . and all the way down here is where Nell Gwyn used to row with the king, with a big picnic with whole pigs and lots of gin, which is made of juniper berries, did you know that?' There was no mistaking Chelle's approaching voice. Ryan made a couple of clumsy bounds and crouched behind a blackberry bush.

He could just glimpse Chelle through the trees. The moustached man they'd met earlier trotted by her side and seemed to be trying to translate her unceasing commentary. Behind them a trail of tanned, dark-eyed teenagers in plastic ponchos picked their way through the puddles of the path, staring at everything around them with incomprehension, misery and loathing.

Chelle lifted her hood with a finger, cast a stealthy glance up the slope and caught sight of Ryan.

'Um, and everybody should look at this bit of the canal,' she added hurriedly, turning away, 'because the poet Ingrid Pollus used to come here to . . . yearn. Because he and his true love used to meet here secretly on different banks, and he would shout his poetry to her, and they would both yearn.' Chelle glanced over her shoulder again, to see Ryan in the embrace of a spray of bramble, and her voice rose in pitch and urgency. 'And . . . while we're looking at the canal you should pay very, very close attention to the ducks, because although they look ordinary they're actually the only ducks in England with . . . teeny-tiny teeth.' The man by Chelle's side translated, and several people took a step away from the canal.

By the time Chelle had moved on to the swans, Ryan had extricated himself and reached the bridge.

'Now up here are the really good bits,' exclaimed Chelle joyfully, and she set off up the wooded slope, oblivious to the protests of several of her charges, who were examining their delicate shoes with dismay. 'This used to be a gallows, and up *here* is the Well of St Margaret the White – and you've got to put a coin in the well and make a wish because it's good luck.'

The moustached man translated for his students, pointing at the well. Word was passed down the chain, and the scowling children fumbled in their bags for wallets and bead purses. Encouraged by the slightly desperate smiles of their guardian, they trooped up one by one to drop in a coin. Ryan wondered how many of them were wishing for a big dry towel.

Chelle watched them with an expression of damp delight.

'Tour over!' she squeaked, as the dismal train started picking its way down again. The man with the moustache called out something to her as she turned tail and ran, perhaps a concerned question, maybe a word of thanks. She did not wait to find out which, but sprinted until she met up with Ryan at the far side of the bridge.

'Teeny-tiny teeth?' asked Ryan as they recovered their breath, and she bared her own teeth in an almost Josh-like grin.

They put up a few more signs along the towpath to guide people to the well. By the time they reached the road again, there was another parked coach, this time full of puzzled-looking old-age pensioners. Chelle and Ryan waved at them cheerfully and pointed towards the steps that led down to the towpath.

'Do you notice something?' whispered Ryan, as they huddled at the bus stop. 'The rain's slackening off.' Indeed, by the time a bus to Whelmford arrived, there was a mere drizzle, and it made them realize how accustomed they had become to the downpour's incessant hammering over the last few days.

Ryan and Chelle found a seat at the back of the bus, so that they could set about planning Carrie's rescue in peace. They were so caught up in their schemes that it was a long time before Ryan noticed that he was idly scratching at one of his warts with the edge of his fingernail. He had grown used to the cold tingle of tenderness in them, as if the top layer of skin had been stripped away. Now, however, his nail was grating over insensitive calluses.

'Chelle.' He held out his hands. His warts were tiny and ordinary-looking, like little lumps of dried glue. 'I can't feel anything through them,' breathed Ryan. 'They're just like . . . warts. I think it's working. The rain's stopping, and now maybe we're losing our powers . . . I think we must have weakened her.'

They were so excited and happy about this that it took them some time to notice that their progress towards Whelmford was slowing. The bus's little bunny-hop motions forwards were becoming increasingly infrequent and, after a particularly long halt, the driver actually sighed and turned off his engine. The traffic ahead was locked solid.

Diversion signs were meant to keep traffic flowing when some roads were blocked. But how bad could it be to move one little sign?

Again and again Ryan caught himself looking at his wrist where he'd once worn his watch. All the time he was making mental calculations, trying to guess how long it would take to rescue Carrie, then bus from Whelmford back to Guildley town centre and run to the library. Could they get back before their parents got worried? Could they get back before the library closed?

In fact, could they get to Whelmford in time to get a bus home at all?

'Down!' Chelle pulled at Ryan's sleeve, and then they peered as a familiar car eased past in the opposite direction, towards Magwhite. In the driver's seat sat Donna Leas, leaning forward for a better view of the flooded road. In the passenger's seat, biting his lips together and scowling over his folded arms, was Josh.

26

The Drowning House

For a moment, Ryan felt a terror that Josh had finished doing something horrible to Carrie and was heading back to the well to report. The next moment he remembered Josh's scowl, and his pulse slowed a little. It was more likely that Josh had noticed his own powers ebbing and was off to Magwhite to find out why.

Ryan's thoughts were in such a flurry that he paid little attention to another car that looked vaguely familiar, nosing through the water after Donna's vehicle. Now once again he suffered the torture of waiting for the bus to crawl its next few feet.

'We're not going to get back before they miss us, are we?' asked Chelle, her voice unusually level.

'No, we're not.' Oddly, admitting the fact made them both feel better. 'All we can do is get to Carrie and get her out of her house before Josh can mend the well.' There was no doubt in either mind that the ever-ingenious Josh would come up with a plan.

'Folks?' The bus driver strained to turn his head. 'There's a diversion up ahead, so it looks like the

Whelmford road is flooded. We'll be taking a left and heading towards Poddington – jump out now if you'd rather take the last bus back to Magwhite . . .'

Ryan and Chelle exchanged miserable glances, and wriggled back into their sodden gear. They jumped down from the bus and trudged along the verge past the long row of cars, some with impatient drivers beating tattoos on their steering wheel. They got a few curious glances as they passed the diversion sign.

The road was a lacework of brown rivulets and puddles, and the sky had an October dullness. By the time they had hiked for a mile, their legs were prickling and shaking with the cold and Chelle was sneezing.

They were grateful when houses started to flank the lane. As the road dipped down towards the river, however, the water level rose, and soon they could not take a step without wading through water. Every window was dark, and most of the cars seemed to have gone. Masking tape was visible around the edges of many front doors. There was little sign of life but for the fat slugs that had sought the high ground of the wall tops, where they glistened like licked liquorice.

'I think everybody's gone away,' Chelle said, 'and I can't hear Carrie's thoughts at all, maybe my powers aren't working right now, but maybe she's gone, maybe the police came and cleared everybody out . . .'

'Not if they went knocking door to door,' Ryan said grimly. 'She doesn't have one, remember?'

Turning into a little alley that ran between two houses down to the riverside, Ryan and Chelle quickly found themselves struggling through knee-high water and feeling a tug against their calves as if the current was trying to discourage them.

The only sign of the riverside walk now was the wire mesh fence which rose from the brown water, sieving a fringe of torn moss and chocolate wrappers. The current bulged and flattened like a tensed muscle and carried past plastic bags and doormats, along with the occasional footpath marker post that had apparently left its station to do its own exploring.

They crossed the little bridge and, to their surprise, found Carrie's gate without difficulty. Beside it, a big, flat rectangular package mysteriously swathed in plastic sheeting leaned against the hedge. Ryan lifted the gate's latch and gave it an experimental tug. It opened.

Maybe Will just looked in the wrong place after all, said the common-sense part of Ryan's brain as the pair of them squelched into the sodden garden, the creeper drawing through their hair like a dank comb. *But then Carrie would still have been able to get out, wouldn't she? Unless . . .* He remembered her shriek when she'd snatched up the phone. *Unless . . .* A pair of new-looking secateurs had been thrown at a marble fawn, decapitating it. *Unless Josh did something so awful that Carrie's really gone mad . . .*

The curtains were drawn behind the French windows.

'Carrie!' squeaked Chelle suddenly. There was no answer but the damp flapping of a carrier bag that had been taped over a rosette-shaped hole in the glass. Ryan gave the doors an experimental tug, but they didn't open. Chelle made spider-patters on the glass with her fingers. 'Carrie!' she called again, and this time there almost seemed to be a sound from the room.

Biting his lip, Ryan pulled his sleeve down his hand and poked it through the hole in the pane. After a moment's fumbling his fingers discovered a key shape and turned it. The door swung open, hushing through water as if resenting the intrusion and pushing back the long corduroy curtain.

The room inside was darker than he had ever seen it before. The bulbs above were lightless. Cloths and picture frames had been used to block out the windows. Many of the boxes that had strewn the floor were now piled on desks and shelves, as if an attempt had been made to rescue them from the rising waters. This attempt had clearly been abandoned halfway, however, and the water now soaked greedily into brown-paper parcels, book stacks, piles of rich cloth. Amid the disarray Carrie sat on a small table, one hand supporting her head, one slippered foot dragging in the wash. Her chin had dropped to her chest, reminding Ryan of the Well Spirit, and as she started to raise her head he was suddenly gripped with a panicky certainty that he would see her eyes open and pour rivulets.

She opened her eyes, and they were her own. It was still Carrie, but a weary, older Carrie that seemed to be looking at him from the far end of a dark tunnel.

'This is Chelle, Carrie,' he said. 'We've come to rescue you.'

The distant Carrie peered out of her mind-cavern and recognized him, then let her forehead slump back to her hand.

'Off you go, Ryan. I'm all right. Close the door after you, there's enough water here already.' Chelle obediently shut the French windows and there was a pause. 'What I meant was, close it with you outside it.'

'Oh, but you can't send us away, we caught two buses, and they both got stuck, and so we got out and we walked and walked up to our knees in river and mud and we're going to be in such trouble when we get back, but we came here for you . . .' Chelle's voice rose steadily in pitch. 'Anyway, we can't leave, we're Angels.'

'Everybody else in the street's gone, Carrie. They've all left.'

'Good,' murmured Carrie. 'That's how I've always wanted it. All I want is peace . . . just to be left alone . . .'

'But you don't want that!' Ryan's voice was a desperate squeak. 'I know that's what you wished when you threw your ring away, but people aren't usually at their best when they make wishes. Making a wish is like saying, "I can't deal with anything, I give up, somebody bigger come along and solve it all instead." But you don't want to give up, Carrie, you brought us in for sponge cakes, and you were fighting your way out of your creeper. You ordered a *door*.'

'It never came,' whispered Carrie.

'Yes, it did!' Chelle's face suddenly came alive with revelation. 'That big package outside, leaning against the hedge, all covered in plastic, it must be your door, so maybe the delivery people just couldn't find your gate . . .'

'I couldn't find it either. It wasn't . . .'

'Well, it is now,' said Ryan gently. 'And so's the door. It's right out there waiting for you.'

Carrie raised her face and looked about her at her antiques, as if seeking their reassurance that she didn't need to leave. Ryan felt suddenly choked by the forest of clutter.

'Please, Carrie, come and look.' He took hold of one elbow, and Chelle grabbed the other, and they dragged her over to the French windows, splashing and stumbling and overturning boxes. 'Look at the water! Can't you see? It's higher on this side of the doors than it is outside.' Carrie's bruised and empty stare took on a new bewildered sharpness. 'You're not shutting the water *out*, you're shutting it *in* and letting the house fill up. The river's flooding, but the water's coming from *in here*.'

'That's impossible.'

'I know the world's full of horrible things and people,' Ryan urged gently, 'but this isn't a safe place to hide, Carrie. It's a place where things wash in and get tangled up and never get out. It's a place where things *drown*.'

Carrie drew close to the pane so that her breath clouded it and her reflection became nothing but two startled eye-stars amid the fog. She trailed her fingertips down it, making little stripes of world through the white veil, and then braced her trembling hands against the French windows and pushed them open. With a sound like a long-held breath being released, water poured out past her shins.

Without warning, Chelle ran up from behind and hugged Carrie, then carried the motion forward to guide her outside.

'We're all going to be in horrible trouble,' she chirruped cheerfully through a faceful of Carrie's cardigan, 'but it'll be OK and firemen will make us hot chocolate . . .'

'Where's the gate?' Carrie asked sharply.

Oh no, thought Ryan as he scanned the unbroken hedge. *Oh no oh no oh no.*

Chelle started, then stared upwards, flinched and wiped something from her eye. 'I just felt a drop . . . Oh no, Ryan, it's *rain*. It's *raining* again. *She* must be waking up . . . we've got to get out of here . . .' Chelle splashed her way over to the secateurs.

'Who's "she"?' Carrie was looking at them suspiciously, almost accusingly.

'She's . . .' Ryan hesitated. 'She's where all the water comes from.'

'So I didn't just cry myself a sea like Alice then,' said Chelle in altogether the wrong tone of voice.

'She reads minds!' Ryan added quickly, seeing Carrie turning to stare at Chelle as if she'd suddenly burst into flames. 'At least some minds, sometimes . . . look . . . can we please talk while we chop?'

'It's a nightmare,' Chelle was murmuring, 'none of this can be happening, I'm really going mad. And anyway, I broke my scythe trying to rip my way out of here and the kitchen scissors were no good . . .'

Carrie stared at Chelle, the colour draining from her face. Then to Ryan's dismay she turned and marched back through the open French windows.

'Carrie, come back!'

There were sounds of ripping cardboard, a clang and a couple of splashes. Carrie strode back out, brandishing what looked a lot like a cavalry sabre in one hand.

'All right, Ryan,' she said a little shakily, 'you talk, I'll hack.'

Many times Ryan had rehearsed in his own mind what he would tell his parents if he was ever forced into the truth. Every time, his stomach had turned to cement at the very thought of having to explain. But, funnily enough, it was much easier telling the story of the well to somebody fighting a magic hedge with a sabre amid rising floods than it would have been on an ordinary afternoon. As Ryan talked Carrie said nothing, but her air of confidence and purpose increased. Perhaps all she'd needed was an explanation, however fantastical, that didn't involve her descending into insanity.

With a stiff pair of secateurs and a bread knife from the kitchen, Ryan and Chelle joined in with snipping and sawing the tough stems. Chelle's face crumpled with effort, but her eyes were bright and clear above the handkerchief that now filled her mouth.

The rain had become a pensive patter, then an insistent rattle, and was now making conversation difficult.

However, when Carrie pushed dank straggles of dark hair out of her face and shouted something, gesturing with her sword, Ryan had no difficulty guessing what she was trying to say.

The hedge was just as thick as before, but the waters were creeping higher.

'. . . anything made of wood . . . rafts . . .' Carrie pointed at the top of the hedge and made an 'up and over' gesture with her free hand. Ryan blinked at her through wet lashes and nodded. The water had almost reached his hips, and Carrie's house had no upper floor to which they could retreat. They struggled back into the living room, where a lot of boxes were now floating.

'Tear open everything!' called Carrie. 'Don't worry about any of it – most of it's stuff I'd never sell anyway! Right, I've got lots of polystyrene packing. Come here and I'll masking-tape it to us to help us float.'

Picture frames, the wooden jackalope plaque, a bicycle inner tyre, a balsa wood aeroplane – all of these were furiously lashed together with masking tape, string and skipping ropes to make little rafts, each just big enough for one person. Back outside, the water was now up to Ryan's waist, and Carrie lifted first Ryan then Chelle so that they could struggle on to their rafts.

Ryan's head twitched. The wind was rising and he thought for a moment he'd heard a soft syllable against his ear, as if the breeze had carried it to him. From somewhere out by the river came the rhythmic, shingling sound of something tearing the surface of the water, in a stride or a swim stroke. Beyond the hedge, someone was approaching.

Ryan had a sudden mental image of Josh striding on the surface of the river, stagnant water leaking from beneath his beetle-eyed sunglasses, and invisible Magwhite leaves wheeling around him. He screamed to Carrie to get out of the water, to get up on her raft, but he knew that it would make no difference. The Well Spirit was waking, and Josh was back.

There was a crash from within the hedge, and the creeper fingers thrashed with new energy. Something was fighting its way through the foliage. Chelle was grasping the secateurs and shouting something, probably Carrie's thoughts. Ryan crouched on his raft, gripping the open kitchen scissors, facing down the hedge as he had the dragon behind the wall.

A pale corner forced itself through the greenery, wrinkled and pimpled with raindrops. A crash, a thrash, and an angular edge emerged, the plastic wrapping around it flapping and clicking and biting off the stems that caught upon it. It seemed to wrestle from side to side, crushing the creeper out of the way.

'Hello?' Through a new hole in the creeper Ryan could see a small fragment of face. 'Is everyone all right in there?'

The angular shape that had thrust through the hedge was Carrie's new door, and peering through the aperture was the nervous, cave-cheeked face of Will Wruthers.

27

Russian Vine

Everybody explained at once, with different levels of shrillness. Since Chelle and Carrie were shouting almost exactly the same thing, they drowned out Ryan fairly easily, but the rain's hammering was loudest of all.

Will shouted something again and wrenched at the door until it was horizontal, a flat surface just above the waterline. Now they could see a little more of him, standing beyond the hedge with water up to his pockets. He reached his hands through the gap above the door and beckoned slightly. Carrie gestured to Chelle, who paddled her little picture-frame raft forward, and wriggled clumsily off it on to the door. Will took her wrists and pulled, while Ryan and Carrie pushed against the soles of Chelle's trainers. She vanished with a squeak of polystyrene as if the hedge had swallowed her, but reassuringly her piping voice could be heard a second later on the other side.

Carrie heaved Chelle's raft over the hedge, and there was a reassuring splash from the other side. 'You next, Ryan.'

Ryan's raft dipped and shipped water as he edged his chest on to the door. The tunnel through the foliage now seemed to have doubled in length. The plastic sheeting slid and rucked under his knees and hands, but he found the shape of the handle and used it to drag himself forward. At last Will's outstretched hands closed around Ryan's wrists, and he too was hauled through to the other side, the creeper scraping at his face and trying to turn out his pockets.

'How many more?' Will was dressed in a heavy black and yellow biker jacket that made his neck and face look even thinner than usual. Nearby, Chelle was doubled over the remains of her raft.

'One,' spluttered Ryan as the two remaining rafts flew over the hedge, one after the other. 'Just Carrie.' He was still clinging to the near edge of the door, and when it tilted under his hand he guessed that Carrie was starting to wriggle through.

'Carrie?' Will leaned in again, and Ryan could just make out her frightened face, a crossword puzzle of light and dark. 'You need to give me your hand.'

Carrie managed a tight nod, smiled nervously and extended her free hand. Even as she did so, the creeper sighed and stirred. The loose stems pulled tight and meshed, cutting out the light, and the door wobbled and tipped sideways. There was a cry as Carrie's silhouette tumbled off the door, crashed into the greenery and disappeared beneath the surface of the water.

Will flung himself forward too late to grab hold of her and leaned across the door, plunging his arms into the brown murk. Chelle was shrieking and shrieking in a terror that wasn't hers, screaming that she couldn't see and couldn't breathe and couldn't move and that something had her by the hair, by the hair. The tip of the sabre broke the surface for a brief moment, circled and then disappeared again.

All three of them lunged towards the place where it had submerged, Chelle and Ryan spilling off their rafts and floundering through the icy water. Ryan clenched his eyes tight, pinched his nose and ducked below the surface, feeling his feet float from the tarmac as he did so. His knuckle-eyes stung with the water as they opened to show him Carrie trussed with green strands, a necklace of bubbles trailing from her nose.

She was twisting in a glowing agate murk while honeysuckle blooms made butterfly-flutters against her neck and creeper strands tried to push serpentine into her nostrils, her ears, her mouth. Sometimes one of Will's legs kicked into view, clad in bulging black leather and trailing a gauze of little bubbles. Then there was only brown murk, but Ryan reached out, felt the flinch of Carrie's forehead and tore the tendrils from her face, ripped them out of the soft flood of her hair. The water was full of other well-meaning hands that brushed his, and limbs that jarred his jaw and knocked the breath out of his chest. A hand, perhaps Carrie's, grabbed at his shoulder, and he kicked upwards reflexively, a terror of drowning suddenly destroying all other thought.

His face broke the surface, the water clicked from his

ears, and suddenly the air was full of snorts, gasps, and churning. There were two faces beside his, no, three – Will blinded by his own hair, his lips pushed out in a blowing expression, Chelle's hair licked up like caramel above her high forehead, and Carrie, sobbing and clinging to Will's shoulder as they kicked away from the hedge.

Will dared the Russian vine just long enough to yank the door free, and they helped Carrie clamber up on to it. Chelle and Ryan scrambled back on to their little makeshift rafts, and Will commandeered Carrie's. They all clung to the wire mesh fence to prevent the current carrying them away.

'What the hell was that?' gasped Will.

'Russian vine,' choked Carrie faintly. 'I . . . I chose it because it grows fast . . .'

'Not that fast it doesn't!' Will sputtered. 'And what's the matter with Chelle?'

Even as he spoke, however, the uncontrolled thoughts that flowed from Chelle's mouth trickled to a halt.

The burst of energy that had set Carrie fighting her way out of her erstwhile refuge seemed to have deserted her. Ryan remembered her talking about her fear of outdoors, the way the sky was too wide and bright. The sky now seemed darker and lower than usual, but he doubted that that would help. There were still long strands of creeper interwoven with her hair, and her arms and thin pullover were covered in sludge like the foam from a chocolate milkshake. Now that she had stopped spilling Carrie's thoughts, Chelle was able to volunteer her own.

'I think she's all, you know, in shock, so I think we have to bath her in whisky but not slap her or anything because that's only if she's hysterical . . .'

'Yeah, she's in shock all right,' Will said uncertainly, and glanced up and down the river as if hoping some help might have materialized. 'Which means she ought to be kept warm . . . which means we have to get her out of here. Hang on . . .' He wrestled off his leather jacket and draped it over Carrie.

'OK.' Will straightened. 'OK.' He seemed to be realizing for the first time that he was the only conscious adult on the scene. 'Everyone else is OK, right?'

'Just a bit cold and chattery,' Chelle said reassuringly, kicking out frog-style behind her.

'OK, good. Um . . . We're going to have to swim and push Carrie's door along in front of us, OK? And let's all tie ourselves together so we don't get separated. The roads are underwater and blocked off for miles – it's probably quicker to take the river to the next town. We'll just wear ourselves out and get nowhere if we go against the current, so we'll go with it, OK?'

For a time they swam along the 'walkway', but then they came to a place where the path stopped and the fence had crumpled. They took to the river proper.

'So what the hell's been going on here?' Will asked at last as the current took them. Having two people explaining something is not twice as helpful as having one, and it was a good few minutes before Chelle and Ryan managed to get across the salient points.

Ryan at last dared to glance at Will's face and found that it was looking thin and grey again.

'You probably don't believe us,' Ryan muttered, flushing. 'I mean, do you want us to tell you about things you were thinking, just as proof? I mean . . . I know there was a kid called Donny Sparks who used to make you buy cigarettes . . .' He couldn't meet Will's eye, but in his peripheral vision he could see a deep flush spreading over Will's face and neck. Ryan wondered how he would feel in Will's place. 'You didn't think anything too bad,' he blurted.

'Just show me your hands,' Will said bluntly.

Ryan held out one hand. His warts were, once again, a cluster of bulges. The percussion from the rain caused the pale eyelids to jump and flicker, exposing Will to half a dozen dark green sliver-stares.

'All right, all right.' Will, who had reached out to take Ryan's fingertips, withdrew his hand quickly. He wiped his plastered hair back from his face. 'That bloody wish!' he exclaimed bitterly. 'I remember dropping the coin in the well. I was *fourteen*. Twelve *years* went by, and my dream never changed or got any closer. That's really sad.'

Ryan did not know what to say.

'So . . .' Will lowered his voice and paddled a little closer to Ryan in order to whisper confidentially. 'You and this other boy have been using Chelle to pick up people's thoughts?' He sounded appalled, but not incredulous. 'Can't you see that . . . a sweet little kid like that . . . there are some thoughts, adult thoughts . . . that she shouldn't have to hear and understand. Not yet, anyway.'

Ryan reddened, but at the same time a warm feeling of relief was soaking through his chest like blotting paper. He didn't mind Will talking to him as if he was an adult who should have known better, despite the fact that he was a year younger than Chelle. Will believed him, and Ryan felt bad for ever having thought of him as floppy.

Will's presence was far more quickly explained. He'd telephoned Chelle's house to let her know that *Silverwing* had accepted his article and had reached her panicky parents, who told him that she had disappeared from the local library. Remembering the 'tea party' invitation, he had decided to attend after all, so that he could warn Chelle that her parents had missed her.

'The Harley got me to the edge of Whelmford before the water got too deep, and by then I was really worried, so I waded the rest of the way.'

'But your Harley!' Ryan stared at him. 'Where is it? Is it OK?'

'Nah, doubt it,' Will said shortly. 'Water in the engine.' He gave Ryan a sideways glance. 'Funny thing is, I'm kind of relieved. It was like I'd expected something to end when I got the Harley, and it didn't. I was just there with the bike looking at me and I knew I couldn't live up to it. Now it's gone I don't have to feel that way.'

Will shrugged, looked around at his bedraggled companions and then smiled reluctantly. 'Anyway, life's all about priorities, isn't it? Let's pick up the pace.'

The water had got into the joints and seams of the world and washed away the glue. Lives and little universes broke their banks, mingling and bubbling over and flowing out to join the river. Plastic tricycles with peeling sticker eyes, photograph albums, biros, washing-up brushes, hair slides, uprooted tomato plants. Comics spun giddily, socks sulked against window sills.

Maybe this is the way the world ends, thought Ryan, *not with a bang, but with a splash*. For a moment he imagined all the people of the world being washed out of their cars and office windows, and swept downstream clinging to shivered timbers, into a great pool where they would be judged.

Then, instead, he thought of the Well Spirit's watery domain claiming village after village. Toilets erupting, cisterns ripping from their frames, road surfaces breaking apart like dunked digestives, flash floods chasing cars down lanes . . . and at every turn a sigh as a vindictive wish was granted. *Destroy my school, my office, the football pitch, the house of the boy that hit me. Destroy Crook's Baddock so they can't make us come here again on coach trips* . . . these would be easy wishes to grant now the floods were rising again. It was no wonder that the waters were growing ever higher and stronger. But what had Josh done to waken the stunned Well Spirit and give her back her powers?

The houses abandoned them, and now they were flanked by hedges where crisp packets and pizza boxes twitched with the wind like the wings of strange birds. The water was so high that they had to flatten themselves against their rafts to pass under footbridges.

Their strange little convoy was just navigating carefully around a great tangle of cables and leaves when voices became audible over the rain. They kicked desperately to escape the current and succeeded in swimming out on to what Ryan suspected was usually a village green.

A row of chipped stone cottages was drinking in the brown flood through every window. Occasional car roofs peeked disconsolately above the surface, and an empty coach stood up to its windows in water. In the middle of the green stood a war memorial, a glistening concrete spire around which metal men in rounded trench helmets waved standards and supported each other. Standing upon two metal shoulders was a single, utterly drenched figure that clung to the spire in an attitude that seemed desperate until she turned and they saw the megaphone in her hand.

'. . . and for the last time, make sure that your electricity, gas and water are turned off at the mains. Turning it off at the switch or tap is not enough. Now has everybody finally understood that or is it just too complicated for some of you?'

It was Donna Leas. Donna with one shoe, and her skirt clinging to her legs, and her make-up long since washed away. Ryan became aware that there were people peering from top windows and listening attentively to the rasp of the megaphone.

'You!' She pointed down at the new convoy and addressed Will. 'Where've you come from? Whelmford? Have they evacuated? You're sure you're the last out of there? Yes, yes, I can see she's in shock. OK, all of you report in at the Rectory. Over there. We've got all the camp stoves and Calor-gas fires in their attic room, and a supply of clean water, hot drinks and dry blankets. I've got the rector taking names so nobody gets left behind, and his wife's on first-aid duty. Hurry up, get those children out of the . . . oh God, it's the *Twilight Zone* twins . . .' Donna's eye had at last fallen on Ryan and Chelle.

'Will,' shouted Ryan, his voice sounding mousy after Donna's electronic bellow, 'can you please get Carrie to the Rectory? We'll be right there, we just have to ask Donna something first . . .'

Only the sight of the rain splashing on Carrie's unresponsive cheeks persuaded Will to go on ahead.

'Be quick, right?' he said. Chelle gave him a reassuring smile.

'Donna crouched and scowled down at the two children in her narrow-eyed witchy way. Rain runnelled off the corners of her bob as if she was an oddly designed gargoyle.

'Donna . . . where's Josh?'

Donna's gaze immediately became unfocused, hostile. 'What did you expect me to do?' She grasped a fistful of her own hair. 'I don't know where he is, all right?'

Ryan's mouth was open to ask what had happened, but the moment was washed away by the torrent of Chelle's voice.

'Donna, it's all right, because we know you took him to Magwhite, we saw you, and then he did something, didn't he, but it's not your fault . . .'

'I don't know!' Donna shouted with the savageness of sheer wretchedness. Her resemblance to a grown woman was dissolving in the rain. 'It wasn't flooding as badly then, but the traffic got bogged down. And we were stuck there, and he just kept on threatening . . . so I finally told him that I didn't care, and he should *get the hell out of my car!*' The last words were almost screamed. 'I don't care if he tells Jeremiah everything, I don't care, and that goes for the pair of you too . . . you little . . . you creepy, freaky little . . . I don't want any part of it any more . . .'

'We're not going to make you; it isn't like that with us. Josh has just gone a bit funny with all his powers, but we're going to make him better only he won't be able to do the things with bulbs for you any more, and Donna . . .' Chelle seemed to draw herself up and took on a more serious and grown-up tone. 'You can really do a lot better than Mr Punzell, you know.'

In dismay, Ryan saw Donna crumple, almost sliding off the soldiers' shoulders. Chelle seemed to have picked the worst possible thing to say. For a long moment Donna watched intrepid drops clambering down the ladders in her tights.

'I know,' she snapped suddenly. She straightened again, muttering something that sounded like 'voodoo' in disgust. Perhaps Chelle had said exactly the right thing.

'Donna,' Ryan asked carefully, not wanting to cramp Chelle's style, 'did Josh say anything about what he was going to do at Magwhite?'

'He was in a nasty mood most of the journey, and then he started sniggering and saying, "I've got her over a barrel," and at first I thought he meant me. Then he started muttering, "She *has* to grant a big wish quickly for power, I can ask whatever I like."'

Ryan was taken aback to find that Josh had worked out so much about the source of the Well Spirit's power. But perhaps she had found a way to tell him what she needed, through something like the Ouija bucket.

'Then he asked how I fancied him as an archangel with lightning coming out of his eyes,' Donna went on. 'And when we argued, he told me that after tonight he wouldn't need me or anybody else, and he jumped out and ran off into the rain.' Donna looked defensive. 'Look – I did go back to find him when I heard the storm warnings on the radio, but my car got flooded out and then there was all this to take care of . . .' She gestured towards the row of rain-lashed cottages.

Part of 'all this' chose that very moment to make itself noisily apparent. Donna leaned out from her pedestal to listen as someone called something from an upstairs window.

'OK, listen, everybody!' she bellowed through the megaphone. 'We've just had contact on the radio and there'll be a helicopter to start winching people out in about half an hour.' She lowered her megaphone to glare at Ryan and Chelle again. 'Both of you, to the Rectory. Right now!' Obediently they started to swim in the direction of her pointing finger.

Donna had clearly thought she was wishing for true love. In fact she had wanted . . . what? *Wanted miserable*, the Well Spirit had said once. Perhaps Donna, who seemed to hate everybody, really only hated herself. She could never let herself be popular or loved because she was unable to believe that she could be or deserved to be. She had to test it all the time to reassure herself, the way she had tested her power at the primary school until everybody hated her. *Well*, thought Ryan, *if she wanted to be miserable, then that explains why she chose Mr Punzell.* In fact, it looked as if what Donna had really needed all the time to bring her into her own wasn't wishes granted, but a full-blown disaster.

'I wish we could go to the Rectory,' Chelle whispered under her breath.

'So do I,' Ryan murmured. 'Hot chocolate . . .'

'And big fluffy vicar towels,' said Chelle with feeling. 'Only . . . we've got to find Josh, haven't we? And besides . . . I don't think *they'd* let us go to the Rectory, would they?'

Ryan cast a glance at the seven little wakes behind

them, arranged in a goose-convoy 'V'. The trolleys were still almost entirely submerged, but they had risen just enough that their weed-trailed orange handles grazed the surface.

'No,' said Ryan quietly, 'I don't think they would. I think she's sent for us.'

28

Mother Leathertongue

'All right. We'll come.'

The trolley formation broke apart, and the two largest approached and submerged, coming up under Ryan and Chelle so that they were encaged but lifted out of the flood. They released their rafts and let them tumble away. Ryan's sleeves and trouser legs were waterfalls. The trolleys began to move forward in a lumpish, lolloping motion, like coin-powered toddler horses.

Out across the fields which were now a lake broken only by an occasional solitary tree. Past a flotsam sign-post that told them that Whelmford was below them and Crook's Baddock was in the sky. The trolleys all caught their wheels in a tall hedge lurking just below the surface and shook the children sick as they tugged themselves free.

To Ryan's quiet terror, they were carried beneath a stalking parade of pylons. But somehow the sheer helplessness of his situation numbed his fear. If he was meant to be killed by a great electric arc, there was nothing he could do about it. But no, it seemed that this was not their immediate destiny.

A wide raft of greenery skimmed towards them over the flood. They reached its edge and found themselves gliding single file into waterlogged woodlands, the ripples of their passing licking at the trunks of the trees. The birds had abandoned them, and instead the boughs were full of trolleys, some antlered with broken branches, some swaying excitably on their perches. The briars bowed under blackberries the size of footballs.

'Where are we?' Chelle hissed as the pace of their convoy slowed.

'Magwhite,' Ryan whispered, watching the liquid moss seething on the tree bark. 'Dream Magwhite. The real Magwhite.'

The waters grew shallower, and the trolley steeds lurched and tangled in brambles. A minute later the ground pushed up through the water, and the little swivel wheels were scooping up great curls of mud and leaf mulch.

'Whoa! Um . . . thank you, we'll walk from here.' Their mounts halted, and Ryan and Chelle scrambled out, Chelle pausing to pat hesitantly at hers and stroke its sodden mane of long grasses. As they climbed the slope that led to the well Ryan could feel his heart banging so hard that it made his vision jump.

Ahead of them, blotted posters in plastic envelopes flitted shyly from tree to tree, then fluttered down to perch on the Well Spirit's throne of roots and litter. The scene seemed deserted at first, but as they drew close Ryan noticed that there was a figure seated on the grille of the well itself, head bowed.

'Is that . . . ?' began Chelle.

The figure wore a long mustard-coloured coat and black patent shoes. Its thin grey hair did not waft, but straggled over its scalp so that every bulge of the skull was visible. The apparition looked up sharply at Chelle's whispered question, and showed them the narrow, sallow features of Miss Gossamer.

For a moment something melted in Ryan's brain, and Miss Gossamer and the Well Spirit danced out of the dark corners of his imagination to become one night-mare shape, but then he recovered his senses.

'Miss Gossamer . . . what are you doing here?' Did she even see where she was, or hear the cricketing of the Coke cans that twisted their metal in warning? Did she think she was sitting on a muddy slope between an ordinary car park and canal? Or had she lost her grip on the ordinary a long time before?

'He's never coming back.' Her voice was a creak. 'It's too late. He can't come back.' She started to laugh in a way that reminded Ryan of the broken sounds on Carrie's answering machine. He suddenly realized that in her hand she was holding a Swiss Army knife with the screwdriver fitting extended. It looked a lot like Josh's knife.

'Josh . . .' Ryan choked on the word.

'I followed them in my car,' continued Miss Gossamer, 'and when he got out, so did I. He ran off ahead, but I knew where he was going. I came here and there he was, kneeling by the well, talking to it, loosening the screws. He kept calling it 'My Lady'. He said that since the only way she could get her power back immediately was to grant a big wish quickly, he'd give her one that was easy to grant. I heard him do it. I heard him pledge himself to the demon of the well in exchange for becoming her 'Chosen One'. He said he wanted every power she could give him. And then he climbed down the well, and I knew I had to be fast . . .'

'Oh no,' breathed Chelle. 'Oh nonononono . . .' Her eyes were fixed on the grille that capped the well and the brown waters licking against it.

'He never heard me put the grille back, the rain was too loud. When the waters started rising, then I heard him trying to climb out. But I sat on the grille to keep it down, and spread out my coat so it would be too dark for him to find handholds, and he never made it to the top . . .'

Ryan's imagination was assaulted by the thought of beating against a grille while air tried to burst from his lungs and escaped from his nose.

'Miss Gossamer, Miss Gossamer, you *can't* do this, you've got to let us take up the grille and see if he's all right.' Chelle's voice had become almost strident with desperation.

'It's too late, he's not coming back.'

Ryan had never realized that triumph could sound so much like despair.

'He's down forever in the cold, dark water, where they sent my beautiful girl.'

'But Josh didn't kill your little girl!' Even the rain hushed for an instant after Ryan's words. 'It was some-body else a long time ago, and they're *dead*. They all went mad and died and their spirits are still trapped and probably will be forever. I mean, how much revenge is enough? Josh didn't kill your baby, and he's not a demon, and he's not a witchy man, and he's not got the answer to everything, he's just *Josh* . . . and he's a kid, OK? There's a kid down there, and maybe he's still alive but drowning . . .' *Maybe we could jump on her and wrestle her off the grille, try to get past the screwdriver she's holding towards us* . . . 'I mean . . . you already know what his parents would feel . . .'

Miss Gossamer suddenly screamed and started tear-ing the buttons from her coat, the locket from her throat, and rings from her ears.

'Don't pretend that you know! You don't know! Nobody pitied my little girl as she sank into the mud without a christening. Do you want to grant a wish? Here!' She dashed the earrings and buttons down upon the grille, so that they bounced and vanished between the spokes. 'Do you know what I wished? I wished him to the hell where they sent my little girl. He's there with her now, forever . . .'

'Are you sure that's what you wished?' Ryan asked gently.

Twenty yards away, the wind stirred the leaves into a spiral, into a column, into the likeness of a figure. It was a little shorter than Ryan, with a bird's egg freckled pal-lor, rosehip-coloured hair and grass-green satin shoes.

A sunbeam smile, a turned-up nose, a dress chequered in shades of dusk and daylight. Miss Gossamer gave a croak and ran to gather the girl-shape in her arms. It collapsed in her embrace, subsiding into a scatter of leavings and litter. Further up the path, the haunting little figure formed and beckoned once more, and again Miss Gossamer scrambled towards her, only to see her tumble to nothing again.

Whatever she claimed, in her unknown heart Miss Gossamer had wished for the return of her child. Not the real baby, but her 'beautiful girl', the daughter-granddaughter that had haunted her imagination. The little girl had never been real, and there was nothing to hold her in one piece each time Miss Gossamer got close to her, so the old woman zigzagged wailing through the wood after the elusive phantom until both were lost to sight.

'Quick!' Ryan scuffled in the mulch for the knife Miss Gossamer had dropped and Chelle cleared the leaves away from the grille's screws.

'He's been down there for ages, Ryan, he's been there since before the rain started so that means he's dead, doesn't it, doesn't it! Unless there was another way out of there, like an underground sewer . . .'

'I dunno. Chelle, can you do this? My contact lens's slid up and I keep slicing my thumb.' Chelle took over and set about slicing her own thumb. 'I just keep thinking, the rain started again, didn't it? So the Well Spirit must have granted his wish to get her power back. So she made him her Chosen One, and she wouldn't let her Chosen One drown, would she? That's what I keep hoping.' At last Chelle sat back sucking her thumb and holding the last screw.

They lifted the grille away, and peered at their reflections in the brimming brown water.

'What about us?' Chelle whispered. 'I mean, we're not as Chosen as Josh, are we, so I guess she won't try to stop us drowning, will she? What are you doing?'

'Taking out my lenses,' Ryan said under his breath. His chest was full of what he had to do, and he knew that it was important not to think about it too hard. He replaced the lenses in their little plastic box and put it in his pocket. He thought of Josh, Josh going down the well the first time to save them all. He thought of Josh's plans, and of James Bond surfing down a snow slope on half a door or somebody's cello case. If only Ryan had a cello case, or even part of a cello case. 'Can you keep an eye out up here and make sure that Miss Gossamer doesn't come back and nail down the grille again?' It was all he could think of to say to keep Chelle safely at ground level. When he stepped up to the side of the well, her eyes widened with an expression of bewildered horror.

'It's all right,' he lied, 'I have a plan.' And then he trusted himself to instinct and jumped into the water.

There was a shock of cold and his knuckle-eyes sprang open. Ryan's vision filled with bubble-flecked brown. His ears licked shut and chimed with depth. He fought against his instinctive need to kick out, to flail with his arms and drive himself back to the surface.

Experimentally he let out a few beads of breath, and drew in another without pain. The Well Spirit had called them to her and apparently would not allow them to drown on the way to her presence. Ryan did not know if she would be so understanding once she had heard what he had to say for himself.

He sank slowly, watching the murky brown light around him change to an eerie emerald. He felt a mounting pain as if someone was pushing fingertips just under his ear lobes, but each time he swallowed it went away.

The walls receded on either side until it seemed that he was dropping into an enormous cavern, and below him he realized that he could make out the flicker of white flames in an enormous hearth. The light glistened on distant walls that seemed to have been made out of a mulch of stone, the way wasps build from chewed paper. One great slab jutted from the rough rock floor like a feasting table, softened to shapelessness by velvety green weed. Every other inch of the floor was scattered and heaped with coins, some bright, some blackened, some frail as shells. Ryan's trainers touched the floor and slithered.

The Well Spirit sat before her hearth, an expressionless silhouette, the flames easily visible through her floating, melting hair. Beside her on a bed of sovereigns Josh lay unmoving, his own short hair obeying the same soft sway. His sunglasses were missing, and Ryan could see that he had gold coins instead of eyes.

My Angels.

The words reached him like a ripple through the water rather than a sound. How strange they were, like the exclamation of a mother or a loving grandmother. But he knew that they were meant quite literally. Angels that belong to me. A moment later he noticed that Chelle was descending slowly behind him, her legs cycling comically, the pinks in her clothing waning into greys.

'Chelle . . .' His voice was a squeak of dismay, and yet he could not help being glad that she was there. He half expected his voice to sound bubbly, but instead it was tinny and muffled.

'I threw the grille in the canal – Miss Gossamer'll never find it.' Chelle's voice was muted, as if she was speaking inside a bottle. She did not seem to need knuckle-eyes to look around her, any more than Ryan had needed them in his dreams. Her gaze fell upon Josh's coin-eyes and she looked at Ryan aghast. Ryan could only mirror her expression and shake his head helplessly. He had no idea if Josh was alive or dead.

Draw closer.

Ryan and Chelle glanced at each other for reassurance, then obeyed the noiseless command. They drift-loped forward like astronauts, their clothes bulging and flourishing around them strangely.

As they drew closer Ryan developed a tooth-twinge feeling that something was wrong, something was different. It was a moment before he realized what it was. The Well Spirit was no longer swinging her head in a slow, thrashing motion as if trying to wake herself from a nightmare. Her head was held steady, and from its angle he guessed that her gaze was directed at Josh. The green-stained fingers of her hand crept over his forehead as if feeling for some bump or injury. And then for a moment he saw something arcing and melting in the firelight, something that was not the Well Spirit's hair.

He snatched at Chelle's arm, bringing the two of them into collision.

'She's changed!' He hissed bubbles in her ear as he pretended to steady himself. 'She has wish snakes now! She never had them before – something's happened to her!' He was not sure if Chelle had understood, but he dared say no more. Hesitantly Chelle and Ryan drew closer and settled themselves on two green-draped rocks.

Disobeyed. Ungranted. Destroyed shri-i-i-ine.

With each word, the firelight flared and their faces tingled with something that was not heat, rather more like the rush of blood after a blow. On the last word, Ryan suddenly felt a choking sting in his lungs, as if the water within had briefly become unbreathable. He was left in no doubt about the likely consequences of giving the Well Spirit an answer she didn't like.

'The other god made us do it,' Chelle suddenly chirruped.

What? Ryan screamed inside his head as the hearth's flames leaped to twice their height.

'Yes, only it's not our fault, because we were trying to grant one of your wishes, the one with the Harley-Davidson, but to do that we had to, um, swim across this lake to get the Harley half of it because you only find them inside a certain kind of apple on this island owned by . . . the Harley Queen, only it turned out that there was a god in the lake and when we were splashing around we scared away the sacred . . . horned rabbits which did his bidding and so he said we had to serve him in their place. So we've been trying really, really hard to serve both of you only it's very difficult . . .'

Name god.

'Um, well if I name him then he'll be really really angry that I told you . . .' The radiation from the fire became almost stinging. '. . . Um, um, but I suppose as a Well's Angel I have to grant wishes for coins, so if I got a coin for the information I'd just be doing my job and he couldn't be angry, could he?'

Slowly one green-fingered hand reached out, felt tenderly across the piles of treasure, selected a large silver coin with a hole in the middle, and flicked it in Chelle's direction. It spun in slow motion towards her.

'Ha!' As her hand closed around the coin Chelle's face brightened triumphantly. 'Ha, got you, penny for your thoughts, ha ha.'

The next second Chelle doubled up, then straightened and opened her mouth. For a moment Ryan thought she was choking, but no, she was speaking. It was a language that he had never heard before, full of gutturals and gasps, lisps and leaning vowels. It was harsh and haunting at the same time. Occasionally a word or phrase was recognizable in the way that faces may be half familiar in dreams.

It was a few seconds before he understood what Chelle had done and why. If the Well Spirit had grown wish snakes, she could become a wisher. And now that Chelle had her ungranted wish coin, Chelle was channelling her thoughts.

As he listened, the words spilling from Chelle's mouth changed and he recognized the language as French, although a lot of the words were lost on him. Another ripple passed across Chelle's expression and the words were suddenly English, although uttered with a creaking slowness as if the sentences were chains jammed with rust.

'. . . and now she echoes me who is this other god steal my servants this other god shall not shall not have them drown them first but not this one he would never betray me I shall not let the other god see him or steal him but why does he not move perhaps cover him with more gold to make him comfortable keep him warm and safe . . .'

Again the green fingers drifted slowly across Josh's brow, and for the first time Ryan noticed a bleached cut near his hairline.

'He's hurt,' he said aloud.

'. . . fell fell from climbing fell against the bricks but I stopped the blood and made him live and I will keep him safe here until better and he will stay with me be my child . . .'

My child. Ryan could suddenly see it all. Josh sniggering angrily at the mouth of the well, telling himself that he'd show everyone now that the Well Spirit had no choice but to make him her representative, the wielder of all her power, her archangel, her Chosen One. Josh had not understood that every wish came in two parts, including a secret part of which even the wisher was often unaware. In desperation the Well Spirit had granted both parts of his wish. No doubt Josh now had all the supernatural power he could want, but this had not been the whole of his wish. Josh wanted to be special, to be the centre of the world for somebody at last. To grant his unconscious wish the Well Spirit had changed her very nature . . . and given him a mother.

'He's not going to get better here,' said Ryan, venturing forward a little. 'It's not right for him – there's no air, there's no light – we're not made for that kind of thing.' He thought he could make out some details of her face, a crease in her neck as she lowered her chin to scowl, a jade sheen on her cheek.

'. . . never fall again safe here . . .'

'Safe isn't enough,' Ryan said gently, suddenly feeling a pang of pity for her. 'Even if you could stop him starving, his muscles would start to waste, and he'd bleach white or blue, and his hands and feet would wrinkle up, and in the end you'd see the coins in his eyes greening over, and then if he ever woke up he'd hardly be able to move. And his eyes aren't supposed to *be* like that.'

'. . . my finest gold . . .'

'I can see that. Only . . . those aren't Josh's eyes.'

'. . . needs me . . .'

'Yes,' answered Ryan softly, 'but he needs air and friends and his life more. You want the best for him, don't you? Then you've got to release him. And . . . not just out of the well. You've got to ungrant his wish and change him back, and release him from being an Angel.'

'. . . ungrant wishes myself lose me my power . . .'

'I know.'

'. . . if I let him go never come back . . .'

'I don't know,' Ryan said honestly. 'No, I think maybe he won't ever come back to Magwhite. But –' he wrestled with his pity and lost – 'but I could. To let you know how he is.'

'. . . needs someone to guard him . . .'

'We can try,' Ryan said slowly. 'Only . . . you've got to release us as well, before we get locked in a loony bin like your last Angels, or we can't.'

The fire ebbed and sighed. At long last Ryan stared into her face. Her eyes were holes through which the water flowed freely, dark and fathoms deep. For a fleeting instant he saw himself reflected in them. He was upside down, and his tiny features were unreadable.

Wish for release when you reach the air. This time I grant. The soundless boom rippled through the hall, and they knew they had been dismissed.

The light of the fire seemed to be dwindling, and in near darkness Chelle and Ryan slid from their stony seats and half crawled, half swam to Josh's side. They each dragged an arm over their shoulders, feeling the chill of his hands against theirs, and kicked away from the stone floor.

As they rose through the black and the green and the brown, Ryan could feel pressure building behind his nose and inside his ears. He heard a hoarse roaring of air. His throat started to tighten and jerk as if at last it realized what it was breathing. Above him, the surface was a capricious, billowing silver disc. He kicked and struggled his way towards it, but it seemed to get no closer. His eyes and nasal passages were stinging, his lungs were lurching helplessly, airlessly . . . and then he smashed through the surface with his face. Suddenly he was spitting and choking water from a stinging throat.

He trod water and supported Josh while Chelle scrambled out, and between the two of them they dragged the older boy out to lie on the mulch. Josh's eyes were closed, but the lids were rounded as if at last they hid ordinary eyes again.

'Wish time,' whispered Chelle, as Ryan climbed out. She extended her forefinger, the tip of which was poked through the centre of the silver coin.

Ryan reached a shivering hand for it and paused. What would his hidden wish be? How could he know? The last week alone had shown him how little he knew himself. Could he be sure that there were no twisted wishes at the back of his mind, mean hopes, vengeful thoughts, secret rages? Who can you trust when you can't trust yourself?

'I think you'd better do it,' he said.

'OK.' Chelle smiled and tugged her finger free. She fluttered her lips in a silent wish, and then dropped the silver coin into the waters of the well.

Epilogue

All three of them were, of course, in trouble. And when Ryan's mum picked Ryan up at last from the hospital where Josh had been taken, she found many new and inventive ways of explaining this to him all the way home.

'You're in the Ninth Circle of Trouble,' she snapped, yanking the steering wheel to take them off the roundabout. 'You'll need a new emergency service to get yourself out of this one.' Ryan tried to feel as daunted as she wanted him to be, but, tucked in the back seat of the car, trouble felt like blankets and brusque, bruising hugs.

'I don't ask much,' Ryan's mother flashed him a look in the mirror, 'but I do expect to be able to trust you.' This was true, Ryan realized, thinking of the way she had taken his word against Miss Gossamer. 'Is this a regular thing for you, running out of the library in secret? Is this the day I have to stop trusting you, Ryan? How many other lies have there been?'

'Just lately there've been quite a lot,' Ryan admitted. 'Mum, I'm really sorry, but . . . it's over now.'

'It's over, is it? "It" is over, is it?'

'Yes. It is.'

'Is it?' his mum asked once more. 'Because I need to know if Josh is going to hurt you again, Ryan.' There was silence but for the *tic-tac-tic-tac* of the indicator. 'Don't assume that I'm stupid, and kindly don't assume that I'm blind. When I came home on the night of the break-in, *objects were moving around by themselves*. I didn't tell the hospital or the police – they'd have decided I was unstable and whisked you off to social services. But I saw it.

'At first I thought Miss Gossamer might have been responsible. But today I went to talk to our neighbour Mrs Milton, the one with the leg and the attic room, and she says she saw Josh in our garden that night, letting himself in through our back door.' She flashed a fierce, rapid glance at Ryan and drove on for a few moments without speaking. 'Reports of poltergeist cases nearly always take place in a house where there's a troubled teenager,' she added at last, in a curt, business-like tone. 'Josh has become a centre for poltergeist activity, hasn't he?'

Ryan's face prickled and his tongue was dry as paper. He hesitated, and then slowly nodded.

'Sort of,' he said.

'And you and Chelle knew about it and have been protecting him, even after he attacked *you*.'

'Josh . . . wasn't Josh at the time, Mum.'

'That boy's disturbed, and I'm not having you suffering for it. Can you take him down from his pedestal long enough to see that?'

Ryan nodded slowly.

'I think I hated him for a bit,' he said after a moment. 'Just for, you know, not being everything I wanted him to be. But . . . even with all the bad stuff he was still my friend. And if your friend's drowning, even if he's *trying* to drown and struggling to shake your hand off his sleeve, you don't let go, do you? He was . . . in a bad place, Mum. We had to go there to get him back, and if I'd told you you'd have stopped me.'

'Damn right,' she said, but her voice sounded less angry. 'So what do you suggest, Ryan? I'm not happy with you spending more time with him.'

'Mum . . .' Ryan rallied his will power. 'He's still drowning. I can't let go. But I promise there'll be no more lies. I swear. On . . . my eyes.'

His mum said nothing for some time, and Ryan waited for her to steamroll his wishes as usual.

'All right,' she said at last. 'I'm going to trust you. I'm going to trust you to tell me if there's any more trouble. I won't pursue Josh over the damage done to the house either. The Lattimer-Stones know now that he sneaked in that night, and I'll leave everything in their hands.' She gave Ryan another glance that seemed to say, *but if he ever hurts you again* . . .

A long silence followed.

'Mum?' The curiosity was too much. 'If you made one wish in a wishing well, what would it be?'

'What? I've never done anything of the sort, how should I know . . . ?'

No, you wouldn't, would you? Too busy rampaging through the world, granting your own wishes . . .

Ryan regarded his mother with exasperated pride as she narrowed her eyes at the odds, and ran a red light.

The Lattimer-Stones passed judgement on Josh the moment he was well enough to see them. As far as they were concerned he had been seeking attention, first by sabotaging electronics around The Haven, then by smashing up the Doyles' house and attacking Ryan, and finally by running away from home and falling foul of the flood waters. He was to go to boarding school in another county, somewhere expensive with good counselling services.

'It's for my own good,' Josh said with a tone of flat disdain. 'They explained that. So I'll be out of the way while they are . . . arranging things.' This was as close as he had ever got to referring to his adoptive parents' divorce.

Chelle and Ryan sat on either side of his hospital bed. Josh's sunglasses had been lost to the well, and now his face looked naked and vulnerable. His eyelids were a little red and stretched from having had coins for eyes, and he was still having some trouble bearing the light. Or perhaps his eyes were lowered to avoid looking at his companions.

'But you'll get there and you'll write to us,' said Chelle as an awkward silence threatened to settle. 'And if they're looking in your mail like in prison then you can use a code and say something like "the ostrich waves from the western tower" to tell us that you need to get away . . .'

Josh grinned. 'And you two'll come, won't you?' He flicked a grey glance at them, then stared down at the fingernails he had broken trying to get out of the well. 'Yeah,' he added quietly, 'bust me out of there . . .'

'Kill the guards . . .'

'Set fire to the school . . .'

'And we whizz away, all on one bike, dropping grenades behind us . . .' Josh looked into an imaginary bag, pulled out invisible grenades with pleased surprise and nonchalantly threw them to the winds. Ryan was glad to hear him sounding a bit more like himself. For now they could play at still being a trio, as if the unsigned pact between them was yet unbroken, and nobody had tried to kill anyone's mother. 'I dunno what I was thinking. I mean, like *we* need powers . . .' Josh gave a grin as hard as glass.

Josh, nobody's child, nobody's Chosen One, and now nobody's hero. The nurses bustling through the ward would have no idea that a god had given up her power just to give him a chance at happiness. Right now, even that chance seemed pretty slender.

The floods had started to recede from the moment Chelle's silver coin had touched the waters of the well. A day or two later, people were able to return to their homes. Flash floods had carried some cars all the way to the harbour and stacked them like dominoes in the mud. In some cases runaway trees had clawed the front walls off buildings in passing. Fortunately, nobody had actually been killed.

The Harley, on the other hand, was quite dead. After the flooding of its engine and its abandonment in Whelmford, it had decided to make one last journey of its own. In his third and last *Silverwing* article in the saga of the Harley, Will imagined it riding the torrent through the county byways, taking every corner more easily than it ever had with him on its back. He described it weaving all the way to Poddington, where it finally buried itself up to its handlebars in a trench of sheep dip, presumably in the hope of preventing Will ever finding and riding it again. Everybody found the article very funny, and *Silverwing* offered Will a small regular column.

Carrie's red door had suffered almost as many adventures. Once she was in the Rectory, the poor door, left outside, had taken off across the flooded fields. Eventually it had been discovered amid the wreckage of someone's greenhouse. The plastic sheeting had done a great deal to protect it from the worst of the water damage, but it had battled with several trees and there were dinks and dents in its paintwork. Nonetheless, Carrie absolutely refused to throw it away, and one month after the day of the floods a tea party celebrated its installation as front door.

'Of course I couldn't abandon it,' Carrie insisted as she poured drinks. 'It rescued me.' She smiled at Will, sitting opposite her at the table. When Carrie had learned that Will was having trouble paying his rent, she had insisted on him taking one of her rooms as a lodger as soon as the flood damage was repaired.

The garden felt less magical and secret now that the hedge at the bottom had been replaced by a little wooden fence, but understandably Carrie had refused to return to the house until the last strand of Russian vine had been torn out.

Will and Carrie seldom mentioned the Well Spirit directly, perhaps out of consideration for each other. However, they both talked animatedly about the plans for new flood defences at Magwhite. They seemed reassured by the idea of a canalside concrete bank which would prevent unsuspecting passers-by from encountering the well.

For several weeks, it was impossible to get away from Donna Leas. She appeared in all the local papers as 'Feisty Flood Heroine Donna' and 'Lady of the Lake'. There were lots of photos, most showing her utterly bedraggled, helping people to put on helicopter winch belts with an expression of impenetrable bad temper on her face, or pulling children out of the water while looking as if she'd rather drown them. When they ran out of other stories, reporters went to Donna to ask her opinion, and only then discovered quite how many opinions she had.

'Do you think maybe she's all fixed now?' Chelle

asked, scrutinizing the paper one day. Chelle was apparently finding it hard to shake the angelic mindset.

'Not all fixed, maybe.' Ryan looked at Donna's face and the bitter angles and lines that the photo had tried to soften. Perhaps some people couldn't get fixed all at once. 'But at least it sounds like she's fixing herself now, not expecting Mr Punzell to do it.'

The magazine that came with the paper also had an interview with Pipette Macintosh, who was shown pouting in front of an urban landscape with a brush in her hand. Pipette had announced that the following year her new authorized biography would be released, written in collaboration with her friend Anne Doyle. When asked if it was true that there had been conflict in the past between her and Anne over an unofficial biography, Pipette 'declined to comment'.

'Mum says what actually happened was that Pipette stormed out of the studio kicking cameras,' remarked Ryan.

'Ooh, ooh, it says here she's hired an "esoteric adviser" to help her channel her energies. I bet that's Mr Punzell – I just *knew* they'd be right for each other . . .'

Ryan couldn't help wondering whether Mr Punzell might get bored of voodoo eventually and find someone else with even more interesting uncontrolled supernatural powers. If so, he hoped Mr Punzell wouldn't mind having his hedge painted pink in the dead of night.

*

Verdigris Deep

All around him lime-green and smoky-yellow moss seethed and bubbled, pockmarked like coral. A few feet away, almost ludicrous in its familiarity, was the Magwhite well, looking just as it always had, the folded crisp packets still jutting from its grille. Somehow now, however, he could hardly bear to look at it. He could not fight the feeling that there was something seeping slowly from the well and hanging in the air above it. It was almost a smell that was almost a darkness that was almost an echo that was almost a bitter taste in the air.

She sat enthroned amid the fanned roots of an enormous overturned tree. The roots knobbed and knuckled, and among them were wedged weird trophies. A child's pink wellington boot choked with ivy, a hiking stick that had sprouted and given bud, the skull of a cat. A hundred bent cigarette butts smoked gently like incense sticks in a church shrine. A bent bicycle wheel spun slowly and unevenly behind her head, a halo for a strange saint. Her gown was studded with fragments of gold foil, punctured in crude patterns, and there was a tarnished, twisted collar of copper wire round her neck.

Also by Frances Hardinge

Fly By Night